DUKE OF DISREPUTE

Dukes of Distinction
Book 3

Alexa Aston

Dragonblade Publishing, Inc. is an imprint of Kathryn Le Veque Novels, Inc.
P.O. Box 7968
La Verne CA 91750
ceo@dragonbladepublishing.com

Produced in the United States of America

First Edition March 2021
Print Edition

ARE YOU SIGNED UP FOR DRAGONBLADE'S BLOG?

You'll get the latest news and information on exclusive giveaways, exclusive excerpts, coming releases, sales, free books, cover reveals and more.

Check out our complete list of authors, too!

No spam, no junk. That's a promise!

Sign Up Here

www.dragonbladepublishing.com

Dearest Reader;

Thank you for your support of a small press. At Dragonblade Publishing, we strive to bring you the highest quality Historical Romance from the some of the best authors in the business. Without your support, there is no 'us', so we sincerely hope you adore these stories and find some new favorite authors along the way.

Happy Reading!

CEO, Dragonblade Publishing

Additional Dragonblade books by Author Alexa Aston

Dukes of Distinction Series
Duke of Renown
Duke of Charm
Duke of Disrepute

The St. Clairs Series
Devoted to the Duke
Midnight with the Marquess
Embracing the Earl
Defending the Duke
Suddenly a St. Clair
Starlight Night

Soldiers & Soulmates Series
To Heal an Earl
To Tame a Rogue
To Trust a Duke
To Save a Love
To Win a Widow

The Lyon's Den Connected World
The Lyon's Lady Love

King's Cousins Series
The Pawn
The Heir
The Bastard

Medieval Runaway Wives
Song of the Heart

A Promise of Tomorrow
Destined for Love

Knights of Honor Series
Word of Honor
Marked by Honor
Code of Honor
Journey to Honor
Heart of Honor
Bold in Honor
Love and Honor
Gift of Honor
Path to Honor
Return to Honor

CHAPTER ONE

London—*September 1808*

WESTON WALLACE, DUKE of Treadwell, tossed back the remainder of the brandy in his snifter. He was pleasantly drunk as he celebrated his upcoming nuptials to Lady Juniper Radwell with his friends. Juniper's brother, Viscount Kingsbury, had hosted tonight's gathering. He had known Monty Radwell from school, more as an acquaintance, since the viscount was four years older than Weston and his tight-knit group of friends.

He glanced to George, the Duke of Colebourne and his closest friend. Their fathers had been neighbors and best friends from their own school days and raised their heirs to be the same. Weston and George had done everything together from the time they could walk and talk and they'd been joined by Andrew once they left their tutors behind and began Eton together. Jon and Sebastian had completed their circle when they'd met at Cambridge. Though Jon was here tonight helping the two grooms-to-be celebrate their upcoming nuptials, both Andrew and Sebastian were far away on the Continent, fighting the menace known as Bonaparte. Weston wished they could be here but he understood war trumped the marriage of school chums, even if they were as close as brothers.

"One more?" Kingsbury asked, dangling the bottle of brandy from his fingertips, his smile tipsy.

Weston shook his head. "No more for me. Not if I am to be standing at the altar tomorrow, pledging myself to your sister." He looked at George. "Are you ready to go home so we can get some sleep?"

George gave him a sleepy smile. He always looked sleepy when he'd had too much to drink.

"All right, West. Whatever you say." He handed his half-finished drink to Kingsbury. "Thanks you for having us."

Everyone else present did the same, setting aside their tumblers and noisily spilling from the library and down the stairs. Weston caught sight of Juniper standing in the shadows, a smile playing about her sensual lips. Lips he adored kissing. Lips that would belong to him alone once they wed tomorrow morning in St. George's Chapel in a double ceremony with George and Lady Frederica Martin. Weston was utterly besotted with his fiancée. She was the most beautiful unmarried woman in all of London.

And she was going to be all his.

Not that she already hadn't been. They'd both been too eager to wait until their wedding night to consummate their relationship. For the last few months, he had been sneaking into her bed regularly, taking precautions so that no little Treadwell would be growing in her womb on their wedding day. His caution would end tomorrow night. Both he and George were eager to start their families. That's why they were marrying young. They'd both ascended to their dukedoms last year when their fathers passed away within days of each other and took their responsibilities seriously. That included making new little dukes to be their heirs apparent.

At least Weston was lucky enough to be marrying for love. He'd chosen Juniper to become his duchess because of her old, solid family name and hefty dowry, along with her immense beauty. It had surprised him when he'd actually fallen in love with her. Juniper was the woman every man of the *ton* worshipped—and she had chosen him to spend the rest of her life with. He warmed thinking of the heat that existed between them when they coupled. His fiancée was like a goddess come to life and she made him feel like a god instead of a mortal man.

He watched his friends file out the door, George the last to go.

"I'll meet you at St. George's Chapel tomorrow," he promised his dearest friend. "Goodnight."

George gave him a knowing wink and retreated down the sidewalk to his waiting carriage.

Weston closed the door and saw Kingsbury move away and enter his study just off the foyer. That left him alone with his fiancée.

Juniper left the shadows and came to him, winding her arms about his neck, pressing her curvaceous body into his. Weston kissed her hungrily. Her hand moved between them, finding his cock and stroking it through his trousers.

Laughing, he broke the kiss. "I've had a little too much to drink, my lady. Perhaps we should wait until after the ceremony tomorrow."

"I don't care," she told him, her eyes gleaming. "I want you. Now."

Taking his hand, she led him up to her bedchamber. She stripped him of his clothes, flinging them in all directions, and then pushed him onto the bed once he was naked. Lazily, he watched as she removed her dressing gown and night rail and then climbed atop him. Within moments, he was hard. She reached under her pillow and removed a French letter, sheathing him and then guiding him inside her, where she rode him with abandon. He watched her, her eyes closed, contentment on her face as they both climaxed at the same time. She fell onto his chest, breathing rapidly.

Then as usual, she moved off him. Juniper wasn't a cuddler, something he hoped might change. She tossed on her night rail.

"You need to leave," she said. "You look far too satisfied in my bed and much too sleepy. It wouldn't bode well if you fell asleep and I couldn't wake you." Grinning, she added, "Think of the scandal that would cause. A groom found in his bride's bed *before* the ceremony was performed."

Weston dressed as she went to her dressing table. He watched her unpin her hair and brush it out. He longed to comb his fingers through it but knew she was right. He needed to get some rest before their big day tomorrow. He went and placed his hands on her shoulders, kissing the side of her neck and then the top of her head.

"Tomorrow at St. George's then?" he asked playfully.

Her eyes met his in the mirror. "Yes, darling. Tomorrow."

"Farewell, my lady." His eyes twinkled. "Or should I say *Your Grace?*"

Her lips twitched with amusement. "Oh, I could get used to that. I think I will make for an absolutely marvelous duchess."

"You will," he assured her, thinking of everything he would lavish upon her once she became his wife.

He left her bedchamber, creeping down the hall. He met Kingsbury on the stairs and grinned sheepishly.

"Goodnight," he murmured. "I'll let myself out."

Weston reached the ground floor and opened the massive door, shutting it quietly behind him. His carriage awaited him at the curb. As he reached it, he realized he'd neglected to put his waistcoat back on.

"I'll be right back," he told his driver and returned to the house.

Normally, it wouldn't matter that he'd left his waistcoat behind but inside its pocket was Juniper's wedding ring. He'd been carrying it with him for a week now, giddy as a schoolboy. It wouldn't do to show up at the altar tomorrow without it. He was afraid if he sent word to her, she might not receive it with all the hustle and bustle of preparing for her wedding in the morning. Even if she did, she would have to get the ring to him. Weston didn't trust that to happen, especially if she gave it to her brother. Monty had garnered a reputation of being irresponsible during their school days and it seemed nothing had changed as he'd matured into an adult. It would just be easier to claim the article of clothing and the ring inside now.

He reached Juniper's bedchamber and decided not to knock and draw undue attention. She always fell asleep quickly and deeply after they'd lain together and was probably already dreaming even now. Turning the knob, he quietly pushed open the door, thinking he could retrieve his waistcoat and kiss her brow before retreating to his carriage.

What he saw caused him to come to a standstill, his mouth gaping.

Juniper was in bed.

With her brother.

Kingsbury's bare back and buttocks glistened with sweat as he hovered over her. Weston could see her legs entwined about his waist. She was making the same noises she made when they made love. Bile rose in his throat. He couldn't stand by idly, though. He strode across the room and shoved Kingsbury off her. Startled, the viscount fell off the bed and scrambled to his feet, a scowl on his handsome face.

Weston tore his eyes from the naked man and focused on his fiancée. She wore a satisfied smile, like a cat who'd been caught licking cream.

"Hello, darling," she said sensually. "Have you come to join in our fun?"

Disgust filled him. He reached to the floor and picked up her dressing gown and threw it at her, turning away. His thoughts were in a jumble. Something touched his shoulder and he wheeled. It was Kingsbury.

"I say, Treadwell, we—"

Weston slammed his fist into the viscount's face. The crunch of broken bone sounded and blood spurted from Kingsbury's nose as he stumbled back. Curses flew from his lips.

"Oh, don't be such a baby," purred Juniper.

He turned and saw her climb from the bed, holding the dressing gown he'd given her. She padded naked to her brother and tenderly stroked his cheek, then used the gown to mop up the blood. Weston's belly soured and he fought the urge to empty all the drinks he'd had, swallowing hard and then holding his breath.

His fiancée came to him. She tried to put her arms about him but he waved her off.

"Oh, come now, Treadwell," she said softly. "You aren't surprised, are you? You know my appetite is voracious when it comes to matters of the flesh."

Anger flushed through him. "Surprised? I'm disgusted. Horrified."

She touched his forearm but he threw off her hand.

"It's only for fun. That's what carnal pleasure is all about. Indulging yourself. Living out your fantasies." Juniper smiled. "In fact, the three of us together will have some interesting times."

"Are you mad?" he hissed.

She shrugged. "We'll try it. You'll get used to the idea. A wonderful, wicked world awaits you. You'll see. You'll try it . . . and like it. I know you will."

"I'll see nothing," he said hoarsely. "There will be no trying. There'll be no *us* to do the trying."

She frowned. "What are you saying?"

"We are not getting married," he told her.

"Treadwell, you must—"

"I must follow my common sense, Madam. Right now, it's telling me to get as far from you as possible."

"You cannot break our engagement," she said firmly. "I've waited for the right man. I wanted a duke. A handsome, wealthy duke. One who enjoys sex as much as I do."

"Not unnatural coupling!" he shouted, not caring who heard him.

She sniffed. "It's in your nature, Treadwell. You are as carnal as they come. You enjoy all the naughty things we already do. There's a world of interesting things to try together. It doesn't have to be with Monty. We can find others. Your friend Colebourne, for example. He's quite dashing. I'm sure he'd be amenable to having some fun with us."

Weston vehemently shook his head in denial. "You are deliberate-ly not understanding, Juniper. I want nothing to do with you or any of your sick games."

Her eyes narrowed. "My reputation will be ruined if you break our engagement."

"Then say you broke it for all I care. I will be a gentleman and keep to myself what I saw this night. Polite Society will never hear of your misdeeds from me."

Her eyes gleamed. She looked like an entirely different person. How could he not have seen what she truly was?

"You must promise you will not speak publicly of this. That you will let me tell my version of the events and not contradict it."

"I promise," he said begrudgingly. "What is the story you will tell?"

"I'll have to give it some thought," Juniper said. "It must cast me in a positive light. I'm afraid, though, it will paint you in quite a bad one." She smiled wickedly. "In fact, you will be totally, utterly disgraced. Of course, society forgives a duke anything. Eventually, that is."

"What kind of lies will you paint me with?" he demanded.

"Lies which will become known as the truth. Ones which will make your new nickname reflect who you truly are, Your Grace." She paused. "The Duke . . . of Disrepute. Yes, that is what I will call you. Disrepute. You will have no respect. No honor. No one will hold you in esteem."

In that moment, Weston didn't care what she said or did. He only wanted to get as far away from her as possible. He had loved this woman. Worshipped her body. Given his very soul to her. Now, he realized the truth. Love didn't exist. Women were never to be trusted. And if he was to be known as the Duke of Disrepute?

Then he would live up to the title and wear it with pride.

CHAPTER TWO

London—April 1809

L ADY ELISE PURNELL waited nervously at the foot of the staircase with her father.

"Why can't Mama ever be on time?" she complained.

He chuckled. "It's not in your mother's nature to let a clock rule her life, my dear. She'll be ready when she's ready. And she'll be beautiful, as always."

"But I'm the one making my come-out!" Elise exclaimed. "If we are late, we won't be able to go through the receiving line. Or worse. All the eligible gentlemen will have already circulated through the ballroom and signed their names to dance cards. I'll be left standing alone, the first designated wallflower of the Season."

Papa came and enfolded her in his arms. "That won't happen, Daughter. You are a lovely person, both inside and out. If the bachelors of the *ton* can't recognize that, then I will take you home with me and keep you as my little girl until the next Season begins."

It felt good to be so loved but Elise didn't want to be her father's little girl anymore. She was eighteen, for heaven's sake. Poised to make her come-out with all her friends. She'd had an entire wardrobe made up for the Season. Taken dancing lessons. Polished her singing and piano playing. She was on the cusp of a new life.

If Mama could choose a dress and make her way downstairs, that is.

"I will go fetch her," she said with determination.

"You'll do nothing of the sort," Papa told her. "Besides, here she comes now." Looking up at his countess descending the stairs, he called out, "My darling, you are a sight to behold."

Mama laughed girlishly, the way she always did when Papa complimented her. "Oh, Shelby, you make me feel young again with that frisky look in your eyes."

Elise grunted. This was not the time for her parents to ogle one another. They were old and married, not two people flirting at a ball, trying to be noticed by the other.

Her father kissed her mother's cheek and, taking her arm, he looked over his shoulder. "Coming, Elise?"

She sniffed and followed them out to the waiting carriage. She sat opposite them, hoping they wouldn't be too late. Even if the receiving line had already begun, they could join it at the end and pretend they'd been there at the same time the others had arrived.

Mama frowned. "Elise, my dear, we haven't talked about this but I want you to refrain from your bluestocking ways tonight. You are not to talk about anything intellectual. No politics or literature. No conversation involving the government or science. Keep to safe topics. Such as the weather," her mother instructed.

She didn't want to change who she was. Elise did want to wed, though. She wanted to find a worthy man and bear him children. She just needed to attract a man who didn't mind that she read voraciously and was interested in the world about her. She found geography and politics endlessly fascinating. Economics. Literature. The sciences.

"Wouldn't it be wise to find a gentleman who shares my interests, Mama?"

"Oh, no. That won't do at all. Men don't want a woman who is smarter than they are." She shook her head. "You are more intelligent than most men in Parliament, Elise, but you can't show it. Men of the *ton* will be put off by that, especially those perusing the Marriage

Mart."

Before she could reply, her mother continued. "Try to dance with as many highly titled gentlemen as you can."

Elise blurted out, "Surely, not the Bad Dukes?"

Lady Shelby's nose scrunched up in distaste. "What do you know of that pair?"

Quite a lot, actually. She had Soames, her favorite footman, save the newspapers for her each day and devoured them. Besides all the interesting articles, she couldn't help but devote a little time to reading the gossip columns. Why, just this week, an unnamed viscount had been caught in bed with his sister-in-law. A certain earl was rumored to have murdered his wife. And the two outrageously behaved Bad Dukes, the Duke of Charm and the Duke of Disrepute, had been involved in three separate antics, causing Polite Society to wag their tongues at the pair.

"I heard a few of my friends mention them," she said meekly, not wanting a lecture from her mother while she protected Soames at the same time. If Lady Shelby knew Elise had been reading the gossip columns, Mama would ban her from reading any part of the newspapers. They were full of information that she gobbled up and she couldn't risk that occurring.

"Oh, I forgot," her mother said. "Take off your spectacles."

"Why?"

"You are tolerably pretty without them. If you wear them, however, no man will ask you to dance."

"You know everything is a blur at a distance when I don't wear them, Mama."

"That's quite all right. You can see up close perfectly fine and distinguish the various men who ask you to partner with them when they stand close to you. Now, put them away."

Begrudgingly, Elise slipped off the small, gold spectacles and slid them into her reticule.

By now, the carriage began to slow and her heartbeat sped up. The driver stopped and let them out and they had to walk two blocks to their destination because the streets were snarled with carriages. She hoped the dust wouldn't cling to her new satin slippers. Thankfully, people were still coming from all directions and they joined the swell. The tide of others swept them into the house.

Once they'd gone through the receiving line, she parted ways with her parents, spying three of her friends and joining them. A footman handed her a programme.

"Did I miss anything?" she asked, but no one paid attention to her as the trio scanned the ballroom so Elise did the same, everything a total blur.

Several gentlemen came up and a flurry of introductions were made. Her programme was signed a half-dozen times and Elise relaxed, knowing she wouldn't be a wallflower tonight.

Then suddenly, the others began whispering loudly and she figured out from what they said that two incredibly handsome men, both tall, were making their way toward them.

"Here they come," she muttered, knowing in her bones it had to be the Bad Dukes, even though she couldn't quite see what they looked like as they approached.

Then they arrived and, up close, they were a magnificent pair. One had a tawny mane of hair and golden skin that made him resemble a lion. The other was sinfully handsome, with dark hair and olive skin. Both were impeccably dressed and utterly confident as they smiled at the group of young women making their come-out tonight.

What would she do if one of them asked to dance with her? It wasn't the done thing to refuse a duke. Would it hurt her reputation? She was a good girl. A very good girl, despite her bluestocking leanings. She always aimed to please others and never thought of herself.

"Good evening, ladies," the Duke of Charm drawled, living up to his reputation with his smooth voice and lively eyes.

"Yes, I second that," the Duke of Disrepute added, looking them over with interest.

His eyes stopped when they came to her. Elise swallowed. They hadn't even been properly introduced to these gentlemen! How could she be embroiled in a scandal before she'd ever set a foot out on the dance floor?

A slow smile spread across his face. "My lady, would you care to dance? I hear the strains of the opening number about to start."

She swallowed again, words beyond her. She'd never lost her ability to speak but he was breathtaking.

When she remained silent, the Duke of Disrepute lifted the dance card she'd tied to her wrist with the ribbon attached to it.

"I see you have this opening number available," he commented, dropping the card. "Cat got your tongue?" He smiled, a dreadfully wicked smile that made her breath catch. "Come along, little kitten."

He took her hand and placed it atop his arm in order to guide her to the ballroom floor.

Finding her voice, Elise said, "Watch out, Your Grace. Even kittens have claws and aren't afraid to use them if they feel threatened."

The duke stopped in his tracks and then laughed. His laugh was rich and deep, something one could become addicted to very easily. It made his gleaming, white teeth look even whiter.

"Oh, Kitten, you have nothing to fear from this wolf."

She sniffed as he took her in his arms as the music began. "I didn't think so, Your Grace. Not only is it well known that you have no wish to wed, but I know you would never want to wed someone like me."

He frowned, seemingly puzzled by her words. "Why do you say that, Kitten?"

She shrugged. "I know I'm only tolerably pretty, Wolf."

Elise looked away, trying to see the other couples on the dance floor and unable to make out anything beyond whirling blurs.

"Why are you squinting?" he inquired, drawing her attention back to him.

"I cannot see any great distance without my spectacles," she admitted. "Only close up. Mama made me take them off in the carriage before we entered the townhouse tonight. She thinks I'm hideous-looking when I wear them."

"Is it your mama who told you that you're only tolerably pretty without them?" he asked gently.

"Yes," she admitted, shocked she was being so open with a man so disreputable.

He smiled. "Well, she's wrong about that. You're very pretty with that russet hair and those violet eyes. I've never seen such an unusual shade as they are. I can't see a pair of spectacles changing your appearance all that much."

Elise felt her cheeks heat and her heart flutter wildly. "Thank you for the compliment, Wolf. I will add it to my list and share with any gentleman who wishes to know that the Duke of Disrepute found me pretty."

She hadn't meant to call him by his nickname, much less sound flippant, but something about dancing with this man emboldened her.

"You are quite unique, my lady. Keep being you . . . and the right man will find you."

They continued to dance though the duke ceased conversing with her. She supposed her talk of spectacles had bored him immensely. He had told her she was very pretty, though. Elise supposed he told every girl who made her come-out the same thing. Still, he'd sounded terribly sincere when he'd said it. If the Duke of Disrepute was this charming, she wondered how much more his friend, the Duke of Charm, could be.

When the music ceased, he led her back to the spot he'd found her. The Duke of Charm was already there and met his friend's gaze. Elise looked up at Disrepute and saw an imperceptible shake of his head. When she looked back at Charm, he was looking at another of her friends and she knew her partner had warned him off her.

"Thank you for the dance, Kitten," Disrepute told her. "The man who captures your heart will land a very beautiful girl, both inside and out."

He lifted her hand and kissed it and then strolled away. Charm followed him.

Immediately, her friends began pestering her for what they'd talked about. Elise blushed and they began teasing her. Feeling overwhelmed, she excused herself and went to the retiring room to escape them and their nosy questions.

Men like this wolf were dangerous. He made her want things that she shouldn't be thinking of. She longed for his arms to gather her up and his sensual lips to touch hers. If he would have taken her outside and pressed her for a kiss, she wouldn't have been able to deny him.

This brief experience made Elise decide she needed to play it safe. She would find a nice, boring man and live an ordinary life. She didn't need the type of excitement and scandal that a man such as Disrepute would bring. Not that he'd ever be interested in marriage, much less with a green girl such as her.

Returning to the ballroom, her next partner approached. Lord Ruthersby was bland in looks but she found him to be quite intellectual. They wound up speaking about several topics and he signed her card again, claiming the supper dance. All throughout supper, they continued to converse. He was sweet. A bit awkward. They had much in common, though.

Elise decided this man would be the one.

Not the wolf.

CHAPTER THREE

Windowmere, Devon—September 1814

WESTON SAT IN the library of the Duke of Windham, a brandy in his hand and the bottle close by. He'd been dragged to Andrew's house by George. His friend feared Lord Ivy, an imbecile who couldn't string two intelligent sentences together, might challenge Weston to a duel.

For sleeping with Ivy's stepmother.

It seemed comical to him because Ivy had also been sleeping with his stepmother—and the woman had apparently mentioned her preference for the Duke of Disrepute over her stepson—thus, Ivy's irritation with Weston. He didn't truly think the fool would issue a challenge. Weston wished George had allowed them to remain in London to find out what Ivy would have done. The choices would have been to either shoot the idiot or ignore the challenge. If he shot Ivy and only wounded him, no harm would be done. If he killed him, as Weston had a mind to do simply because the young man annoyed him to no end, a scandal would ensue—and that meant fleeing London. With Bonaparte still causing havoc throughout Europe, it would limit the scope of places to live in exile for a few years, until the matter was forgotten.

On the other hand, he could dismiss the challenge. Disregarding a challenge would be possibly an even larger scandal and would certainly seal his fate forever as the Duke of Disrepute. Weston toyed with the idea of returning to London without George and seeing how the affair played out. This house party Andrew and his new wife, Phoebe, was holding had no appeal. The Duke of Disrepute found house parties limiting and boring, being confined to one place with a set number of guests.

He took another sip of brandy and admitted to himself what was really on his mind.

George's troubling declaration.

His longtime friend had joined Weston for the last six years in cutting a swath through society after their broken engagements. The Bad Dukes, as they were known, lived for debauchery. They indulged in every known sexual pleasure and drank and gambled to excess. They broke every rule of Polite Society and lived their lives with no goal other than achieving enjoyment. They'd even come up with rules of their own making to guide them on their hedonistic journey through life.

Rule Number One had been easily agreed upon. They never stayed overnight with a lover. It was one thing to bed a woman but to wake up beside her in the morning light was quite another. Women were difficult creatures and could become very possessive. Finding a man had remained with them all night put odd notions in their heads. Ones that Weston and George didn't care to deal with.

Their second rule allowed them a wide field of choices. They could make love to any willing woman between eighteen and eighty. Younger than eighteen was like robbing the cradle, and therefore, forbidden. Over eighty would be unthinkable—although he could think of one countess who had passed eighty and still looked a good twenty-five years younger.

They parted ways on the third rule, which was perfectly fine with Weston. He chose to have sex with a woman only once. One time was enough for him to get a taste for her and satisfy his curiosity. More than that led to that air of possession again, which he avoided at all costs. George, on the other hand, limited himself to three encounters before he moved on to someone else. Weston couldn't remember why but it seemed to work for George. It probably had something to do with charming his lover and leaving while things were still sweet between them.

Rule Number Four was *de riguer*. They must come home and bathe after any encounter. Not having the smell of a particular woman on them—or their sheets—was important. Their home and personal bed must always remain their sanctuary, which led to their final rule.

Never, ever, ever allow a lover in your own bed.

The only exception occurred at a house party. Both he and George had gone to women and brought prospective lovers back to their beds when they were away from home, experiencing entertainment in the country. Since it wasn't their actual bed but a guest bed instead, they eased the rule whenever they found themselves away from London.

These rules had served the both of them well. Until now. Out of the blue, George opened up to him on their carriage ride to Devon. That, in and of itself, shocked Weston. They never talked about anything having to do with their emotions. Though they were closer than brothers, they never allowed the personal to come into their conversations. They drank and gambled. Raced their phaetons and boxed and hunted. The closest they came to discussing anything personal was comparing various lovers they'd shared.

Then George had gone and ruined it all. He'd bared his soul to Weston, telling him he was tired of the years spent in emptiness. The loneliness and waste of time. How he wanted only one woman in his life and a family with her.

And then he'd mentioned Samantha.

The thought of his sister caused guilt to rush through him. Once, he and Sam had been the closest of siblings. Then she'd wed a boring, harmless viscount and moved far north while he'd lived with the aftermath of Juniper breaking their engagement and the creative lies she'd spread about him. He tried to live up to and beyond those lies, running wild amidst society. Weston had never recaptured his closeness with his sister. He'd seen the disappointment in her eyes when they crossed paths during the following two Seasons. Then she'd stopped coming to London. He hadn't written or visited. He had nothing to say. Nothing that would explain his actions. He'd promised himself long ago that he would never reveal what he had seen in Juniper's bedchamber. Not even George knew why Weston hadn't married his fiancée. He'd merely joined in the fun once his own bride jilted him in front of hundreds of guests at their wedding.

Closing his eyes, he continued sipping the brandy, wanting it to dull his pain. Of all things, Sam had turned up at the Windhams' house party, the last place he would have expected to find her. He dreaded the confrontation that would occur between them. Then he noticed a change in the air and knew he had company. He wearily opened his eyes and saw his sister seated in a chair next to him. He steeled himself for whatever she would say, knowing the time had come for him to pay the piper.

Giving her a rakish smile, he said, "I always have time for my favorite sister." He brought the brandy to his mouth and downed what was left.

"Considering I'm your only sister, I have to wonder about that statement." She took a deep breath. "Weston, why did you abandon me?"

"What? I don't know what you mean." He reached for the bottle and poured himself three fingers, hoping if he drank enough he could forget the past.

"You do know exactly what I'm speaking of. Put that drink down," she commanded.

He did as asked and settled back into the chair, knowing from the moment he'd learned that she was at the house party that this showdown was inevitable.

"I want to understand what happened to you. To us."

He shrugged, keeping a tight rein on his feelings. "You wed. I didn't. You moved to the north with your husband. I remained in London, a bachelor sowing his wild oats. You're a woman, which means you came out of the womb writing letters. I'm a man and can't be bothered to write them."

She shook her head. "You have an answer for everything. Not ones I'm pleased with, though."

He studied her a moment. He loved her so much, despite the wide gulf between them. "Accept my apology, Sam. I know I've been a terrible brother. I'm not a very good person and haven't been for some time. I thought you'd washed your hands of me after wedding Haskett. You never gave me the cut direct but you ignored me at *ton* events. I did try and write a time or two but I had little to say." He ran a hand through his hair. "How do you tell the little sister who worshipped you that you've become a scoundrel of the worst kind?"

"I suppose you dip the quill into the ink and move it across the page," she snapped.

Weston frowned. Sam had been a sunny child and had grown into a young woman full of optimism. He took her hand. "What's wrong? Where is all of this anger coming from? Yes, I didn't write to you much. I'm sorry I lost contact with you. But you had a husband, Sam. A new life. A new family. I was the idle, worthless brother you'd left behind. I know you're ashamed of me and what I've become."

"You never checked on me," she accused. "I was miserable in my marriage. Lady Rockaway ruined every day I spent at Rockwell. Haskett was under her thumb and wouldn't take a step without her. The sweet, sincere, awkward gentleman I thought I'd married became a stranger once we returned to Rockwell. His mother was unhappy he'd wed me and bullied me to no end."

Samantha jerked her hand from his. Even with the contact broken between them, her pain radiated from her. "Then I lost my baby. You don't know how devastating that was. My husband rarely visited me in my bedchamber before that occurred. He barely spoke to me after it happened and never touched me again."

She stood and began pacing the room.

Weston came to his feet and hurried to her as she gripped the mantel and stared into the fire.

"I was so lonely," she said, her voice small. "So alone. No one comforted me. No one cared if I lived or died. I wanted my big brother to come rescue me, especially after Haskett's death. To take me away and bring me home, where I would be safe."

"What do mean—safe?" he asked, wanting to get to the heart of the change he sensed within her.

She remained silent. He wondered if her secrets were as ugly and deep as his.

"Why didn't you just leave after Haskett's death? I would have welcomed you."

"Because I . . ." Her voice trailed off.

Weston placed his hand on her shoulder, wanting to offer her comfort. She jerked away.

"You let me down," she accused, her tone harsh. "You disappoint-ed me. You abandoned me." Her eyes narrowed. "I don't know if I will ever forgive you."

"Sam." He pulled her into his arms and stroked her hair. He didn't know how to make it up to her. How to be the brother she wanted. She was broken, almost as much as he was. He knew in that moment that she could heal. With George's help. His friend loved Sam. He would take care of her much better than Weston ever could.

He released her and she stepped back, crossing her arms protec-tively in front of her.

"Maybe you need George as much as he needs you."

"What do you mean by that?" she asked.

Weston shrugged. "I don't know what happened, but the entire carriage ride here he went on and on about how he despised his life and wanted to change it. That he was ready to settle down and how much he wanted a family. And a wife." He shook his head. "He talked about *you*, Sam. I think he'd already made up his mind to leave Windowmere after the house party and go directly to Rockwell to see you."

He saw that his words stunned her. Good. She needed to be shaken out of the depths of her misery. Relief filled him. He knew he could leave—and she would be in good hands with the man he trusted beyond all others.

"At least George was thinking about me," she said. "You never did."

"You're right," he admitted. "I was a selfish bastard who forgot about you once you left London. You were someone else's responsibility. Not mine. And I relished that. I was tired of being decent and honorable and always doing the right thing. So, I stopped doing it. You weren't around to see my fall. When you returned the next Season, it had already occurred."

Weston released a long sigh. "I've dug myself deep into a pit, Sam. An abyss of my own making. I didn't want to drag you down with me. I thought with you gone, I could do whatever I wanted."

She touched his arm. "Why, Weston? What happened between you and Lady Juniper? What could be so awful that it would make you hate yourself and everyone around you?"

He shook his head. His shame would stay with him. "No. You'll not get that out of me. Thank God she's dead and gone and I never have to see her again,"

He couldn't hide the bitterness. The only good thing that had happened since he broke from Juniper was hearing of her death. She and Kingsbury had been racing their phaetons in Hyde Park three years ago and Juniper had lost control. The resulting crash had taken her life. In his grief, her brother went straight home and shot himself.

Polite Society mourned their deaths, two young, vibrant souls being taken far too soon. Weston had celebrated by getting soused and staying that way for a week.

He saw the concern written on Sam's face and couldn't stand the thought of her pitying him. "I am what I am now, Sam. I won't have a change of heart. Not like George. He might be able to save himself. *You* might be the one to help him. I'm just a blackguard of the worst kind. I have no heart or soul left."

Weston placed his hand over hers. "I do love you. I always will." He leaned to kiss her cheek. "But I never should have come to Windowmere. Say my goodbyes to everyone."

He smiled sadly and left the room, thinking he should go and tell Wilson to pack. Instead, he went to his room and gathered up what coin he had and made his way to Andrew's stables, where he asked for a horse to be readied. As he rode the mount toward Exeter, he decided he desperately wanted to fix himself. George thought he could do so by marrying Sam and having a family and Weston was all for that. The two people he thought the most of would have a good life together. For him, one woman wouldn't solve his problems. He didn't believe in love and would never wed. He was tired of his life, though. Tired of wasting it. Fed up. Exhausted. Jaded by his experiences.

What if he chucked it all—at least for a little while?

No more mindless encounters with women. No more being the Duke of Disrepute wherever he went. Or even the Duke of Treadwell. What if he escaped and had the time to discover himself, who he truly was and who he wanted to be in the future? Nothing held him back. He could walk away and give himself the gift of time. He knew he would never totally heal. The scars cutting through his heart could never be erased. But he might figure out what he wanted in life and make a fresh start. He couldn't face decades of the life he now lived, else he'd go mad.

Reaching Exeter, he rode to an inn he had stayed at before and dismounted, leading his horse to the stables next door. He found a groom and asked for the horse to be put up for the night, giving the man ample coin to see to its care and asking that the groom return the horse in the morning to Windowmere.

"I'd be happy to do so, my lord."

"Thank you."

With that, Weston walked through the city and continued south.

CHAPTER FOUR

Briarcliff, Devon

ELISE OPENED HER eyes and inhaled slowly, enjoying the silence surrounding her. Claire, her daughter, snuggled close beside her. The girl had her mother's rich brown hair and violet eyes and Elise supposed she had looked much like Claire did when she was the same age. She would have asked her parents but they had never seen their granddaughter, despite the fact that Shedwell was only fifty miles from Briarcliff. They—meaning her mother—had washed her hands of Elise the day of her wedding to Lord Ruthersby. Though she had written to both her mother and father several times, Lady Shelby had finally replied that they were too busy with their new lives, now that they had raised their daughter. She was now Ruthersby's responsibility. Not theirs.

That was the last piece of correspondence Elise had received from her mother, a woman too vain to admit she was old enough to have a married daughter, much less that the daughter had also given birth to a child. In it, Lady Shelby had told Elise not to write again unless it was grave news. A birth. A death. Nothing in-between needed to be spoken of. The harsh words on the page still haunted her.

Her father continued to write her, however, though he asked her to direct any letters to him to their local clergyman, who'd see them delivered directly to Shelby's hand when they met once a week. She could never understand why her mother controlled every aspect of the relationship between her and her husband. Once, her father had briefly spoken of how Mama was the most beautiful girl to make her come-out that year and how surprised he'd been when she chose him to be the suitor she would marry. It was as if Papa spent every day on his knees, grateful to have wed Mama, and did her bidding in everything.

Mama loved wearing pretty gowns and being told how beautiful she was. She only became practical when it came to telling Elise what to do. At least she didn't have to suffer those lectures anymore. Not that her life was any better at Briarcliff. Oh, it had been ideal for two and a half years. Norwood Blakeney had been a dear husband, very considerate and thoughtful. They'd conversed on many topics and he'd been delighted when she found herself with child shortly after their wedding. Claire had been born a year after their marriage and was the light of their lives.

Then the accident had occurred. Norwood had been at his club, which was very close to their London townhouse, so close that he enjoyed walking to and from it every day they were in town. He had told Elise that he would stop on his way home and purchase a new book for Claire. Elise had spent that afternoon at the modiste, being measured for new gowns for the upcoming Season. When she arrived home, she went to wake Claire from her nap, knowing Norwood would be home soon for tea. The three of them would sit with Claire between them and read together.

Instead, a doctor arrived with the awful news that a carriage accident had occurred. A Lord Borwick and his young son had been killed, along with Norwood. The doctor had been passing by the scene and rendered aid as best he could but he wasn't able to save anyone. He had given Elise the book of nursery rhymes that was found next to her husband. She read from it every night before she tucked Claire into bed, always telling her daughter stories about how kind her papa had been and how much he loved his little girl.

When Elise fainted after the funeral, a doctor was sent for. He determined that she was with child. Norwood's younger brother had been most displeased. He'd already moved his family into the London townhouse and claimed the title. With the possibility of Elise carrying Norwood's heir, they had to wait until the birth to see who the true Earl of Ruthersby would be. She had delivered a boy, whom she named after the child who'd perished in the carriage accident, learning his name from the newspapers. Unfortunately, Nathan only lived a short while. He was found in his crib, dead after three days. The doctor consoled her, telling her that crib death was common and nothing could have been done to prevent it. Still, Elise watched the new Lord Ruthersby with fresh eyes. She wouldn't have put it past him to sneak in and smother her baby but she had no proof and kept the accusation to herself. The law favored peers of the realm. Even in the case of murder. With no proof and no male protector, Elise held her tongue.

After Nathan's death, though, she felt adrift. She'd written to her father, who explained that it wasn't a good idea for her to come home, especially with a young child. She was still hurt that her parents had not attended Norwood's funeral and now fumed when she wasn't allowed to return to them. As the dowager countess, she had the option of staying on with her husband's family and informed the new earl that she'd decided to do so. He had agreed—but it was Ruthersby's wife who was the real power in the family. Her sister-in-law had made Elise into the family nanny for their two boys.

She turned onto her side and smoothed Claire's hair. She supposed every mother thought their children to be perfect. Lady Ruthersby certainly did. Joseph and Josiah were holy terrors and had already run off three nannies before Elise became the latest one. She couldn't understand why her sister-in-law had named the boys as she had, the names resembling one another so closely, but she rarely understood anything the woman did. She only knew that her staying was depend-ent upon keeping Joseph and Josiah in line.

Unexpectedly, she had pulled off a miracle. The boys, who'd been badly behaved during her entire confinement, were now merely high-spirited. Trouble still seemed to find them but she had established a firm yet loving relationship with her nephews. What worried her now was the fact that Joseph had just turned seven and Josiah would be six next spring. The older boy would be sent off to school next autumn and the younger would follow the year after. Elise wondered if she would still be allowed to remain at the family residence, caring for the boys when they returned on school holidays. It terrified her what might happen to her and Claire if she were asked to leave.

That thought had kept her awake many nights in the last few weeks. If Lord or Lady Ruthersby did ask her to leave, she would be forced to return to her parents, whether Mama liked it or not. Perhaps her father could give her a small income that would allow her to rent a cottage in the country nearby or even a few rooms in London.

Claire began to stir and Elise slipped from the bed, quickly performing her morning ablution and dressing for the day. Then she went to the bed and gently shook her daughter.

"Good morning, my lovely," she said. "Are you ready for another day?"

Claire opened her eyes and smiled. Elise lived for the girl's smiles.

"Good morning, Mama. I love you."

She kissed her daughter's brow. "And I love you, my precious. Come, let's dress and braid your hair and then you can go to the schoolroom. You may read while I ready your cousins for the day."

Once she had Claire settled with a book, Elise went to the room Joseph and Josiah shared. Both boys were grumpy in the morning and it took twice as long to get them out of bed and dressed than it did Claire. Once up, though, they were in better spirits. Joseph ran and opened the door that led to the schoolroom. The small bedchamber she shared with Claire was on the other side of the schoolroom.

As they entered, a maid came in with the breakfast tray.

"Morning, my lady," she said brightly. "Morning, little lords and my lady."

The children greeted her politely. Manners was one thing Elise had stressed from the beginning with her new charges. It had taken a while but now both her nephews were responsive and kind toward the servants.

She helped distribute the breakfast and as they ate, they discussed their lessons for the day. Claire, having no nursery governess of her own, sat in on the boys' lessons and could already read as well as Josiah, despite the fact that she would only be four in a few days. She could also do simple sums and locate several countries on the various maps in the atlas. The atlas was Elise's prized possession, a wedding gift from Norwood, who knew her well. Where most brides would have longed for jewelry, the atlas let her know her groom truly understood her.

They were just finishing up when the butler appeared in the doorway. He never ventured to this part of the house. She noticed he held a letter in his hand.

"My lady, this came for you in the morning post. I thought you would like to see it at once."

He brought it to her and she thanked him. She recognized the handwriting as that of her father, though it appeared a bit shaky. Slipping it into her pocket, she watched as the children finished their breakfast. She'd lost her appetite.

A different maid appeared and took the tray away and Elise re-trieved the books they would be using today, along with three slates for them to figure sums and parchment and pencils for writing. She had Joseph start by conjugating simple Latin verbs, while Josiah worked on copying spelling words. Claire already had her nose in a book.

With her pupils all busy, she retreated to the corner and broke the seal on the letter. Several pound notes lay within, raising her curiosity.

She glanced down and began reading.

Dearest Elise —

I write this with a heavy heart. Your dear mama is gravely ill with the pneumonia. She has fought like a champion but the doctor says she is too weak to recover. I need you here, my child. She wants no one else to care for her but you. She has begged for me to send for you.

Please come at once. Bring Claire if you will. I have waited a long time to meet my granddaughter. I am sorry it's under such circumstances. I've enclosed traveling money if you need it. I know from what you've said that Lord Ruthersby is quite stingy with you.

Hurry, Elise. I pray you will be in time.

Your loving Papa,
Lord Shelby

She folded the bank notes and slipped them into her pocket. She didn't want her brother-in-law to know about them. She could use the money to buy new material so she could sew a few new gowns for Claire, who had hit a growth spurt. New shoes, too, since her daughter had said only yesterday that hers pinched her toes.

"Children, I must go downstairs for a few minutes to see Lord and Lady Ruthersby. Will you be all right?"

"Yes, Auntie," Joseph said. "I'm the oldest. I'll watch over everyone."

She patted the boy's shoulder. "That's a good lad. Finish your verbs and start your reading if you'd like."

"I could read to the others," Joseph said eagerly.

"That's an excellent idea," she praised. "Finish the conjugations first and then you may do so."

Elise went to the door and saw all three children engaged in their work so she left and went downstairs. Lord Ruthersby would still be at breakfast, reading his newspapers and sifting through his correspondence. His wife would still be asleep for a few hours and would take breakfast in her bedchamber before rising and dressing for the day. The earl she could handle. The countess was another matter. That's why she needed to speak to her brother-in-law now and gain his permission to leave before Lady Ruthersby knew what was afoot. If things worked out in Elise's favor, she and Claire would already be packed and gone by the time the countess was awake.

Entering the breakfast room, she stopped a few feet from him and cleared her throat. "My lord, might I have a brief word with you?"

He glanced up. Sometimes, it startled her when she looked him in the face because she saw so much of Norwood there. The two men had the same eyes and nose though this Ruthersby had a cruel mouth and supercilious attitude. Where her husband had been kind to a fault, this man didn't know the meaning of the word. She hoped he was in a good mood and would honor her request. And provide transportation, as well.

"What is it, my lady?" he asked.

"It's my mother. She hasn't long to live and is asking for me. My father begs me to come as soon as I possibly can."

He pondered her request. "You have never gone to visit them that I know of."

"No, my lord. I haven't. My mother and I are estranged. I do write my father regularly, though, and he replies each week. He is beside himself with worry. He loves her very much and wants to make her last days peaceful ones. I feel by asking for me that Mama wants to put aside our differences."

"I see." He took a sip of his coffee and set the cup down. "How long would you be gone? I know you tutor and watch over our boys."

"Not long, my lord. Papa seems to think Mama hasn't got much time." She paused. "He's also asked that I bring Claire with me."

"I see," he repeated. He closed his newspaper. "Very well. You may go."

"Might I use the carriage?"

"Oh." He looked astonished as if he hadn't thought of how she would get to Shedwell. "I suppose so. How far is it?"

"Around fifty miles."

"Hmm. Well, once the coachman drops you off, have him and the horses rest and then he is to return at once. Your papa will have to escort you home after your mother's funeral. It's only fair for him to resume that responsibility."

She blew out the breath she'd held. "Thank you so much, my lord. I will leave as soon as I've packed."

Ruthersby glanced to the butler. "Have the coach brought around and tell the driver where he's to go."

"Yes, my lord."

Both Elise and the butler left the breakfast room and the servant said, "I'll send a maid up to pack for you, my lady."

"That won't be necessary. I can do so myself. I could use a footman, though, in half an hour. He may bring my trunk downstairs and load it onto the carriage."

"Very well, my lady."

"Would you please send up the housekeeper? We'll need to talk about who will watch the boys while I am gone."

They parted and she hurried upstairs to the schoolroom. When she arrived, Joseph was reading to the other two. She knew he couldn't have completed his verbs but thought it sweet that he'd been eager to read aloud. She reached to the table next to the door and picked up the atlas Norwood had given her. It was the only thing she had of her husband and she would not leave it behind.

Since the children were busy, she hurried to her bedchamber. Her trunk sat in a corner and she wrestled it over and opened it. Elise pulled gowns from the wardrobe for both her and Claire and began packing. She'd almost finished when the door flew open, startling her.

Lady Ruthersby stood in the doorway.

"What are you doing?" she asked shrilly.

"I am packing, my lady. My mother is gravely ill and hasn't long to live. She is asking for me."

The countess smirked. "Lady Shelby always thought she was so young and beautiful. That she would live forever. You do know she never really claimed to be your mother? I overheard her several times telling others you were sisters."

That didn't surprise Elise in the least. Her mother had flirted her way through social events, acting as a woman half her age.

"You do realize how inconvenient it is for you to leave," her sister-in-law pointed out.

"How so, my lady?" she asked, already knowing the answer.

"You're abandoning my boys," was the reply. "Who will act as their governess? Who will keep them occupied during the day? See to their lessons?"

"Joseph and Josiah are both bright boys. A short break in their lessons will not do them any harm. Besides, they both love to read. I'm sure they'll do plenty of that while Claire and I are gone."

"Oh. You're taking her with you."

"Well, I certainly wouldn't leave her. Papa is eager to meet her."

The countess' lips thinned. "I'm sure he is. Still, who will watch my boys?"

"I've sent for the housekeeper. I thought she and I could discuss that."

"*You* sent for her? You are not the lady of this household and haven't been for some time. *I* will meet with her and decide who will supervise my boys in your absence."

Elise bowed her head. "As you wish." She kept it down until she sensed Lady Ruthersby leave.

A last glance around caused her to place her small mirror and comb and brush inside the trunk. She dropped to her knees and reached under the bed, feeling for her satchel. Retrieving it, she slipped in the satchel, a few books, and a stuffed rabbit that Claire slept with every night. She took the bank notes from her pocket and tucked them inside her reticule.

A knock sounded on the door. "My lady, is your trunk ready?"

She turned and saw the footman. "Yes, it is." She closed and fastened it shut. "Thank you."

She went through the connecting door to the schoolroom. Joseph was just finishing his story. He looked up as she came in. Claire and Josiah applauded.

"Cousin Joseph read us a story, Mama," Claire said. "He's a very good reader."

"He is," she agreed. "I want to talk to you all."

Joseph closed the book and pushed it aside. All three children looked at her curiously.

"Claire and I are going to go away for a little while," she explained. "My mother is ill. We are going to go take care of her."

"Will she die?" Joseph asked.

"Yes, my papa thinks she will."

"I don't know her," Claire said, her bottom lip thrusting out in a pout.

"I know. She is your grandmother, though. She and your grandfather would like to meet you."

"And then she'll die?" Josiah asked.

Elise nodded, knowing none of the three children had any experience with death.

"You will come back?" Josiah asked, a worried look on his face.

"Of course, I will. For now, though, you'll have a little break from your lessons."

"No more Latin?" Joseph asked.

"Not until we return."

He blew out a breath, causing her to laugh. "You may read as much as you like, though. I'll also talk to the groom and see if you can spend more time on your riding lessons."

Both boys cheered at that idea.

Elise stood. "Get Miss Molly, Claire."

While her daughter retrieved her only doll from its chair in the corner, she held out her arms. Her nephews came to her and she enfolded them.

"Now, be especially good for the servants who watch you. And your mama and papa," she told them.

"We used to be bad," Josiah said. "But we're good now."

"You both are very good boys. I will miss you."

"I love you, Auntie Elise," Joseph said.

It was the first time he'd said so. Josiah echoed his brother's words and Elise found herself tearing up.

By now, the housekeeper had arrived with a maid. "Go ahead, my lady. We'll look after the little lords. Have a safe trip."

"Thank you." She held out her hand and Claire took it, Miss Molly under her arm.

They went downstairs, where several of the servants told her goodbye. She asked the butler to let the groom know that the boys were to spend more time riding while she was away.

"I'll see to it, my lady. We'll miss you. Have a safe journey."

Elise left the house she had come to as a bride and now lived as an upper servant. Though her life had changed greatly since her husband's death, she still had a roof over her head. And she had Claire. Her daughter curled up next to her.

As the carriage pulled away, Claire asked, "Will Grandfather and Grandmother like me, Mama?"

"They will do more than like you, my darling. They will love you."

Elise only hoped that was true.

CHAPTER FIVE

Brixham, Devon

WESTON HAMMERED THE last nail into the barn and then took a few steps back to survey his work. He and Neal Digsby had built the structure from scratch over the last few weeks. It had felt good, spending the majority of his days outdoors, using his hands. Though he had accumulated and honed muscles from countless sessions of boxing at Gentleman Jack's in London, working as a laborer had refined those muscles and added new ones. He felt stronger than he had in years. Capable of doing whatever he wanted.

Even being a duke again.

He'd spent almost three months avoiding who he was. He'd begun walking south from Exeter, his destination unknown. He'd lost his fancy coat and waistcoat in a card game but gained his money back soon after. The coin had gone into his pocket and not to purchase new clothing. By now, his hair was growing out and his beard thick. He continued pushing southward, deciding he wanting to be near the water for a time. He'd always experienced a tranquility whenever water was nearby and often walked along the Serpentine in London for hours. Since he didn't own any properties by the water, Weston decided when he did return to his other life, he would be sure and invest in one and use it as a retreat.

He'd hitched a ride with a farmer traveling south. Digsby had journeyed north from his small farm near Brixham for the reading of his father's will. He'd been estranged from his parents ever since he'd wed one of the family's parlor maids and been ordered to leave his home. Katie, his new wife, had family in Brixham and the couple had gone there, eventually inheriting the farm after Katie's father passed. With Digsby's own father dying, the farmer returned to his childhood home for a brief spell. His older brother inherited the title and estate but Digsby received one hundred pounds in the will, which made it well worth his trip.

Weston had stayed on with Neal and Katie, who belonged to the handful of farmers in the area. Most men who lived this close to the coast were fishermen, sailors, or shipbuilders. Neal had tried to hire on a hand to help and couldn't convince anyone to stay on land. When Weston heard about his plight, he offered to remain for a bit. He'd rebuilt fences and repaired the roof of the family abode. Learned to milk a cow and how to slaughter a pig. Building a new barn had been the biggest task and now that it was complete, a sense of pride filled him. All it would need now were a few coats of paint.

He went to the well and washed up, knowing as it grew dark that the family would be eating soon. Though the food was plain and simple, with none of the fancy sauces he was accustomed to, Katie was a fine cook. He enjoyed her company as much as Neal's. Though he'd given up all trust in women long ago, he found himself wavering, seeing no guile in Katie.

More than that, he'd fallen in love with the two Digsby children. Maisy, at eight, had golden ringlets and more enthusiasm than a dozen children put together. Mark, her brother and younger by two years, was dark-haired and quiet like his father. Both children were intelligent and polite. As Weston entered the cottage and took his seat at the table, a deep yearning filled him. He wanted to be at his own table, with a wife and children. He realized it had been foolish to let Juniper Radwell ruin his life for so long. Why should a dead woman still rule his world, making his heart as heavy as a stone?

His former fiancée had spread so many lies about him that it was hard to tell where the truth actually began and who Weston really was. Like George, he'd suddenly tired of playing a role and being placed in a cage for all of Polite Society to gawk at. Once, he had been loyal and honorable. He had wanted to be a good duke and care for his tenants and workers. He'd believed in the good that lay within men. Until he'd seen Juniper with her brother. The sight had broken something within him. But no longer. He'd hit rock-bottom, dragging George down to the depths of despair with him. They had risen as phoenixes from the ashes, each creating a new persona and living up to their nicknames of Disrepute and Charm, debauchery becoming not just their way of life but a way to survive all the pain and frustration.

The concerns George experienced after years of such a wasted existence had planted seeds of doubt within Weston, which had driven him away from his friends. Truly alone for the first time in his life, the solitude had given him clarity, which was reinforced by seeing how loving Neal and Katie were toward one another and how devoted they were to each other and their children. Desire grew within Weston, along with hope that he could make the radical changes necessary. He would never be able to be the same young, idealistic man he'd once been—but with experience and maturity, he thought he might return to one who was honorable. Gone would be the shame and humiliation and ennui. Instead, he would find purpose in life.

And a wife.

The right one, of course. He'd partaken far too long in the pleasures of the flesh. He didn't want to live like a monk. It would take a special woman, though, to cause him to commit to her and her alone. If he were to have children—which he wanted very much—he wanted not only to be a good father to them but a good example. That meant no catting about. True, a majority of the married men of the *ton* had mistresses. If Weston wanted to alter his entire life and become totally separate from the man he'd been for years, he would need to commit fully to change. That meant promising himself in both word and body to one woman.

Now, all he had to do was find her.

"How is the barn coming along?" Katie asked as Weston slipped into his seat at the table.

"It's done. All Neal has to do is help me paint it," he replied, glancing to his new friend.

"You've finished? My stars, that went fast," Neal said.

"You helped build the bulk of it. It didn't take long for me to finish up."

"Can we help paint, Papa?" Maisy pleaded, her large blue eyes capable of melting the sternest of hearts.

Mark perked up. "Can we, Papa? Mama? I can do it. Mr. Wallace can show me how."

Weston hadn't let on to his title or background and merely gave the family surname when he'd met Neal.

"We'll see, children," their father said.

Maisy's bottom lip thrust out in a pout. "We'll see means no," she said, already wise at her young age.

He thought how much more she could do with a bit of schooling. Katie was teaching both children to read but she didn't have much time for it with all of the cooking and cleaning and sewing she did to keep the Digsby household running. Glancing at his friend, he knew as a viscount's son that Neal had a good bit of schooling himself and probably longed for better opportunities, including education, for his children.

Impulsively, he said, "Might we speak after supper? It's important."

Neal nodded. "Of course."

Katie encouraged the children to clean their plates and after the meal, she cleared away the dishes, which she and Maisy would wash. Mark went outside to start the final milking and Weston promised he'd join him soon.

With the two men alone, he said, "It's time for me to leave."

Neal sighed. "I knew you wouldn't be with us long, Weston. I'm only grateful for the work you've put in."

"You have taught me more than you know, Neal. I was at a cross-roads in my life. It's not so much what you've said but how you lead by example."

"Me? A simple farmer?"

He frowned. "You're far more than a farmer and you know it. You are a gentleman's son. Well-spoken and educated. Isn't that something you want for your own children?"

Neal shrugged. "Wanting and getting are two very different things, I'm afraid. Although I wanted my Katie. I knew by marrying her that I would be cut off from my family. My parents were terrible snobs. They always carried an air of superiority about them. Their son wedding a parlor maid was unthinkable."

"Yet you did so."

"How could I not?" Neal smiled. "I think I loved Katie from the moment I saw her. It was hell trying to stay away from her. I didn't want to be one of those men who pursued a helpless servant." He chuckled. "I became the helpless one. I couldn't think straight whenever I was around her. I finally worked up enough courage to converse with her and found her delightful. It didn't take long for us to realize that we wanted to be together, no matter where that together would be lived. I'm grateful we were able to return here and have a roof over our heads. Farming may not pay much but it's decent, honorable work."

"What if you could do more? For both Katie and your children?"

Neal eyed him with suspicion. "I'll not do anything illegal, Weston. I know of the smuggling that goes on along the English coast. I refuse to be a part of that, despite the fact that there's huge financial reward in it."

"I'm a duke," Weston said abruptly and gave it a moment to sink in.

"You're . . . a duke?" Neal sputtered.

"Yes. The Duke of Treadwell. My primary estate is Treadwell Manor, about thirty miles northwest of Exeter."

Neal whistled low. "I knew you were more than a man who could swing an ax or hammer." He studied Weston. "Why on earth have you lived with us for the last couple of months?"

He decided only honesty would suffice. "Because I had lost my way. It's a long, ugly story. One I will never repeat. I've discovered I am finally ready to return to society and be the man I am meant to be. Living here gave me time to think and clear up the many questions I had. I know now that I am capable of doing whatever I put my mind to."

"Then I am happy to have had your company, Your Grace. When will you leave?"

"In the morning. You once offered me employment. I'd like to do the same to you. My steward at Treadwell Manor, Mr. Starling, is getting on up in years. He's squawked about retirement before but I put him off. I think you would be an excellent replacement."

Neal shook his head in disbelief. "You want me. To be you steward. The steward of a grand, ducal estate."

"You certainly are intelligent enough. The position comes with a good-sized cottage close to the manor house. Maisy and Mark could be schooled in the village with Reverend and Mrs. Clements. Katie could keep house for you or I could see if there's a position she might be interested in."

"I am dumbfounded, Your Grace," Neal admitted. "But your offer is very tempting."

"Talk it over with Katie. And the children," Weston urged.

"I will but I'll tell you, my Katie will want us to seize such an opportunity."

"If you agree to accept the position, I know it will take time to sell the land and animals."

"When would you need me?"

He laughed. "The sooner, the better. Old Starling will be delighted to be able to finally retire."

Neal thrust out a hand. "We will be there as soon as the land sells, Your Grace."

Katie came up, curiosity written across her face as she placed her hand on her husband's shoulder. "Be where? And why are you teasing Weston? *Your Grace*. I hope you're having a good laugh about that."

Neal placed his hand atop his wife's. "We're not bantering, my love."

She laughed and then suddenly stopped, eyeing Weston. "You mean . . . you . . . are a *duke*?"

"Have a seat, Katie," he suggested.

Neal pulled her onto his lap. "Not only is he a duke, but His Grace has asked us to come work for him. And Maisy and Mark will go to school."

Between them, the two men explained the situation to Katie, who gazed at Weston in awe and said, "A duke has been eating my cooking. Imagine that!" Then looking to her husband, she eagerly asked, "When do we leave?"

"We'll need to paint that barn first," Neal said. "And then sell the land and the animals. Finding a buyer might prove difficult, though. No one around here wants to farm."

"I know who would buy us out. Sir Winston," Katie said eagerly. "His land is adjacent to ours. I've heard he wants more for grazing." She giggled. "If he buys our land, he'll probably tear down that fine barn you've built, Your Grace."

"Let him," Weston declared. "Do you really think Sir Winston is in the market for more land?"

"I know so. I heard it at church only last week. From not one but two others."

He knew the gossip mill among women steadily turned out news, as much in the country as it did in the city.

"If that's the case, it means you could come to Treadwell Manor sooner," he pointed out. "We'll go into Brixham tomorrow and find a solicitor to draw up the documents and then pay Sir Winston a visit with them in hand. If he's eager for more land, the transaction would be quick."

He left the couple as they excitedly discussed what their new life would be like and went to sleep in his newly-finished barn. Exhilaration filled him at the prospect of going home and beginning a new life. Like a snake shedding its skin, Weston was ready to embark upon the rest of his life. One of his choosing. He would no longer allow Polite Society to place him in a cell and gape at him as if were on display. He would become a model for what a good duke should be. He believed that would be easy because he'd been raised right and only fallen into bad patterns because of his immaturity in handling the unfortunate experience with Juniper Radwell.

Becoming an exemplary duke would be the easy part. It was finding his duchess that worried him. Every woman of the *ton* knew what a rake and scoundrel he'd been for years. Weston prayed he would find someone who wouldn't judge him on his past. A woman who would accept him, flaws and all, and help him build a strong future with her by his side.

CHAPTER SIX

Shedwell, Devon

E LISE WAS TIRED of being in the coach, the second day in a row. At least they would be at Shedwell soon. Claire was slumped against her, her long lashes dark against her pale cheeks. She had tried everything she could to entertain her daughter during the past two days but Claire had been as grumpy as her cousins when they arose each morning. She couldn't blame her. The roads had been rough, with the winds especially high, rocking the carriage more than usual.

She wondered how ill her mother truly was and if the illness was a ploy by her father to try and reconcile mother and daughter. Papa had said Mama was dying. Elise hated to be hard-hearted but she would believe it when she saw it with her own two eyes. She also didn't want to speak to her mother with Claire in the room. It was one thing for her mother to spew venom Elise's way but she wouldn't have Claire subjected to one of Lady Shelby's tirades.

On the other hand, she was eager to reunite with her father and have him meet his granddaughter for the very first time. She knew the two would fall utterly in love with one another. Elise had always been her father's shadow and she believed Claire would be the same during their short stay at Shedwell.

The carriage rolled to a halt and, a moment later, the footman opened the door, helping her and Claire out. Elise leaned back in to retrieve the satchel, holding the books and all-important stuffed rabbit that her daughter couldn't go to sleep without. Miss Molly already rested in Claire's arms.

The front door opened and she saw the local doctor exiting the house. When he saw her, he smiled.

"Lady Elise! How good it is to see you after all this time."

She didn't correct him since he'd called her that from her childhood. It might be nice to be Lady Elise for a few days instead of Lady Ruthersby, the dowager countess who didn't really belong in society anymore because she was a glorified servant.

"Dr. Wilbourne, I am happy you are here. If you have time to come inside again, I would like to discuss my mother's case with you."

Sorrow crossed his face. "Of course, my lady." He glanced down and, once more, a smile lit his face. "And who is this young sprite?"

Claire's brow furrowed. "What's a sprite?"

"This is my daughter, Claire. She will be four tomorrow. This is Dr. Wilbourne, darling. He brought me into the world years ago."

Claire frown deepened. "Where were you, Mama?"

Elise laughed. "I'll tell you sometime. Let's go inside. It's cold."

By now, the Shelby butler had appeared and two footmen hovered. "Hello, Baines. Could you have the footmen bring up our trunk?"

"Yes, my lady. You will be in your old room, of course. Lady Claire will be next door."

She shook her head. "No, she will sleep with me, Baines." Turning back to Dr. Wilbourne, she said, "Come inside. I want to find Papa and then discuss my mother's illness together."

Holding out her hand, Claire took it and they went inside. Baines asked if they would like to go to the library, while the housekeeper said she would take Claire to the kitchen for some milk and bread.

"I wanted her to meet Papa first."

Mrs. Baines looked startled and she began stammering.

"Allow Mrs. Baines to take Claire with her," suggested Dr. Wilbourne. When Elise started to protest, he said, "I insist, my lady."

She supposed their discussion would be too mature for her daughter's ears and nodded in agreement. Bending low, she looked Claire in the eyes and said, "This is Mrs. Baines. She has some warm milk and bread for you. You said you were hungry."

Claire nodded sleepily. "I am, Mama."

"Come along with me, Lady Claire," the housekeeper said. "Once you've eaten, we'll put you to bed."

"She'll stay with me in my room, Mrs. Baines," Elise said.

Baines led them to the library, where a fire was lit. She went to stand before it, holding her hands out, seeking its warmth. Dr. Wilbourne poured them each a brandy. She noticed he did not pour a third glass.

"Why isn't Papa joining us?" she asked, shedding her cloak and gloves and placing them on a chair. "Is Mama so ill that he won't leave her side?"

"Sit, my lady," the doctor ordered, handing her a snifter.

She took a sip, the amber liquid burning a path down her throat and pooling in her belly. They seated themselves in two wing chairs and she looked at him expectantly.

"Your mother is severely ill. I fear she hasn't long. When the pneumonia reaches this stage, there's nothing to be done except keep the patient comfortable."

"I see," she said, taking another small sip.

"Your father is also ill."

Fear trickled through her. "Is it also the pneumonia?"

"No," Dr. Wilbourne said, shaking his head. "It's his heart."

His words startled her. Her father had always been lean but robust, walking and riding on a daily basis.

"He had a heart attack six days ago. He is very weak, I'm afraid. I don't think he'll outlast Lady Shelby by much."

"You mean—he'll die?"

"Yes, I am afraid so. Very soon."

She began trembling. All her life, her father had been her rock. Even though she hadn't seen him in several years, their weekly correspondence had kept the relationship strong. The thought of him gone made her feel as if she were adrift at sea without any oars.

"I want to see him as soon as possible. Is that allowed?"

"Of course. I fear he has been hanging on in order to catch a glimpse of you. And Claire."

Elise decided she would see him alone first. Claire was already tired and irritable and in good hands with Mrs. Baines. Once she assessed his condition, she would decide whether or not to allow her daughter into the sickroom.

She rose. "I'll go to him now." She downed the rest of the brandy, as much for its warmth as the courage it might bring her.

"I'll remain here in case you have any questions for me after your visit."

"Thank you, Doctor."

She left the library, finding it difficult to put one foot in front of the other. Her father was dying. It was as if a part of her curled up and died, as well. He'd always been so kind and jovial. Now he would never have any kind of relationship with Claire. Selfishly, Elise had thought once her mother passed that her father would insist that she and Claire return to live at Shedwell. On the journey here, she'd fantasized about what they'd do together, Claire always with them. She thought her father could teach Claire to ride a pony in the pasture. Show her how to plant flowers. Read to his granddaughter.

None of that would happen now.

The thick carpeting muffled her steps as she walked down the corridor to his bedchamber. Pausing, she gathered her strength and courage before turning the latch and pushing the door open. His valet sat next to the bed and turned his head when he saw her. He rose and came to her.

"I'm glad you came, my lady." Tears swam in the servant's eyes. "I'll give you a moment alone with his lordship."

"I'll try not to tire him," she promised.

The valet sadly shook his head. "It's beyond that."

She made her way to the bed and saw the sunken shape lying there. For a moment, she only stared, trying to reconcile the man before her with the image of her father she'd carried in her head for so long.

The earl had lost a good bit of weight. His usually ruddy cheeks were sallow. His hair seemed to have fallen out in odd patches. His eyes, always so bright and lively, met hers. They were dull and listless.

She perched on the seat and captured his hand in hers, bringing it to her cheek and closing her eyes.

"My dear girl," he said, his voice cracking.

Elise kissed his hand and then kept it next to her cheek. "Hello, Papa."

"The doctor says it won't be long." His breathing seemed uneven. "I'm so tired. So very tired."

"I brought Claire to meet you," she said, hoping to tempt him to stay alive.

He tried to smile but the effort was too much. His eyes closed for some minutes. She would have thought he'd already passed except his hand remained warm.

Finally, he opened his eyes again. "I would like to see her. Tomorrow."

"I will bring her to you," she promised.

"Go see your mother. I . . . haven't been able to. Not since my heart gave out."

Elise kissed his hand again and lowered it to his side. "Rest now, Papa."

She watched his eyes close again and sat for several minutes, reluctant to leave him. She supposed she owed it to him to go see Mama.

The valet waited outside. "I'll be with him all night, Lady Elise. If I think it's the end, I'll summon you."

"Thank you."

With a heavy heart, she moved down the corridor to her mother's rooms. Opening the door, she saw an unfamiliar servant sitting at the bedside and supposed it was Mama's lady's maid. She went through a good three or four each year, thanks to her demanding nature.

"I would like to sit with my mother a few minutes," she said.

Without a word, the servant rose and left the room.

Turning her eyes to the bed, she saw her mother looking old. Much older than when she'd last seen her on the day she'd wed Norwood.

"Mama?" she said softly.

The countess opened her eyes. A sour look crossed her face as her mouth turned down.

"Why are you here?" she asked and began wheezing. Her eyes were bright with fever and a sheen of sweat covered her face. Her hands, folded on her chest, displayed blue nails that matched the blue of her lips.

"I came home to see you and Papa," Elise said.

"I don't want you here," Mama said testily. "I never wanted you." She stopped speaking only because a dry, hacking cough began and lasted for several minutes.

When it stopped, her mother glared at her. "I never wanted girls. Girls are competition for their mother. I wanted boys. An heir for Shelby. That never happened."

The coughing began again and her mother snatched a handkerchief lying on the bed and held it to her mouth. When she pulled it away, Elise could see the bloody mucus on it.

"You were always too pretty and too smart," her mother complained.

The words shocked Elise. "You always said I was only tolerably pretty."

"I lied."

For a moment, she remembered a long-ago dance with the Duke of Disrepute. He had told her she was very pretty.

"Go away," Mama said. "Go sit with your father."

"Do . . . do you know Papa is very ill?" she asked.

"Yes," her mother said, exasperation obvious in her tone. "We'll both die soon. It's a race to see which one of us will land in the grave first."

Her mother would never change. Elise would not allow Claire to meet this querulous woman. She had never had a good thing to say about her own daughter and certainly wouldn't about her granddaughter.

"Goodbye, Mama," she said, leaving the room.

She intended never to return.

CHAPTER SEVEN

WESTON HAD STAYED two days longer, meeting first with a solicitor in Brixham and then having the two of them call on Sir Winston without an appointment. He wanted to keep the old codger off-balance, fearing he would lowball the price if he knew how eager the Digsbys were to leave the area. Using his ducal charm and insistence, despite his rough appearance, Weston negotiated the sale in a matter of minutes. Having already had the Brixham solicitor draw up papers with the specific price, Weston urged Sir Winston to sign on the spot—else he might lose this opportunity. Flustered, the baron did as asked.

It didn't take long to pack up the Digsbys' belongings. All their clothing went into their lone trunk. When Katie wanted to bring along chipped dishes and worn linens, he had discouraged her, telling her to leave everything behind since they'd have all the items they needed in the steward's house. Reluctantly, she agreed and so they'd set out for Treadwell Manor. Weston rode on a horse he'd purchased in Brixham, using the last of the funds he'd set out with, while the Digsbys traveled in a wagon, drawn by their lone horse. Neal had seen that one of Sir Winston's tenants would take on the few animals they left behind.

The group now left the highway and turned down the lane. After a few minutes, Treadwell Manor came into sight. His throat grew thick at the sight of his childhood home. This is where he would raise his own children, emulating his father as much as he could. The duke had taught his son many good lessons, ones which Weston had ignored for several years now. He wanted to close the door on that chapter in his life and look to the future.

As they drew closer to the house, he glanced to his friends and saw disbelief in their eyes. Yes, they knew he was a duke and had begun addressing him correctly but seeing his grand house now had most likely made the situation real to them.

"Are we going to live here, Papa?" asked Mark.

"No, Son, His Grace will provide a lovely cottage for us."

"It's actually more than a cottage, Neal," he said. "It has seven rooms."

"Seven?" cried Katie. "It will take me forever to clean it." Then she grinned. "But I'll be thankful for all the elbow room just the same, Your Grace."

"Why do we call Mr. Wallace *Your Grace* now?" Maisy piped up.

"Because it's a polite way to acknowledge my title," Weston told the young girl. "I am a duke. Dukes are called Your Grace or His Grace. A duchess is called Your Grace or Her Grace."

"Do you have a duchess?" Maisy asked.

He laughed. "Not yet. But I would very much like to have one. Then she could give me children as smart and lovely as you and Mark."

Maisy grinned. "We are smart. Mama says we're going to go to school here."

"You will," he assured her. "It's a week before Christmas so most likely, you and Mark will begin your schooling after the new year comes."

"Will we get to read?" Mark asked.

"That and much more." He glanced to Neal. "Bring the wagon around to the right of the house. We'll leave it at the stables."

They turned and bypassed the house and came to a standstill at the stables. A groom came out, a frown on his face.

"Can I help you?" he called.

Weston dismounted. "Yes. See to my horse and the one attached to the wagon. The wagon can be brought into the stables."

"See here," the man began, taking a few steps forward and then came to an abrupt halt. "Your Grace? Is that you?"

"It is. Have a couple of footmen bring the trunk into the house."

The groom stammered and then a voice behind him spoke.

"We have no footmen, Your Grace."

Weston turned and saw the longtime family butler standing there. "Hello, Pratt. It's good to see you. What's this about no footmen?"

"I let them go, Your Grace. They had nothing to do with you never here and no guests coming to visit. We're down to this lone groom and two housemaids."

"I see. What about Mrs. Pratt and Cook?"

A shadow crossed the butler's face. "Mrs. Pratt passed in the spring, Your Grace. Cook is still with us."

He felt guilty not knowing any of this. "I'm sorry, Pratt." He motioned for the Digsbys to join him and said, "This is Mr. and Mrs. Digsby and their children, Maisy and Mark. Pratt has served the Wallace family since I was a boy."

Greetings were exchanged and he said, "Mr. Digsby is going to take Mr. Starling's place. Starling has written to me twice about his wish to retire. Mrs. Digsby, would you consider becoming our new housekeeper?"

She gave him an eager smile. "It would be a pleasure to serve you, Your Grace."

"Good. Pratt, you and Mrs. Digsby will see to hiring a full slate of servants. Footmen. Grooms. Parlor maids. Scullery maids. I plan to spend a good deal of time at Treadwell Manor from now on and want the house up and running as soon as possible."

Pratt beamed at him. "That is very good news, Your Grace."

"Show Mrs. Digby and the children to some rooms. They will be taking over Mr. Starling's house once he is gone. Then give her a tour of the house. Mr. Digsby, come along with me. We'll visit a bit with Mr. Starling."

As they moved toward the house, his valet came running out.

"Oh, my goodness! Is that you, Your Grace? Of course, it is. No one but you and your sister have eyes like that. But you look a mess. Where on earth have you been?"

"It's good to see you, too, Wilson. This is my valet, Mr. Digsby. Wilson, this is my new estate manager. Speaking of my sister, is she here—or is she going by Her Grace these days?"

Weston had figured in the time he'd been gone that George would have made quick work of things.

Wilson smiled. "Her Grace wed the Duke of Colebourne shortly after you left the house party, Your Grace. They are in residence at Colebourne Hall now."

"Have hot water brought up. I want a bath to wash the dust of the road from me and then I want to go see them."

The valet snorted. "You will need far more than a bath, Your Grace. Your hair needs barbering something awful. The beard also needs to go."

He chuckled. "I forgot how you always seem to boss me around, Wilson. So, you don't like my beard?"

Wilson's nose crinkled in disgust. "Not a bit. And neither will the ladies."

"See to the hot water. I'll be up once we've spoken to Mr. Starling."

Weston led Neal through the house, stopping at the steward's office. They entered and found Mr. Starling fast asleep, his loud snores filling the room.

"Mr. Starling," Weston called. "Mr. Starling."

The old man snorted and opened his eyes. He peered at Weston a moment and then came to his feet. "Your Grace?"

"Yes, it's me. And Mr. Digsby, your replacement. I've received your letters, Mr. Starling, and am at last ready to grant you your fondest wish. You may retire in the next few days, once you've brought Mr. Digsby up to snuff."

"Ah, thank you, Your Grace. A pleasure to meet you, Mr. Digsby."

"Likewise, Mr. Starling."

"You'll need to pick out a cottage on the property, Mr. Starling," he said. "I'd like to give Mr. Digsby and his family the house attached to the steward position."

"No need for that, Your Grace. I've made plans to join my brother in Bristol. He's a widower. We've decided we started life together and will end it that same way."

"Then I will see to your pension. You know you have been an important part of Treadwell Manor for many years and I appreciate your service. For now, share a little about the estate and tenants with Mr. Digsby. Tomorrow, I will take him riding about the property."

"Very good, Your Grace."

Weston left them poring over ledgers and went upstairs. Stepping into the duke's rooms made him feel like an imposter. These rooms had been his father's. He'd only spent a brief time in them because a majority of the last several years had been lived in London. He would have to get used to the idea that he was the Duke of Treadwell and take up the responsibilities he'd neglected for so many years.

Going to the mirror, he looked at the reflection of a stranger staring back at him. His hair, always thick and unruly, was wild. Coupled with the beard, he looked quite rough, much as he imagined a pirate might appear. It surprised him that this was the man who'd been able to strike a deal with Sir Winston. Fingering the beard, he knew Wilson to be right. Women would not care for it. It gave him a devil may care look, the very thing he wanted to divorce himself from. It was going to be hard enough convincing Polite Society that he had turned over a new leaf. The beard would definitely have to go.

Once his bath was readied, he sank into the hot water gratefully, soaking a bit before scrubbing the dirt from him. Wilson cut his wet hair and shaved him. When Weston gazed into the mirror, he recognized the man peering back at him.

"You did have a few clothes here, Your Grace," the valet said. "I plan to burn the ones you arrived in."

He chuckled. "Do as you see fit."

Wilson dressed him and Weston felt like his old self, though even more confident. He was on the right path now and would see that nothing lured him from it.

"I'm off to see my sister and Colebourne."

"They will be very happy you've come home, Your Grace."

Returning to the stables, he only had his choice of two horses, not wanting to use either one which had come the long way from Brixham. He would need to add to the stables over time. Mounting a large bay, he rode the two miles to Colebourne Hall and was met by a groom and the butler in front of the house. The butler signaled for the groom to take his horse and then greeted Weston.

"It is a pleasure to see you, Your Grace. Please, come in."

"I am looking forward to seeing Colebourne and my sister."

"Their Graces have just gone into the library for tea," the butler said as they entered the house.

"I'd like to surprise them. Let's forego announcing me," he suggested.

The butler bit back a smile. "A capital idea, Your Grace."

Weston bounded up the staircase and went down the corridor to George's library. As he reached the door, a maid exited.

"I plan to stay for tea," he informed her. "Bring another cup if you would."

She bobbed a curtsey, her eyes wide. "Yes, Your Grace."

He entered the library and saw Sam and George on a settee, their backs to him. Creeping toward them, he leaned down and wrapped his arms around Sam from behind.

She gasped and turned. "Weston!"

He released her and came around to greet her. Sam flung herself at him, squeezing him tightly. Over her shoulder, he saw George rise, a huge grin on his face.

"If it isn't the Devil himself come to call at Colebourne Hall," his friend joked.

Weston soundly kissed Sam and then threw his arms around George, slapping his back. "It's been too long, old friend."

"Where have you been?" Sam demanded. "You missed our wedding, you know."

He released George and took her hand. "I am sorry for that. You'll have to tell me all about it. How this oaf charmed you into marrying him."

One eyebrow arched. "This oaf is the man I love. And he loves me."

"Madly," George agreed. "Sam is the only woman for me."

She pulled Weston down and sat beside him. George took the nearby chair.

"It was a small wedding, performed by Reverend Clements. Andrew and Phoebe stood up with us. Jon and Elizabeth came," Sam said.

"My bride looked lovely," George praised.

"Well, I was a bit bedraggled," she said, a look passing between them. "At least we wed on the day we planned to. And we've been deliriously happy ever since."

Weston could tell there was something more to the story. He'd get it out of George later.

"I'm glad to hear it. I always thought you two would wind up together."

"Where did you vanish to?" George asked. "I came looking for you in Exeter. You never replied to the letters we sent to London."

The maid arrived with the extra cup and Sam poured out for them. Over tea, he described where he had traveled and the work he'd done on the Digsby farm.

"Being away from everything helped clear my head," he told them. "I, like George, discovered that I was merely existing and unhappy beyond words. I am ready to be the duke I should have always been. One who would make Father proud."

His sister's eyes lit up. "Does that mean you will be at Treadwell Manor more often? And better yet, that I may have a sister-in-law?"

He nodded. "I plan to make Treadwell Manor my primary residence so you'll be seeing a good deal of me. As to a wife? Yes, I've put away all the darkness. Juniper Radwell has held me in her clutches long enough. I tried to live up to her lies and be someone I wasn't. Now, all I want is to settle down and raise a family. That means finding myself a duchess. The hard part will be convincing the *ton* I'm no longer a scoundrel."

"You'll have to be careful," George advised. "Once Polite Society sees you are serious about marrying, all the frantic mamas will come out of the woodwork and foist their daughters upon you. An eligible duke doesn't come along that frequently. You'll have to weed through those who only want to wed you for your title."

"I know." Weston sighed. "Frankly, I dread going through the Season and perusing the Marriage Mart." He brightened. "Who knows? I may be lucky enough to find my duchess before the Season ever begins."

CHAPTER EIGHT

E LISE STARED AT the two coffins sitting at the front of the church as the clergyman droned on. He'd said several nice things about her father but when his remarks starting praising what a saintly, Christian woman her mother had been, Elise refused to listen.

She'd had but a single day with Papa. The day after she arrived, she had introduced him to Claire, having told the child how sick her grandfather was. Claire had climbed into the bed and snuggled close to him. The smile on her father's face had been worth the journey there. Moments later, he passed away, the smile remaining on his lips.

She hadn't gone back to visit her mother. She saw no sense in punishing herself. Elise didn't know who had told Lady Shelby of her husband's death but the countess hadn't lasted but a few hours after her husband's passing. That had led to their double funeral, with all their tenants and servants in attendance, along with her cousin and his family and people from the village. Cousin Leonard, whom she hadn't seen since childhood, would now be the new Earl of Shelby.

The funeral ended and those gathered left the chapel, with only the family going to the graveyard. Elise had not wanted Claire to attend a funeral at such a young age. Leonard also had two children, a boy and a girl, and they were also left behind at Shedwell. The skies overhead threatened rain any minute, which was why she suspected the good reverend kept his remarks brief. He came and offered his sympathies to her while the new earl and countess made their way to the waiting carriage.

She thanked the clergyman and then hurried to the vehicle as cold rain began pelting her back. A footman saw her inside and closed the door behind her.

"Nasty weather," Cousin Leonard said. "It's good things ended when they did."

Not knowing what to say to that remark, Elise remained silent.

"Will you be leaving soon?" asked the countess.

Her plans of asking Papa to allow her to live at Shedwell had been shelved. Leonard's wife had made it obvious she was only tolerating Elise and Claire being there.

"I suppose we will leave in the morning," she said cautiously and then added, "I will need your carriage to return. Since I didn't know how long I would be at Shedwell, Lord Ruthersby asked that I send his carriage home as soon as I arrived."

"Oh," Cousin Leonard said, blinking rapidly.

"That would be most inconvenient," Lady Shelby said, making Elise think the woman cut from the same cloth as the new Lady Ruthersby. *Inconvenient* seemed to be both women's favorite word, especially when it came to Elise and her actions.

"It would only be four days," Elise said. "Two there and two back. As you are in mourning, you won't be accepting social invitations."

"About that," Lady Shelby said. "We won't be in mourning, you see. Shelby hadn't seen your parents in ages."

"My father thought Uncle a buffoon," the earl added, angering Elise. "I hadn't seen Uncle or Aunt in a good two decades or more. My wife and I see no reason to mourn people she never met and I barely knew."

"I see."

Elise would mourn her father in her heart but she didn't have the coin to buy—or make—a mourning wardrobe. As for her mother, she was relieved never to have to speak to her again.

"You'll understand then that we cannot give up our coach for you," Lady Shelby said. "I wish to meet our new neighbors as soon as possible and become a part of things."

She gazed pointedly at her cousin. "Then how am I supposed to get back to Briarcliff?"

"I'll think on it," he said.

She wanted to pin him down instead of allowing him to be vague, especially if she and Claire were to leave in the morning. It made her nervous being away from Briarcliff for as long as she had been. She felt she needed to make herself necessary to Lady Ruthersby in order to continue to have a roof over her head, and Claire's.

They arrived at Shedwell and hurried inside, the rain now coming down in torrents. Mourning guests awaited them in the drawing room and they went to receive them. Elise spoke to all of the estate's tenants, happy to see so many of them after her long absence. Claire was present and she enjoyed introducing her daughter and showing her off a bit. The girl was well-spoken and polite and very clever for her age.

Once their guests left, she asked Baines for a supper tray to be brought to her room. Both she and Claire were tired and she planned for them to eat and then go to bed.

"Where is Grandpapa now?" Claire asked as they dined on a hearty soup and warm bread.

"He is in Heaven with your papa."

"Papa watches over me."

She smiled. "Yes, he does. He loved you very much." She didn't add that she hadn't loved Norwood, though she had liked him a great deal. They'd had a pleasant relationship but she'd felt no excitement or desire for him. She had done her wifely duty in the bedroom, thrilled that Claire was the result of their awkward couplings.

"Then why did he leave us?"

"I've told you, my darling. He was in an accident. The doctor tried to fix him but your papa went to Heaven instead."

"Will Grandpapa have a hard time finding Papa?" Claire asked worriedly.

She ruffled her daughter's hair. "Not at all. Your papa met him at the gates."

"Will they be friends?"

"I'm certain they shall."

Claire frowned. "Will Grandmama also go to Heaven?" she asked worriedly.

Elise choked on her soup. She sputtered and coughed and then regained her breath. "Where did you hear about Grandmama?"

Her daughter shrugged. "The servants were talking about her. Was she mean? They said she was mean."

She always wanted to tell her girl the truth. "Yes. She was very mean."

"Grandmama didn't like you, did she, Mama?"

"No. She didn't."

"And she died."

"She did. And now, it is time for bed. Enough talk about dying and Heaven. Let's get you into your nightclothes and I'll read you a story from your special book."

After she got Claire settled into bed, Elise packed their things. She sat in a chair for a long time, thinking about how her life hadn't turned out anything like she thought it would. Years ago, her father used to tell her she would grow up and find a wonderful man to wed. They would have lots and lots of children and live happily ever after. She had found a nice, shy man to be her husband but they'd had far too little time together. Even now, she had trouble sometimes recalling Norwood's face. She would look at the current Ruthersby and see bits of Norwood in him but she couldn't quite recall exactly what Norwood looked like when he was alive.

Unhappiness washed over her. She had no idea how to change the course she was set upon. She would love to marry again and give Claire brothers and sisters but that didn't seem possible. She'd been in mourning for Norwood two years ago and hadn't gone to London for the Season. Last year, she had accompanied the Ruthersby family to town—yet it was assumed she would stay home and watch Joseph and Josiah while Lord and Lady Ruthersby attended balls and routs and the theatre. Even if by some miracle they thought to include her next spring, she hadn't the clothes to wear to the many social events. If she couldn't participate in the Season, she would never find a husband.

And never escape the path she walked.

She thought about the men in the neighborhood surrounding Briarcliff. All but two in her social set were married. One was a widower and thrice her age. The other was a young man who still had two years left of university, far too young for her to consider. Even if she waited for him to finish, he would be like all young men his age and partake in several Seasons before settling down to wedded life. By then, she would be far too old for him to consider. He would only have eyes for the young, fresh girls making their come-outs. Her eyes brimmed with tears. She was only three and twenty but it seemed as if her life were already over. Elise stood and returned to the bed, slipping in and breathing in Claire's scent. It was time to stop being so selfish. She had her daughter. That's all she needed.

No matter what the future held.

THE SOUND OF thunder filled the carriage. Elise glanced out the window and saw the flash of lightning.

"Mama, I'm scared," Claire said, burrowing her face into her mother's side.

She stroked the girl's hair. "It will be fine," she assured her daughter.

Worry filled her, though. The heavy rains had slowed their journey, along with the rickety carriage Cousin Leonard had provided. She'd recognized it as one from her childhood, surprised that her father hadn't gotten rid of it. She doubted it had been used in years. It rolled along unsteadily, lurching as they hit holes in the road. Her fear was that a wheel would come off and they would be stuck in the middle of nowhere.

Elise wished now that she had refused to ride in the vehicle. She should have had one of the grooms use a wagon to take her and Claire into the village, where they could have taken a mail coach south. It might have been packed with riders but at least the coach would have been sturdy.

They hit another deep rut and the vehicle wobbled and shook. The carriage went on another few seconds and then it collapsed to the right. Claire clung to her as it came to a stop. Elise glanced out the window and saw the driver had left his post and was leaning over, inspecting a wheel. Moments later, he opened the door. Wind blew the rain in and she urged him to climb in and shut the door.

He did so and said, "My lady, the front right wheel has come off. The rear two aren't in much better shape. The roads are almost impassable for a carriage in good condition, much less one so poorly maintained. I can't risk us going on."

As Claire trembled in her arms, Elise asked, "What do you suggest?"

"We're at an intersection with a wide lane so I'm certain an estate lies at the end of it. If they've a blacksmith, he might be able to repair the damaged wheel. I've pulled the coach to the side of the road so if anyone is out in this treacherous weather, they will be able to safely pass by. In the meantime, you and your daughter should remain here, my lady, out of the elements. I'll have a good walk ahead of me and it would be a hard one for you to make."

She looked out the window, barely able to see the lane he had mentioned, much less any house at its end. It would be a long, cold, wet walk if they got out. The coachman could move much more quickly if they didn't accompany him.

"All right. We'll stay here," she agreed.

The driver exited the vehicle and slammed the door as another loud thunderclap sounded. She watched him start up the lane and soon lost sight of him. The December wind continued to howl as the rain pelted the roof of the carriage. Elise pulled the carriage robe about her and Claire and tucked it in. She didn't know how long the coachman would be gone, much less whether he would bring back a blacksmith to repair their wheel. She was cold and miserable as she rubbed Claire's back, trying to keep her daughter warm.

The minutes dragged by, the storm never letting up. She hoped the driver had reached his destination and would soon bring back help. The wind rocked the vehicle, which already tilted perilously to the right and she tightened her arms about Claire. Then the loudest thunderclap she'd ever heard sounded, causing her to gasp. Before she could say something to try and comfort Claire, the inside of the coach lit up like fireworks had gone off. She turned and saw lightning had struck a nearby tree, sparking a fire. As the blaze climbed, the tree rent in two and she saw the top half falling in their direction.

It was too late to escape the carriage. Elise pulled Claire to her and ducked her head as the tree crashed into the carriage.

CHAPTER NINE

WESTON CLOSED THE ledger he'd been studying and sat back in his chair. He'd been at Treadwell Manor a week now and was settling in nicely, getting used to the ducal suite and finding himself happy being away from the artificiality of London. It amazed him he'd remained so caught up in that life for so many years. He'd forgotten how he enjoyed the simplicity of the country and knew his time with the Digsbys had been well spent, bringing him back to his true self.

He had taken Neal around the estate on two occasions, helping familiarize his new steward with the land and tenants. Mr. Starling had left yesterday, telling Weston that everything would be in good hands for the next several decades, praising Neal's affinity for numbers and good nature.

Katie had taken to the position of housekeeper as if she'd trained for it her entire life. Quickly, she and Baines had assembled a new staff and they were putting the house to rights. Rooms were being opened and aired. Carpets cleaned. Furniture and silver polished to a fine shine. He almost was sorry he'd agreed to spend Christmas Day with Sam and George at Colebourne Hall since he was ready to show off his own home.

He glanced out at the dreary day. The heavy rain had kept him from walking or riding this morning. He'd hoped it would let up this afternoon but the rain continued and the day remained almost as dark as night, though it was but three o'clock. A little early for tea but he was ready to take a break before burying his nose in the ledgers again. He was studying which crops had been grown and harvested during the last decade and what animals had been bred. He still was interested in adding to his stables and would do so in the coming year.

Suddenly, a figure caught his eye. Weston stood and went to the window, surprised to see someone trudging up the lane toward the main house. No guests were expected. Curiosity had him leave his study and head to the foyer to see who the man was and find out why he was out in such a storm. He arrived in time to see Baines admit the drenched visitor, who stepped into the foyer, watering puddling under him.

"Good afternoon," Weston said. "I am the Duke of Treadwell. What brings you out on such a wet, blustery day?"

The man pushed back the hair from his brow and bowed. "I'm Mixon, Your Grace. I serve the Earl of Shelby at Shedwell, which is near Barnstaple. I'm driving the Dowager Countess of Ruthersby and her daughter back to their home at Briarcliff. It's close to Plymouth. We've hit a bit of a problem. The carriage is quite old and one of the wheels has come off. Two others are in poor condition. I was hoping you had a blacksmith on your property so he could help us out."

"I do," he assured the man. "It could take a while to finish the repairs, though. How are the roads in this weather?"

Mixon shook his head. "Hard to navigate, Your Grace."

"Why don't I send my carriage out to the dowager countess and her daughter? It's already past mid-afternoon and quite dark. Even if my blacksmith can help repair things, it's too late for you to continue traveling. You can stay the night and then set out first thing tomorrow morning. Hopefully, the weather will be more cooperative by then."

"Oh, Your Grace, that would be a godsend," Mixon said, relief on his ruddy face.

"Here, I'll go with you. We'll take the carriage out to the main road and I'll bring the ladies back to Treadwell Manor."

Already, Pratt had Weston's greatcoat in hand. The butler helped slip on the coat and handed him an umbrella.

"Thank you, Pratt. Come along, Mixon. We'll see the blacksmith first and then head to the stables."

Weston led the servant through the house and they exited a back door off the kitchen. They stopped at the blacksmith's shed and Mixon described the problem.

"We never should have left in the vehicle," the coachman confided. "It hasn't been used in years, not since the recently deceased earl was a much younger man."

"Then why did you set out on such a long journey in it?" Weston demanded.

Mixon looked sheepish. His eyes dropped to the floor. "I follow orders, Your Grace."

He wondered why those orders had been given but didn't want to put the servant in an awkward position.

"I'll get what I need and load it in a wagon," the blacksmith said cheerily.

"I'd be happy to help," Mixon said. "And then I can ride with you."

The three men parted. Weston headed to the stables and told John, his head groom, that he needed the carriage readied for a brief trip, explaining the stranded travelers he needed to collect and bring back to Treadwell Manor.

"Right away, Your Grace. I'll drive you myself."

Quickly, two other grooms appeared and the three men hitched the horses to the coach and Weston climbed inside. He recalled the Countess of Shelby, though not the earl. The countess was a handsome woman but acted half her age, flirting with both married and unmarried men of the *ton*. He hadn't liked how aggressive she behaved toward him and had never pursued a night with her. The coachman had mentioned the old earl being deceased and Weston wondered when the man had passed away. As for the Dowager

Countess of Ruthersby, no image came to mind. Since the woman was traveling with her daughter, however, he wondered about her. Would this daughter be of a suitable age? He'd told George and Sam that he dreaded hunting for a bride on the Marriage Mart next spring. What if his future wife now appeared upon his doorstep in need of help? Glancing out the carriage window at the pouring rain, Weston thought it a good thing that he was rescuing the pair. Just in case the daughter did prove to be eligible.

He knew Sam would berate him for thinking in such a manner. His sister and George were totally smitten with one another. She would want a love match for her brother. Weston was too smart to seek that again. Once, he'd imagined himself head over heels in love with Juniper Radwell. He had been taken in by her tremendous beauty and seductive ways, never knowing what evil was hidden beneath her surface. This time, love wouldn't play a part of any decision regarding a wife. He wanted a woman with intelligence and depth. One who was kind and could carry on a decent conversation. A woman who could effortlessly host an event and also birth him a good number of children. He hoped they could become friends. That they would respect one another.

But love? It would have nothing to do with his marriage. He planned to guard his heart and never suffer the kind of pain he'd been through with his former fiancée.

His carriage came to a halt and Weston bounded out just as thunder sounded so loudly that it hurt his ears. Then he was almost blinded by a lightning strike. Blinking, he saw a huge tree light with fire, despite the heavy downpour. Suddenly, half of it toppled over.

And slammed into the center of the crippled carriage.

He ran toward it as the horses screamed, trying to fight their way from the massive, burning trunk. Something snapped and the horses galloped down the road, three still hitched together while another one dashed away into the woods.

"John! Help me!" he shouted over his shoulder and the groom scrambled down while Weston arrived at the damaged carriage. The tree had crushed the vehicle. He only hoped its occupants were alive and unharmed. At least coming into contact with the carriage and then heavy rain had all but put out the fire.

"Hello?" he called. "Where are you? We've come to help."

A muffled sound came as he climbed up onto what was left of the coach and then someone called, "We're here. Please. Help."

A woman's voice. Low. Fearful.

"I'm coming."

Weston moved carefully, peering inside what remained of the vehicle, which now lay on its side. He saw a shape moving and realized a blanket covered the occupants. Pulling it off, he saw it was a young woman, bent protectively over a child, whose foot protruded at an odd angle. Whimpers sounded and he believed the foot might be broken.

"Hand her up to me," he urged.

The woman's head turned, looking up at him. Large, violet eyes gazed into his. Eyes in pain. Filled with worry. Ones which stirred something within him, some memory he couldn't place at the moment. He shoved it aside and reached out.

"Give her to me."

"I'll try," the woman said, her voice steady, which he found remarkable under the circumstances. "My wrist is injured, though."

She relaxed her arms but the girl clung to her mother.

"It's all right, Claire. This man has come to help us. I'm going to push you up and he'll hold fast to you."

"I'm scared, Mama. My foot hurts."

"I am a little scared myself but help has come. We must take advantage of it."

"We aren't dead, are we, Mama?"

"No, baby."

"We aren't going to Heaven with Papa and Grandpapa?"

"Not anytime soon, Claire," the mother said reassuringly.

He leaned closer. "My name is Weston. I'm going to help you and your mama get out. Then we'll go to my house and have some warm milk and biscuits. Would you like that?"

The girl nodded through her tears.

"What's your name?" he asked, though he'd heard the mother call the child Claire.

"C-C-Claire."

"Well, Claire, you'll have to hold your hands out to me. I'll clasp them and bring you out."

"Will you also get Mama?"

"Of course. I'm sure she'll want some milk and biscuits, too." He gave her a smile. "In fact, I shall keep careful watch over her so she won't steal any of yours."

Claire giggled. "What if you try to steal some?"

He chuckled. "You'll have to see if I do. Come on now. There. That's a girl."

Claire lifted her arms to him. Weston was able to grab her wrists and pulled. The carriage rocked and he prayed he would keep his balance and not drop the girl, causing her further injury. He glanced down and saw John ready, his hands also stretched high.

"I'm going to lower you to John, Claire. He's my head groom and a lovely man." To John, he said, "Watch her leg."

Weston eased the girl down until the groom's hands circled her waist and he released her.

John brought her close. "Hello, little lady. Let's get you inside the carriage where it's nice and dry."

"Miss Molly!" the girl cried and squirmed. "I need her. And Mama."

"I'll get them both," Weston promised and stepped back so he could peer inside the broken carriage.

"Miss Molly is her doll. It's here somewhere," the woman said. "Here." She handed the doll up and said, "I need to find my satchel."

"Forget it," he said, tossing the doll to his groom. "We need to get you out. The coach is unsteady. It could collapse at any minute."

He watched her fumble around with one hand. "Found it!" she called and lifted the satchel toward him.

It must have been heavy because she couldn't hoist it very high. Quickly, he reached as far as he could and grabbed it, bringing it up and tossing it to John, who caught it and set off for the ducal coach.

"Now, you, my lady. Are you hurt anywhere besides your wrist?"

"I bumped my head but I think my wrist is all that's injured."

"Push yourself up with your good hand," he instructed.

The coach tilted as she moved and he prayed he would be able to get her out before it crumbled. She shifted and sucked in a loud breath and then moved again. Somehow, she got herself closer to him. His hands encircled her waist and he pulled her from the interior.

"John!" he cried and the groom came running. "Take her. It's shift-ing."

He handed the woman off and then leaped to the ground just as the vehicle collapsed into itself. His heart beat incredibly fast as he took her healthy wrist and pulled her and his groom away from the accident. Sweeping the woman off her feet, he carried her to his carriage and set her inside, leaping in and closing the door behind him. Moments later, the carriage started up.

"Mama, my foot hurts," Claire said, clutching her doll.

Weston saw that John had stretched the girl's legs across the seat. The mother went to her knees on the vehicle's floor and smoothed her daughter's hair.

"You'll be fine," she assured the young girl and winced.

"Mama, are you hurt?"

"A little."

His hands captured her waist and brought her up to sit beside him on the opposite cushion. "Sit here. Claire's leg needs to stay as straight as it can and she needs to keep her foot still. I'll send for the doctor once we're back at Treadwell Manor."

"I'm not sure he'll want to go out in this storm."

"He'll come," Weston said with assurance, knowing everyone did their best in order to please a duke.

"Thank you," she said softly, those violet eyes shining at him.

"I feel we've met," he said. "Though I'm not sure where."

"The satchel!" she cried, panic on her face. "Oh, we must go back."

Weston rapped on the ceiling and the vehicle slowed and then stopped. He opened the door. "Did you get the satchel?" he asked.

"Yes, Your Grace," John replied. "Got it right with me. Figured it was important."

"Very good." He closed the door. "John has it. You need not worry."

He saw relief fill her. Her shoulders sagged. Without thinking, he placed his arm around her and pulled her close. He caught a faint floral scent. That and wet wool, which caused his nose to crinkle.

She squirmed against him and tried to pull away.

"You have had a bad scare, my lady. You and Claire both. I don't want you to go into shock. Just be still."

She quit struggling. He wanted to take her hand but that seemed too forward. Inexplicitly, he was drawn to her.

"Your man, Mixon, told us about your damaged carriage wheel. He and my blacksmith will see to it. He said . . . you are the Dowager Countess of Ruthersby?"

"Yes. I lost my husband two years ago," she said quietly. "In a carriage accident."

He wondered if she had been in that carriage with him. To live through that and then today and another carriage mishap would be unthinkable. He glanced at Claire and realized she was probably too young to remember her father.

"You and Claire will stay the night at Treadwell Manor. The doctor will see you both and we'll make sure your carriage is mended. If it can't be, I'll transport you myself to your home." He paused. "I do think we've met. Might you recall the occasion?" he asked, still drawn in by the unusual shade of her violet eyes.

"I do, Your Grace. You danced with me several years ago. It was my come-out. My first ball." She swallowed. "My first dance."

Weston remembered as if it were yesterday, all the years and scads of women falling away. She was the young woman whose mother had called her only tolerably pretty. He had thought his curvaceous dance partner very pretty and believed she would grow into quite a beauty. Her innocence had touched him and he'd decided to stay far away from her, even warning George off.

"My mother had warned me not to dance with you or . . . your friend."

"I remember your mother not being very kind to you."

"You recall that?" she asked, her surprise evident.

"I have an excellent memory, Lady Ruthersby." He smiled. "And I am happy to make your acquaintance again."

CHAPTER TEN

THOUGH FLUSTERED, ELISE hid it. The Duke of Disrepute's carriage had arrived at his home. He helped her from the vehicle, handing her the satchel which his driver had passed along, and then carried Claire in himself, talking to her in a calm, reassuring manner.

"Pratt, send the carriage to Dr. Cherry. He's to come at once."

"Certainly, Your Grace."

A woman hovered nearby and Elise thought she must be the housekeeper.

"Mrs. Digsby, we have guests," the duke told her. "This is Lady Ruthersby and her lovely daughter, Lady Claire, who has injured her foot or ankle. Everyone is wet and cold and tired. Have hot water sent up for baths and rooms prepared."

"One room will do for Claire and me," she said quickly. "We share one at Briarcliff."

"Is there a trunk, Your Grace?" asked Mrs. Digsby.

"We had one," Elise said. "I don't know if it survived the crash."

"Pratt, have two footmen retrieve Lady Ruthersby's trunk. We can see if any of the clothes are salvageable. Four horses escaped so have our grooms comb the woods and road for them."

The butler nodded and left the foyer, along with the housekeeper, leaving only the three of them as they dripped on the tiled floor.

"Do I still get milk and biscuits?" Claire asked hopefully.

"Plan on it," His Grace said emphatically. "But first, my lady, we must get you dry and warm. Your teeth are chattering. For a moment, I thought you'd turned into a magpie."

Her daughter giggled. Elise thought how very undeserved Disrepute's nickname was. He had been kind to her upon their first meeting and was exactly the same now, years later. She didn't think many dukes would be so solicitous of a child who was a stranger.

"If your clothes are damaged, we can check my mother's wardrobe. She passed away many years ago. The gowns would be out of fashion but would give you something to wear for now. I will have Mrs. Digsby place you in her bedchamber."

The butler returned and the duke said, "Young Lady Claire may have a broken foot or ankle, Pratt. Do you remember when my sister fell out of the tree and broke her leg?"

"I do, Your Grace. Lady Samantha was quite determined to do everything you and His Grace did."

"I seem to recall a chair that could be wheeled around. It had something that braced the leg, which allowed Sam to rest her leg and keep it straight and elevated."

"I do recall the chair, Your Grace. I'm sure it's in the attic. Shall I have it fetched for Lady Claire?"

"Yes. Bring it to my mother's rooms. The hot water should be sent there and to my rooms."

The duke turned to her. "Let's go upstairs. The sooner we get the two of you out of your wet clothes, the better. I don't want you catching a cold. Or worse, pneumonia."

Elise thought of the duke removing her clothes and felt her cheeks flame. No man had ever seen her unclothed, not even Norwood. When they had coupled, it had always been in the dark. He would hitch her night rail to her waist and had done the same with his dressing gown. She thought of how clumsy they'd both been, even after a couple of years of marriage. She had never gotten over her embarrassment of what went on between a man and a woman. For his part, Norwood performed the act quickly, giving her a kiss and then slipping his manhood inside her. It never lasted very long and she always felt relieved when it was over.

Something told her coupling with the Duke of Disrepute would be an entirely different experience. Ever since they had met at her first ball all those years ago, she had followed his and Charm's exploits in the newspapers. It was the rare gossip column that did not mention one or the other. From what she'd read, it was apparent Disrepute had been with more women than any man in England. He must know some secret for so many women to allow him into their beds.

As they went up the stairs, he kept asking Claire questions to take her mind off her pain, which endeared him even more to Elise.

"So, my lady, do you have any brothers or sisters?"

"No. I have cousins. Joseph and Josiah. But I can read. Better than Josiah."

"You can read? My, you must be very clever for your age."

She held up several fingers. "I'm four."

"Four? That's a marvelous age to begin reading. And how old is Cousin Josiah?"

"Six. Joseph is seven. We live with them since Papa went to Heaven."

"My mother and father live in Heaven, too. I'll bet they are friends with your papa."

"And Grandpapa. He just went to Heaven. Mama said Papa is waiting for him. They watch over us."

"Then they'll see if you steal my biscuits," he warned playfully.

Claire's eyes widened. "Oh!"

The duke laughed. "Better mind your Ps and Qs."

"What's that?"

"It means you better behave."

"I'm a good girl. Mama says I'm always good. My cousins used to be bad but Mama makes them behave now. Especially at lessons."

The duke flashed a grin at Elise as he opened a door. "I'm sure your mama is very good at that."

Mrs. Digsby must have been following them upstairs and said, "Is this the bedchamber you'd like Lady Ruthersby to use, Your Grace?"

"Yes. Comb through the wardrobe and see if you can find anything suitable for her to wear." He turned to Elise. "I'll leave you in Mrs. Digsby's capable hands and go bathe and change myself. Hopefully, Dr. Cherry will arrive by then."

"The weather and roads are miserable," she told him. "He might not come."

The duke cocked an eyebrow. "Oh, he'll come. If you'll excuse me."

Hot water arrived and the tub in the deceased duchess' dressing room was so large, Elise and Claire both fit into it with plenty of room to spare. Mrs. Digsby helped both of them bathe and wash their hair since Elise's injured wrist didn't allow her to assist.

A maid entered. "Here's the nightdress you wanted, Mrs. Digsby. The fire's been lit and the trunk is also here. That tree busted it up something good and the clothes inside it were all wet. The laundress will see to them being washed and then you can check to see if Lady Ruthersby can wear anything or not."

"Thank you," the housekeeper said. "See that the warm milk and biscuits are brought up now for Lady Claire."

The housekeeper lifted Claire from the tub and wrapped her in a huge bath sheet. "I'm going to put you in one of my daughter's nightdresses, Lady Claire. My Maisy is eight and it will be large on you but it's the best we can do for now. I'm going to take you to sit by the fire in the bedchamber. Mr. Pratt has the special chair waiting for you so we can keep your foot propped up."

Mrs. Digsby returned after getting Claire situated and helped Elise to dry off.

"I've found a few gowns we can try on, my lady."

"Thank you, Mrs. Digsby. You've been most helpful."

"Oh, there's nothing more I like than to help others. His Grace helped my family and I want to always take care of him and his guests."

She wondered how the duke had helped this woman's family but didn't want to ask.

Soon, she sat next to the fire. Mrs. Digsby combed Elise's hair, fanning it out to dry more quickly. A maid did the same for Claire. The gown she'd been given was tight in the bodice, which didn't surprise her. She'd grown breasts that were larger than most women had and had always been self-conscious about them. Mrs. Digsby had found a fichu and tucked it in so that they weren't on display.

The warm milk and biscuits arrived and Claire nibbled on them while the maid worked the tangles out of her hair.

A knock sounded at the door and the duke and another man entered. He was short and rotund, with sparse hair.

"This is Dr. Cherry," the duke said. "I've told him about the carriage accident and how he needs to look at your wrist and head and Lady Claire's ankle and foot."

Elise rose. "Please, see to my daughter first, Dr. Cherry. She never complains but I can see how her injury pains her." She went and took Claire's hand.

The doctor smiled and went to his knees next to Claire. "It's a good thing you've got this chair, Lady Claire. I am going to feel your ankle and foot and see if either is broken. Is that all right with you?"

The girl nodded.

The physician rotated the foot, causing Claire to whimper. Elise tightened her fingers, wanting to reassure her daughter.

Dr. Cherry said, "We won't have to manipulate it to restore it to its natural position. The ankle is not broken. Merely sprained. A severe sprain, all the same, but infinitely better than a break. Now, let me see your wrist, Lady Ruthersby."

He rose and Elise extended her right arm to him. He prodded her wrist and turned it and proclaimed, "Another sprain, though yours is much less severe than your daughter's. Having passed by the carriage—or what was left of it—it's a miracle nothing is broken between the two of you. You were lucky to have escape with but minor injuries, my lady."

"His Grace is to be thanked for that," she replied. "He rescued both of us from the carriage moments before it collapsed."

"Then I commend Your Grace on your quick actions," the doctor said approvingly.

He then examined the small bump on her head and said it was nothing to be concerned about. Dr. Cherry then discussed the care they would need. They both were to expect swelling and in Claire's case, bruising, as well as inflammation and loss of movement. Dr. Cherry wrapped both Claire's ankle and Elise's wrist in linen, telling them it must be snug but not overly so because if too tight, it would restrict blood flow and inhibit proper healing. He also recommended placing ice against the injuries for a quarter-hour every hour.

'I doubt you'll need laudanum, my lady, and your daughter is far too young for me to administer any to her. She will be in some pain for a day or two. Rest for you both will be crucial. As for you, after a day, you might do some light stretches when the wrist begins to stiffen. A mild sprain will respond to a bit of exercise three times a day. It will help increase the blood flow and flexibility."

"What should I do?" she asked.

"Place your palms together, as if in prayer." Dr. Cherry demonstrated by bringing his hands in front of him with the elbows bent. "Put pressure against your hands by raising your elbows slightly until a nice stretch occurs. Hold it for half a minute and relax again. Remember, that's in a day or so. For now, you and your daughter must get rest. Lady Claire needs a light diet. I will return to Treadwell Manor in two days and see what progress you've both made. In the meantime, I will place your arm in a sling. Lady Claire will need to remain off her feet and stay in bed. If she tires of it, she can sit in the invalid chair."

"Thank you, Dr. Cherry, for coming to tend to us in such a frightful storm."

"Not a problem, my lady. It's not every day the ducal carriage comes for me. I was happy to assist."

He removed a sling from his medical satchel and helped slip it around her neck and placed her arm in it.

"Having your wrist elevated will also promote healing. Pillows can be used to prop up Lady Claire's ankle whenever she is in bed."

"I'll walk you out, Doctor," the duke said and glanced about. "And be back to see that Lady Claire has finished her milk and biscuits."

As they left, Claire yawned loudly. "I'm so tired, Mama."

"I know, darling. It has been a hectic day. Why don't we put you into bed? I'm sure you'll sleep until tomorrow."

"You'll be here with me?" Claire asked anxiously as Mrs. Digsby lifted her from the chair and placed her in the bed.

"I will." She handed Miss Molly to Claire, who held the doll close and asked, "Where's Ralph?"

"Oh, he's still in the satchel. I'll fetch him."

Elise went and opened the waterlogged satchel and pulled out the stuffed rabbit, which was damp.

"Ralph will need to sit by the fire and dry some before he comes to bed," she proclaimed and set the rabbit next to the hearth. She also removed the book they read from each night and placed it with its pages open next to the rabbit. Finally, she removed the atlas. It had protected everything in the satchel, taking on the most water. A lump formed in her throat. It was most likely ruined. She braced it against the wall next to the fire, not having the heart to turn the pages and see the damage.

"You will need something to eat, my lady," Mrs. Digsby said. "I'll stay with Lady Claire. Would that be all right, my lady?" she asked

Claire. "Your mama can get a bite to eat and then she'll be with you."

"Watch your biscuits, Mama," her daughter warned. "His Grace might steal one."

Elise kept a straight face. "I will do so." She kissed her daughter's brow as Mrs. Digsby placed a pillow under Claire's ankle and then brought the bedclothes up.

"She'll be fine, my lady. I'll tell her a story or two," the housekeeper promised. "Ones that my girl and boy enjoy."

"Thank you, Mrs. Digsby." Then she touched her hair. "Oh, it's not quite dry yet."

"Leave it down, my lady, until it does."

She didn't know if that was appropriate, especially around a duke. Before she could disagree with Mrs. Digsby, the duke entered the bedchamber again.

"I see you're all settled in, Lady Claire."

"Mama needs to eat. But don't steal her biscuits."

The duke clutched his heart. "Ah, my plans have been foiled. Oh, well." He perched on the side of the bed. "I will see to your mama now. Tomorrow, when you tire of your bed, I will roll you about Treadwell Manor so you may see my house."

"We cannot impose upon you, Your Grace," Elise protested. "We should continue on to Briarcliff." How they would get there, though, was a mystery. With Claire's injury, the thought of the two of them riding in a cramped mail coach seemed impossible.

The duke faced her. "You heard Dr. Cherry, my lady. Both you and your daughter need plenty of rest to recover from your injuries."

"It's almost Christmas, Your Grace. I don't think—"

"You don't have to think, Lady Ruthersby," he replied, an enigmatic light coming into his eyes. "I will take care of that for you." He turned and pressed a soft kiss upon Claire's brow.

"Goodnight, Lady Claire. I will see you in the morning. Sleep well."

Elise's throat grew thick with emotion at the duke's sweet gesture. It had been so long since anyone had showed Claire—or Elise, herself—any kindness. The two had depended only upon each other. Now, a veritable stranger's simple gesture tore at her heart.

He stood. "You look famished, my lady. Let's go downstairs and see what Cook will bring us."

With that, the Duke of Disrepute took Elise's arm and guided her from the room.

CHAPTER ELEVEN

WESTON HAD SATISFIED his curiosity about the young woman he'd danced with years ago by plying her daughter with questions. He had wanted to take the child's mind off her aching ankle but was rewarded with knowledge every time she replied.

So, Lady Elise had had wed Ruthersby. He remembered the earl, who had been a few years behind him at school. A very scholarly type, with absolutely no social skills. How he'd landed such a curvaceous beauty was beyond Weston. He vaguely recalled meeting the new, haughty earl and countess last Season. The countess had flirted outrageously in front of her husband, something he didn't approve of. Because of that, he'd never pursued her. He was glad now that he hadn't.

Because he most definitely wanted to pursue Elise Blakeney.

Not for a night, as he would have in the past. For all the nights to come. He couldn't think of a more suitable match. She wasn't some featherhead straight from the schoolroom. She carried herself with a dignity and grace. She wasn't tongue-tied around him. Most likely, she had been the one who had taught her daughter to read at an extremely young age, which meant she had a love of books and knowledge. She would be interesting. Unassuming. She was already a good mother, based upon the interaction he'd seen between her and her daughter. And she was more than tolerably pretty.

Elise Blakeney was downright beautiful.

Her hair, which had been drying when he and Dr. Cherry arrived, remained down, falling about her shoulders and almost to her waist. It was a burnished brown with a slight hint of red in it, rich and thick. Her skin was like cream, with a faint blush touching her cheeks every now and then. Her rosebud mouth cried out to be kissed. More than anything, he was taken in by the luminous, violet eyes which had compelled him to ask her to dance at that ball so long ago. She hadn't lost her trim waist after childbirth and he was itching to pull the fichu from her gown's neckline and gaze upon the ample breasts he remembered.

All in all, Lady Ruthersby was duchess material in his eyes. She would be a good companion. A wonderful mother to their children. A marvelous hostess.

What he had to decide was how to convince her to marry him.

He didn't know if she had been in love with her husband. He doubted it. Most marriages in the *ton* were arranged or decided upon to further a family's wealth or social standing. She wouldn't have a dowry this time around but the lack of one wouldn't stop him. As one of the wealthiest men in England, he didn't need it. He would need to sound her out about her marriage. Learn exactly when her husband passed away. From what she had said earlier, it seemed Ruthersby had been gone long enough for Lady Ruthersby to consider wedding again.

Then he recalled the child mentioning her grandpapa dying. That meant Lady Ruthersby would be back in mourning. The thought irritated him. Weston had never been one to wait on anything. What he wanted, he took.

And he wanted Elise Blakeney before someone else snatched her up.

He would need to tread lightly and discover what he could about her father's passing. He also remained curious about something Claire had said. How her cousins were poorly behaved but that Mama made them behave now at lessons. Coupled with learning that Claire slept with her mother, he had an idea that the new Lord and Lady Ruthersby were using their sister-in-law as an unpaid governess for their sons.

It surprised him how much the thought angered him.

They reached the winter parlor and entered. He indicated for her to sit while he rang for Pratt. Normally, he'd want Katie but she had remained at Claire's bedside.

"We missed tea but her ladyship is rather tired after her journey and accident, Pratt," he told the butler. "Have Cook prepare a supper for us. It's to be brought here."

He liked the winter parlor for its intimacy, knowing the food would be rolled in on a teacart and no footmen would be hanging about, listening to their conversation.

"I'll take care of it at once, Your Grace," the butler said and left.

Weston turned and saw she'd risen, going to the fire. She held her palms out to the blaze. His mother's dress was a bit tight on her, revealing her curves. The tempting mass of hair that tumbled down her back called to him as a siren. He longed to run his fingers through it.

Joining her, he also held his hands out. "It's very cold for December in Devon. The rain and wind make the cold's bite even worse."

Her hands fell and she returned to her chair. "Yes. I've lived in Devon all my life, except for time spent in London. I don't remember a colder winter, much less one coming so early."

He took a seat near her. "Claire said both her papa and grandpapa were in heaven. How long has it been since they passed?"

"My husband died three years ago come March. A carriage accident in London."

"March, you say? My friend, the Duke of Windham, married a widow who lost her husband and child in a carriage accident around that same time."

Her eyes widened. "Lord Borwick? And Nathan?"

"Yes. It must have been the same accident. Phoebe, the former Lady Borwick, wed my friend this past summer and is now the Duchess of Windham."

He thought to plant in her head that widows do remarry. Especially when it's to a duke.

Tears now welled in her eyes. He reached for her hand and squeezed it. "Did I say something wrong?" he asked gently.

"No. I . . . had just learned that I was with child when Ruthersby died. We had to wait months to see if I birthed a boy or girl in order to see if the babe would become the new Earl of Ruthersby." She swallowed. "I had a son and named him Nathan, after the boy in the accident. I thought that little boy hadn't lived but a part of him could live on through my Nathan."

Tears spilled down her cheeks. Without thinking, he reached up, his thumbs wiping them away. The contact sparked something within him. Something he hadn't felt before. From the look on her face, neither had she. He lowered his hands and fumbled, finding a handkerchief in his coat pocket and presenting it to her.

"Thank you," she said softly and pressed it to each cheek. Then she added, "My boy only lived three days. That meant my husband's younger brother became the earl."

Weston could see it now. The man and his obnoxious wife, hovering about, waiting to see if he or an infant would become the next Earl of Ruthersby. The baby's death had proved convenient.

"So, you've been a widow for a while now. I don't recall seeing you last Season. Isn't it time you began to circulate in society again?"

A shadow crossed her face. "No. I am too busy for that."

"Doing what?" he demanded.

She looked taken aback by his question. "I . . . help care for my two nephews. They need me. Their parents . . . aren't . . . well, they are busy themselves. The boys need attention and understanding."

"You act as their caregiver? Their governess?"

She nodded.

"I suppose they pay you no salary."

Lady Ruthersby bit her lip. A frisson of desire rippled through him. *He* wanted to be the one sinking his teeth into her full, bottom lip.

"They do provide a home for Claire and me." She shrugged. "Besides, my father passed away a couple of days ago. I will be in mourning for him."

"I knew your father slightly," Weston said. "He was a kind, jovial man. A man who would want his daughter taken care of. Your brother-in-law isn't doing so. You need to participate in the Season, my lady, and find yourself a new husband. Besides, those boys are almost old enough to be leaving for school. Where will that leave you?" he asked. "You need to think of your daughter. You are a good mother. You need to find her a father."

Her eyes narrowed. "She had a father. She doesn't need another one."

"You know what I mean," he protested. "You—and she—could benefit if you get out of that household and move on."

She shook her head, anger spotting her smooth, porcelain cheeks. "You men think it's all so easy. I'll tell you, it's not. I'm in a precarious position with the boys close to going away to school. Cousin Leonard and his wife, the new Earl and Countess of Shelby, already made it clear they don't want me or Claire at Shedwell. You see how little they think of us, sending us out in a carriage that should have been scrapped years ago. And even if Ruthersby and his wife agreed I could participate in the Season, I haven't any funds for gowns. I also haven't been to any social events in London since before my husband's death. Who would issue me invitations? What would I wear?"

Lady Ruthersby stood and began pacing. "I am doing the best I can, Your Grace. Hanging on by a thread. Trying not to rock the boat and have it capsize on me. Yes, I do have Claire to think of. Yes, I would like to wed again someday. But I can wish all I want and none of that will ever come true. I am dependent upon relatives who think little of me. I'm not going to alienate them and have them toss us to the street, especially when I know my cousin and father's heir wouldn't bother to take us in."

He sprang to his feet and came to stand in front of her. He took her elbows in his hands. Being so close to her, he could smell the soap from her recent bath. The scent of rosemary rising from her hair. No woman had tempted him since Juniper.

Until now.

Weston lowered his mouth to hers. Their lips touched and electricity raced through him. He fought the urge to plunge into her and brushed his lips against hers instead. She was a wounded little bird and he couldn't scare her off. He had plans for her and needed her cooperation.

Then a knock sounded at the door. She jerked away from him and hurried to the fire, her back to the room.

"Come!" he called, irritated beyond words.

A footman rolled in a cart of food. "Where would you like it, Your Grace?" he asked.

Lady Ruthersby turned, her face drained of color.

"I find I am feeling ill, Your Grace," she said. "You'll have to eat without me."

She fled the room.

He was an idiot.

ELISE HURRIED FROM the winter parlor, her heart pounding violently. She found her way back to the massive staircase and hurried up it and down the corridor to the bedchamber where Claire awaited. No servants were in the hallway so she paused, leaning against the wall, trying to compose herself on the chance Claire might awaken and see how upset her mother was.

The Duke of Disrepute had kissed her.

And she had wanted him to.

From the moment he'd pulled her from the carriage and she'd recognized him, an odd sense of yearning had filled her. It was ridiculous, of course, to think a wayward, handsome as sin duke would look twice at a widow with a child. When he'd scooped Claire up and chatted with her, it tugged at her heartstrings, this big, wealthy, titled gentleman talking to her little girl, teasing her like a father would. It made Elise want even more to wed again. To have children. To have a husband who would be a companion. Someone to take away the deep loneliness that filled her.

When the duke had escorted her downstairs, the scent of his sandalwood soap filled her, along with a clean, masculine smell that made her want to cling to him. She'd never experienced such a physical attraction before. At least, not since the last time he'd held her in his arms and danced with her.

"Blast," she muttered to herself.

She was delusional. He was the Duke of Disrepute. He bedded women left and right. She happened to be available. Of course, he would try to worm his way into her good graces and then slip into her bed. Worse, she wanted him there. She knew from what the gossip columns reported that he only spent one night with the women he chose. They only came together the one time and then he moved on to the next female who caught his fancy.

Tonight, the Duke of Disrepute would come to her. She knew it in her bones. He would make love to her and discard her. Come this time next week, he wouldn't even remember her name, much less their encounter.

Well, this was one widow who would turn him down. It might be the hardest thing she ever did, but she *would* do it. She had to. First, she had Claire with her and couldn't leave her daughter alone and go with the duke to his bed. Second, though no one else seemed to value her, Elise had to value herself. That meant no casual tryst of one night. The next time she gave herself to a man, it would be to the man who was her husband. She wasn't a merry widow who would allow men to hop into her bed for a brief spell and then abandon her.

The duke had convinced her of one thing, though. It was time to find Claire a father. Or rather, stepfather. She needed a man who would be kind to her daughter and treat her as his own. She longed for more children and that meant marrying again. She had thought it impossible since she'd never go to *ton* events again—but she didn't have to in order to find a husband. She didn't have to wed another earl. She didn't need a man who possessed a title. She only needed one with a good heart, a man who could provide for her and Claire. She could wed a barrister. A doctor. Even a clergyman. Simply because she was the daughter of an earl, she didn't have to remain in her own social class. By broadening her choices, she would be able to find what she was looking for.

Elise took a deep breath and continued down the corridor, opening the door to the former duchess' quarters. She spied Claire asleep in the large bed, Mrs. Digsby sitting in the chair watching over her.

Going to the housekeeper, she said, "Thank you for staying with her."

"My pleasure, Lady Ruthersby. She's a little love, that one."

"You said you have a daughter."

"Yes, my Maisy. She's eight and Mark, my boy, is six. They are my pride and joy." Mrs. Digsby paused. "I know you are tired, my lady. Let me help you from your gown. I've found a night rail and dressing gown for you. I can also plait your hair if it's dry."

The housekeeper aided Elise, even helping her into bed and placing a pillow beside her and gently lowering Elise's wrist to rest upon it.

"I'll check on your gowns now, my lady, and Lady Claire's, too. Hopefully, some can be salvaged from what was inside your trunk."

"Thank you, Mrs. Digsby," she murmured as she drifted off to sleep.

And dreamed of dancing with Disrepute.

CHAPTER TWELVE

THE NEXT DAY, Weston headed to the breakfast room. He wanted very much to go see his two guests but didn't think it appropriate showing up at their bedchamber so early in the morning. Dr. Cherry had said both patients needed rest. Resting meant staying put.

And he was determined they would stay.

So much that he had sent Mixon back to Shedwell on one of the stray horses they'd rounded up. A Treadwell groom accompanied Mixon, with both men leading the remaining horses that had been located. Weston had also sent a footman to Briarcliff with news of the carriage accident that had occurred, informing Lord Ruthersby that his sister-in-law and her daughter would remain at Treadwell Manor for the next week or so as they recovered from their injuries.

When he reached the bottom of the staircase, he met Katie, who held a tray in her hands.

"Are you taking that to our guests?" he asked.

"Yes, Your Grace. Lady Ruthersby is already up and I've helped her to dress. Lady Claire is still fast asleep, though. I thought it would be better for them to have a quiet breakfast in their room."

"I agree. Do you think I could stop by and check on them later this morning?"

She smiled, her eyes gleaming with the same mischief Maisy's had in them when she was up to something.

"Oh, I think that would be a grand idea, Your Grace," she said loftily. "In fact, I'll make sure Lady Ruthersby is ready to receive you. Shall we say ten o'clock?"

"Very well."

He breakfasted and then went to his study. The same ledger he'd pored over yesterday was open. It had been less than a day since he'd sat here and spied Mixon coming up the drive. Less than a day since his world had turned upside down.

It was the uncompleted kiss that had kept him up half the night. He'd barely touched his lips to Elise's when they were interrupted. He'd lain awake, wondering what the feel of her skin was like. What she might taste like. How soon it would take him to persuade her to marry him.

Her reaction sent him mixed messages. He believed she had wanted the kiss. She certainly didn't push him away or turn her head aside. Then again, he'd barely begun when their supper had arrived. Had she wanted him to kiss her or not? Would she have let him go further than a kiss? She'd walked out abruptly, making him feel as if he'd done something wrong. Perhaps he had acted too quickly. They'd hardly spent any time in each other's company. He was a known rake, one her own mother had warned her about years ago when she'd made her come-out. If she'd read any of the gossip rags, she would know about his adventures in the bedroom.

He was different now. George had challenged him regarding the way they'd lived their lives. Weston had taken the time to truly think about what he really wanted out of life. Who he wanted to be. The kind of duke he knew he could be. No one in London knew that. Not the members of the *ton* or the London newspapers. Only Sam and George knew what lay in his heart. That Weston was weary of being Disrepute and longed to be a family man.

It would be important to bide his time. First, he had to keep Elise here for a little while. She had to see him for himself, not the cartoonish character lampooned in the newspapers. She might even be a little afraid of him.

And afraid of feeling anything for him.

She couldn't deny the spark between them, though. She might not know she desired him—but her body betrayed her. Now, he would need to walk a fine line, balancing between being a perfect gentleman and host with hoping to finally get her alone at some point in order to explore whatever connection they might have.

He did his best to immerse himself in the ledger and read about crop rotations and profits and losses. It proved to be ridiculous. He only wanted to concentrate on the way Elise Blakeney smelled. He sat back in his chair and closed his eyes, fantasizing about a true kiss with her. Touching those magnificent breasts. Burying himself in her.

Quickly, he sat up. Christmas was two days from now. She would still be here. He dashed off a brief note to Sam, explaining that he had unexpected guests turn up and that he wanted to bring them with him for Christmas Day dinner. He chuckled at how vague he was. Sam would think it might be Jon and Elizabeth who'd turned up at Treadwell Manor. He grinned. She would get the surprise of her life when he came in with a beautiful woman and her enchanting daughter. He would add to that surprise by telling his sister of his plans to marry the widow.

Summoning Pratt, he told his butler the letter was to be delivered at once to his sister, despite the fact that the rain was still falling.

Only moments after Pratt left, a knock sounded at the door and he said, "Come."

Lady Ruthersby entered. She wore what had to be one of her own gowns. For a moment, he was disappointed, liking her far better in one of his mother's tight concoctions. He noticed the gown was a deep green.

Was she in mourning? Or not? The color did not speak to that state.

"Good morning, Lady Ruthersby," he said cheerily, rising behind his desk. "Won't you come in and have a seat?"

She did so and said, "Mrs. Digsby said you were coming up to see us. I thought I would come to you instead so you wouldn't be inconvenienced."

"Nothing concerning you inconveniences me, my lady." He almost cringed. His words sounded far too flirtatious to his own ears. Who knew what they sounded like to hers?

"I wished to discuss with you—"

"Did you sleep well last night?"

"I . . . well, I suppose I did. As well as could be expected with my throbbing wrist. Claire wasn't her usual, restless self, thrashing about the bed. She must have been very tired."

"She is a lovely girl. I am very taken with her. I have always seen myself with daughters."

"You . . . you want . . . children?" she sputtered. Her cheeks flushed with color.

"Oh, I most certainly do. Several daughters whom I believe will wrap me about their tiniest fingers. And a few sons thrown in, for good measure. After all, a duke does need an heir."

"But I thought . . . that is . . . oh, forgive me, Your Grace."

"For what? Reading the gossip columns in the London papers?"

The pink heated to a cherry red, washing across her cheeks and splashing along her neck.

"No need to apologize, my lady. For too long, I have played the scoundrel. George, too. That is, the Duke of Charm," he said with a smile. "George and I grew up together. His estate is adjacent to mine. It took longer than most but we've finally sown all our wild oats."

"All of them?" she asked, doubt in her eyes.

"Quite. George wed my sister recently. I believe I mentioned that to you. Seeing wedded bliss is a powerful thing, Lady Ruthersby. It has given me the urge to wed myself."

The lady was now red to her roots. "I see. I wish you well in that venture, Your Grace. All the eligible ladies in London—and their mamas—will set their caps for you. I would advise you to be discriminating."

That was it, he thought. He could ask for her help in finding a bride. She wouldn't know it was to be her. Of course, that would mean waiting until the Season. It was only four months away. Still, it would be enjoyable, having her advise him, all the while drawing her in.

"I thought you might help me in this endeavor, my lady."

"Me?" she squeaked. "Oh, you'll need no help at all, Your Grace. You cut quite the dashing figure. You have the physique and outstanding looks that women are attracted to. You are also a duke and possess unimaginable wealth. Finding a woman to be your duchess won't be any problem at all."

He came around from behind his desk and sat on its edge. She was right in front of him. He was close enough to catch the whiff of rosemary.

"That is where you are wrong, my lady. I have never looked for the right kind of woman to be my duchess. I am afraid I have indulged in pleasure. I need guidance so that I don't rush into things. The perfect woman is out there for me. I just need assistance in finding her."

She looked a bit panicked and hastily said, "I am certainly not the one who could do that for you, Your Grace. As I informed you last night, I don't even attend the Season anymore."

"I know." He waved a hand in the air. "No clothes. No invitations." He paused. "What if I could remove those obstacles?"

She sniffed. "I don't see how."

"You expressed your desire to wed again. I want to do the same. I can easily place a few words in the right ears and you will be invited to every event held. As for clothes, I have a seamstress at Treadwell Manor. I'd be happy to loan her to you. She could make up an entire wardrobe for you."

At least, once he found a seamstress, Weston would hire her so she could share her services with Lady Ruthersby.

He leaned forward, fighting the urge to kiss her. "You see, my dear Lady Ruthersby, you are an experienced woman. One who has already been wed and widowed. You will have a more discerning eye than I ever could as far as this entire process goes. You could help me evaluate the eligible ladies this Season. You have a good head on your shoulders. I would value your opinion. By doing me this favor, you would also be able to move freely through Polite Society and find a husband of your own."

She sat, stunned, so he continued.

"We could meet on a daily basis. You could give your assessment from the night before and guide me toward the women you believe would best suit me. By the end of the Season, we both will have made our perfect matches."

Of course, he planned to win her so they would wind up being the match they each sought.

Weston gave her his most charming smile, knowing how it affected women. "So, what do you say, my lady? Would you be willing to help me in this endeavor?"

He saw her wrestle a moment, weighing the pros and cons of the arrangement.

Finally, she said, "I believe we could aid one another, Your Grace. Your proposition is very tempting. Unfortunately, I don't think Lord and Lady Ruthersby would find it convenient for them."

"You let me worry about them, my lady. Casting them aside, do you have any further objections?"

"None," she replied. "If you could make this happen, we both could come out very happy indeed."

"Very well. I will take this up with Ruthersby next week. When I see you and Lady Claire back to Briarcliff."

She began shaking her head back and forth. "No, Your Grace. That is why I came to see you this morning. I need to return as soon as possible. My nephews are already very high-spirited boys. With all the excitement of Christmas, they will be almost impossible to control. It is my duty to see that they—"

"Your duty is now to me, Lady Ruthersby. There will be no more of this unpaid position of governess for you. You will need to prepare for the upcoming Season. With my seamstress. Reading the gossip columns. Going back early to London to renew old friendships or at least writing to women you were close to and letting them know you'll be in attendance this Season. I, too, will return early. We can meet daily to plan our strategy for how I will go about perusing the Marriage Mart."

He smiled again, wanting to put her at ease and allow her to see he was harmless. "I will also go to my clubs and begin assessing which men might be a good match for you. Any bachelors close to your age that might be worthwhile suitors. Or possibly a widower or two. You wouldn't be opposed to marrying a man who already has a child?"

"Not at all," she assured him. "I think a heart has love enough for as many children as are in a household."

"Very well then. Have we reached an agreement?" He thrust out his hand. "My influence for your guidance?"

Lady Ruthersby smiled, revealing a most delightful dimple in her right cheek. She took his hand. For a moment, her eyes widened slightly and then she inhaled deeply, slowly exhaling.

"You have yourself a bargain, Your Grace. May we both be engaged by the Season's end."

Weston smiled broadly. Oh, they would be engaged, all right.

To each other.

CHAPTER THIRTEEN

E LISE COULDN'T BELIEVE what she had just agreed to, striking a bargain with the Duke of Disrepute.

"As I begin reacquainting myself with old friends and perusing which young ladies will make their come-outs this year, do you have any particular characteristics in mind, Your Grace?"

He grew thoughtful. "I'll be very choosy. That's for certain. First, I need a woman with keen intelligence. I become bored easily and if I'm to spend the next fifty or more years with her she must be clever and interested in a wide variety of topics."

She frowned. "That doesn't sound like many women of the *ton*. What about her family name and dowry?"

"Pish-posh on that, Lady Ruthersby. My name and title are plenty old and I couldn't care one whit about a dowry—or lack of one. I have estates too numerous to count and untold wealth. No, I want other things."

His words intrigued her. "Such as?"

"Besides intelligence, I need a woman who can make decisions quickly and without questioning herself. I have a large household for her to run. She will make numerous decisions on a daily basis. She'll need to be firm with servants but not to the point where they don't like her or their jobs. She must be an excellent hostess, able to plan soirees and dinner parties and their menus with ease."

The duke's list was certainly growing. "Anything else?" she asked, worried that there would be.

"I want her to enjoy the activities I enjoy since we'll be spending so much time together."

"Such as?"

"Riding, for one. I'm never happier than when on a horse. Unless it's walking. I can walk for hours and do so frequently in London. I enjoy the theatre. Playing chess. Of course, I also spend a good deal of my time at Gentleman Jack's. My duchess won't have to box, however-er."

She snorted. "Well, that's certainly a relief."

"She will also need to be kind. Compassionate toward others. A sense of humor would be nice. And naturally, she'll need to adore children."

"Your Grace, your list is growing by leaps and bounds. I'm not certain any of the young women making their come-outs would—"

"Oh, it doesn't have to be some young miss straight from the schoolroom, Lady Ruthersby. In fact, I doubt any of them will do. I don't mind if my future bride has a few Seasons in her past."

"You want that Town polish."

"I do." His eyes gleamed. "Debutantes don't have that."

"I beg to differ. A few do from the start. I'll daresay there are half a dozen who have been raised by their mamas to become a duchess should such an opportunity arise."

"Still, I am almost thirty. Ancient to those newcomers. I require a lady of sophistication and maturity. She'll need to not only be my friend and companion—but an eager, willing partner in the bedroom."

Elise felt herself go hot all over. "Surely, you don't think I can assess such a thing, Your Grace." Her face felt on fire.

"No," he said, a wicked grin touching his lips. "You can leave that to me."

Curiosity filled her. "You can tell by looking at a woman if they would be . . . that is . . . that they . . ." Her voice trailed off in embarrassment.

"No, not by merely looking. But there is always something in a woman's eyes that signals her desire." His gaze lingered on her and her body heated.

"I didn't think so," she stammered. "That a man could merely look at a woman and determine her experience in the bedroom."

"My bride doesn't have to be experienced, Lady Ruthersby. I have experience enough for us both. I'll admit I am a carnal man and have indulged in pleasures of the flesh for the past decade. I will want to wed a woman who doesn't mind exploring her desires for me *with* me. Since I wish for someone with a bit of maturity, perhaps we should limit my scope to widows. They would have some knowledge."

Though she was a widow, Elise had no idea what Disrepute was talking about. Even having given birth to two children and knowing what the marital act consisted of, she felt as green as any girl making her come-out.

"I am glad that you will handle that portion of the selection of your bride," she said primly, wishing her face and flesh would cool. "There are a handful of young women—women in their twenties— who married older men and have now been widowed. I will definitely help you consider them but I don't think you should rule out any females who are making their come-out, Your Grace. There may be that rare flower who would surprise you."

Disrepute smiled. "Oh, I do like a surprise."

Elise went hot all over again.

"Remember, though, the qualities I've discussed. Compassion. Grace. Intelligence. Love for children and a willingness to have a great many of them. If we can find those characteristics, I can teach my bride what I want and need in a lover."

Their entire conversation was completely inappropriate and yet she was fascinated by it. By him. She would have to watch herself around him. Already, the duke appealed to her a great deal. She couldn't go falling in love with him. Not when she was supposed to find him his bride.

"You mentioned a love for children, Your Grace. What about love for you?"

He shrugged. "I don't believe in love, my lady. Neither does most of Polite Society. Oh, I'll grant that every now and then, someone makes a spectacular love match. My sister and Colebourne, for instance. And my friend Windham and his wife. I don't need or require love, Lady Ruthersby. I fear I'm already demanding enough in what I'm looking for in a duchess. Love will play no part in my marriage. I'm happy to settle for friendship."

"I see."

He studied her. "Did you love your husband?"

"No," she answered honestly. "I liked him a great deal. He was very sweet. He understood me and my bluestocking ways. He was an excellent father to Claire. I didn't require love, as you've said. It was enough that we were compatible."

She rose. "You've given me quite a bit to consider. I hope that we will find a woman who meets most of your requirements."

"*All* of them, my lady."

"But surely, Your Grace, you must understand that you can't have the perfect woman. I doubt anyone in society would fit all of your lengthy requirements. Most women are not pressed to explore their intellectual side."

"You seem very intelligent."

She chuckled. "That's because I read a great deal, much to my mother's confusion and disapproval. I can promise you that I will do my utmost to help find you a suitable bride. In the meantime, I need to check on Claire."

"I hope you will also let Lady Claire be a part of this."

"What?"

"I long to be a father but haven't a clue how to go about it. While you and your daughter are here, I would like to spend time with her. Get to know how to speak to a child. How to behave around one."

Elise couldn't help but smile. "You have already done very well in that regard. As for spending time with her, I came to discuss with you returning to Briarcliff."

"You heard Dr. Cherry, Lady Ruthersby. You and Lady Claire require rest in order to heal. Not riding in a freezing coach over unpassable roads so soon after you have both been injured."

"But I am expected. I sent word after my parents' deaths. Lord and Lady Ruthersby will be upset if I do not arrive soon."

He frowned sternly. "I've told you that you're no longer to be at their beck and call. Besides, I sent Mixon back to Shedwell this morning and a footman south with a letter from me to Ruthersby."

"You what?"

"I explained to the earl about the dreadful carriage accident and how you and your daughter suffered injuries."

"They are minor injuries," she pointed out. "Nothing that would interfere with travel."

"Still, you don't need to rush off until both of you are completely well. I told Ruthersby I would escort you home in a week's time."

"That is quite thoughtful but very unnecessary, Your Grace."

His gaze penetrated her, causing a tingle to rush through her. "It's very necessary, my lady. I want to meet in person with your brother-in-law to make sure he understands our arrangement and that you will be needed in London, a very active participant in the Season."

"He won't like any of this," she said, shaking her head worriedly. "In fact, I sincerely doubt he would approve of my attending the Season. Lord Ruthersby is not a man who likes to be inconvenienced. He and Lady Ruthersby will expect me to remain in the country with my nephews as I always have."

Elise swallowed hard, hating that she had allowed herself to entertain thoughts of returning to Polite Society to find a husband when she all too well knew the harsh realities of her life.

"I am sorry, Your Grace. Though I agreed to help you in finding a bride, the fact is that I misspoke. Lord and Lady Ruthersby would never agree to bringing me to London with them, much less having me live in their townhouse as an equal. Though you thoughtfully agreed to provide a seamstress, I simply do not have the funds to pay for the fabrics required to make up the many gowns which would be required."

She blinked rapidly as tears formed in her eyes, willing them not to fall. Meeting his steady gaze, she added, "I do thank you for your kind offer, Your Grace, but I must think of the welfare of my daughter above all else. I refuse to anger Lord Ruthersby, who provides a roof over our heads. My brother-in-law would not approve of this scheme."

"He won't have to. He'll do exactly what I say." The duke grinned. "I am a most persuasive man."

She thought about how he'd kissed her. How he could have talked her into doing much more if they hadn't been interrupted. It still surprised her that he was interested in marrying, especially because he had kissed her. Perhaps that was merely a reaction to his old nature. She didn't think herself to be very tempting but he was buried in the country in December, with no female companionship available.

Despite the fact he had briefly kissed her, Disrepute did seem sincere in his mission to acquire a wife. No, she must stop thinking of him by such a silly nickname. The duke had been nothing but kind to her. She truly liked him as a person.

Perhaps too much.

"I hope you will convince Ruthersby," she said. "If you'll excuse me."

"My lady?"

She turned.

"I also sent word to my sister that you and Lady Claire would accompany me to Christmas dinner at Colebourne Hall."

"Oh, no. We couldn't possibly intrude on your time with your family," she protested.

"Nonsense. By going to Colebourne Hall, it will allow my servants to celebrate their own Christmas earlier than usual, with no one to wait upon. You wouldn't want to delay that, would you? Besides, Sam will be delighted to meet you and Lady Claire."

"I briefly meet Lady Samantha during my come-out. She was wed to Lord Haskett then."

"You will like her much better now," he confided. "She's happy in her life and her marriage and wasn't before. I have a feeling the two of you will become as thick as thieves."

"I doubt it. She's a duchess."

"What does that have to do with anything? I am a duke and that hasn't bogged down our conversation."

"Yes, but . . . it's different with women. A duchess doesn't have a need to be friends with a dowager countess who has few connections."

The duke laughed. "Sam isn't like that at all. I guarantee that you will become friends. Just wait and see. In the meantime, I have a request."

"More than finding you a wife?" she asked, her brows arching at him.

He laughed again. "Since we are to spend so much time together, I would like you to call me Weston."

Shock filled her. "No! I cannot do that, Your Grace. That wouldn't be fitting at all."

"I only meant in private. You may call me Treadwell in public but I would very much like to be friends with you. And my friends call me Weston. Except for George. He's called me West from the beginning."

She bit her lip, unsure how to reply.

"Come, now. Is it that so unreasonable? Your Grace before others. Weston when we're alone."

"It would be difficult," she admitted.

"But not impossible," he said. "May I call you Elise?"

The sound of her name on his tongue caused her to go warm again.

"Yes, Your Grace. Weston," she corrected.

He gave her a charming smile, one that she was sure he used as a reward if someone pleased him. Elise very, very much wanted to please him suddenly.

"Then I will see you later, Elise."

She bobbed her head and fled the room.

CHAPTER FOURTEEN

E LISE WAS SITTING with Claire, who'd just finished eating, when Dr. Cherry and Treadwell entered the bedchamber. She'd done her best to quit calling the duke by his nickname in her mind, working hard to think of him as Treadwell.

Or Weston.

She liked his Christian name and felt it suited him. She just didn't know if she could use it aloud. First names implied an intimacy which would be inappropriate between them, especially since she was charged with finding him his duchess.

"How are my patients today?" the physician asked. "Ready for Christmas?"

"It's tomorrow," Claire said promptly.

"Indeed it is, my lady."

"His Grace said we will go with him to church and then . . . where?" Her brow wrinkled.

"To my sister's," the duke prompted. "Her Grace, the Duchess of Colebourne."

"Colebourne," Claire repeated. "I like that name. What is your name, Your Grace?"

"Treadwell. Give your attention to Dr. Cherry, my lady," the duke urged.

"How is your ankle feeling, Lady Claire?"

"Better. It doesn't hurt. Mama made me sit in the chair and I haven't walked at all."

"That's excellent news." Dr. Cherry sat on the bed and lifted Claire's ankle, turning it slightly. "How about now? Does it hurt?"

"A little. Well, not hurt. It feels . . ."

"Different?" the physician asked.

Claire nodded.

He manipulated it some more and then said, "Either I was mistaken and the ankle wasn't as badly sprained as I believed or it's the healing powers of the young. They seem to bounce back more quickly than the rest of us."

"What does that mean, Doctor?" Elise asked.

"I'd suggest another day in bed or the invalid chair and then Lady Claire may begin putting a bit of weight on it." He looked at his patient. "No running, my lady. Just walking around the bedchamber a few times the first day. A little more the next. Within a week, I think you'll be up and about, moving with ease."

"Oh, that's very good news, Doctor," Elise said.

"Let me see your wrist, Lady Ruthersby. I see you've abandoned the sling."

"I didn't need it after the first day," she told him.

He moved it gently, circling it in one direction and then reversing. "Any pain?"

"None."

"Are you doing your exercises?"

"I have been."

"Keep up with them another week. Try not to lift anything too heavy. Other than that, I would say you are fine."

"Thank you for coming, Dr. Cherry," the duke said. "I wish you and Mrs. Cherry a very Happy Christmas."

"The same to you, Your Grace."

The physician left—but the duke remained behind. His presence brought a heightened awareness to Elise. Everything around her seemed more vivid in color. Stronger in smell. Physically, he seemed to take up much of the room, with his height and broad shoulders. Her stomach fluttered and she swallowed, tamping down the odd feelings stirring within her.

"Shall I read to you, Lady Claire?" he asked.

She nodded. "From my special book. It's my favorite."

Elise went to retrieve it and handed it to him.

"Why is this book special?" he asked, surprising Elise as he climbed into the bed next to Claire.

"Papa gave it to me. But it got wet."

He rifled through the pages. "I can see that."

"Mama's atlas got wet, too. It made her sad."

His eyes met hers. "Is it ruined?"

She felt tears sting her eyes as she nodded and looked away.

He turned back to Claire. "Which is your favorite story? We'll read that one together."

Claire turned to it. "Read this one."

"I will try to do as good a job as your papa did," he promised.

"Papa didn't read me this book. He died," Claire said solemnly, causing Elise's heart to ache.

"I heard about that. It's good that you have your book to remember him, though."

Claire didn't say anything so the duke began reading. Elise went to sit in a chair by the window and stared out. The day was dark and overcast, with skies that threatened to open up again. If the rain didn't end, she wasn't sure they could make it to Christmas dinner at Colebourne Hall. She was still torn about accompanying Treadwell to a family dinner but knew it would be selfish to stay behind and have his servants wait on her and Claire when they could begin their own holiday celebration in the servants' hall.

The duke's voice soothed her and she became lost in thought. Suddenly, it stopped. She looked up and saw him easing from the bed, tucking Claire's stuffed rabbit next to her. He brought the bedclothes over the girl and then bent and kissed her brow, moving Elise. She rose and came closer, reluctant because she didn't want to smell him. He had a clean, masculine scent that seemed to fill her every time he was near.

Treadwell handed her the book. "She seems worn out."

She clasped the book to her bosom. "She has been tired ever since the accident. I'm just happy to hear that she is recovering nicely."

"Did you give her the book and tell her it was from her father?"

Her grip tightened on it. "No. Ruthersby purchased it at a bookstore. He was on his way home after that when the accident occurred. The doctor who tended to him discovered it nearby and brought it to me, along with the news of his death."

He stepped closer to her, placing his hand atop her shoulder. "I'm sorry. I cannot imagine how difficult that must have been."

His touch did terrible—no, wonderful—things to her. His warmth seemed to permeate her, causing her to come alive. Quickly, she turned away to break the contact and placed the book on a nearby table. When he touched her, it put foolish ideas into her head. Ideas that shouldn't be there.

"Where is your atlas?" he asked.

Elise retrieved it from where it rested and handed it to him. He opened it and the pain struck her anew as she saw the ruined pages.

"It was in my satchel. It was large enough to protect Ralph Rabbit and a few other books. I suppose I should throw it out."

"No. That would be unwise. It was a gift from your husband. Obviously, one you cherish."

She sighed. "All my life, I wanted to go places. Not just to London but to see the world. Or at least the Continent. I read about far-off places, such as Egypt and the Far East. I imagined sailing to the Caribbean or to America. Ruthersby understood how much I wanted to travel. He was not the least bit adventurous himself, so I knew we would never leave England, but as a wedding gift, he gave me this atlas."

"Most women would expect jewelry upon their marriage," he noted.

Her gaze met his. "I am not most women."

"No. You aren't," he said softly. His hand reached out and took hers. He laced his fingers through hers.

Elise thought he might kiss her again. She desperately wanted him to do so and yet warred with herself. What good would it do? He was looking for a woman with a multitude of fine qualities. Ones she didn't possess. He would never consider her for his duchess. He needed a woman far more important than she was. One of beauty and wisdom and everything she would never be.

The duke squeezed her fingers lightly and then released her hand. Disappointment flooded her even though she understood his gesture to be one of kindness toward her.

"I don't know what it feels like to lose a spouse. I am very sorry for your pain. It seems fresh even now."

Tears misted her eyes. "I miss the companionship I had with Ruthersby. I miss being able to share my day with someone. I think the atlas became a symbol of what I once had. A dream of the places I wanted to go but never would. Losing it is like losing a part of him again. I fear Claire already has forgotten him. I've tried to keep his memory alive for her but she was so young. I don't remember my own father at her age."

"You were close to him?"

"Very much so. I followed him about every day. My mother never had time for me but Papa always did."

"You mentioned both your parents passing recently."

She dug her nails into her palms. "Yes. Papa died of a weak heart. He'd had a heart attack days before I arrived. My mother got the pneumonia. She wasn't happy to see me. She had washed her hands of me after my wedding and returned to live a life of gaiety, without a grown daughter to remind her how old she truly was. I'd foolishly thought when she passed that Claire and I could return to my childhood home and live with Papa." She shook her head. "It wasn't meant to be."

Treadwell reached for her hand again. When he held it, she felt secure. As if all the problems of the world melted away.

"I'm sorry you lost your father, Elise." His gaze was tender. "You have led a difficult life. Suffered hardships more than most. I assure you that is over. You will find a husband who will always take care of you. Cherish you."

She attempted to smile. "I'll hold you to that part of our bargain, Your Grace. I will do my best to find you a woman who will make you happy. In turn, you can help find me a husband who will keep Claire and me safe."

He raised her hand to his lips and pressed a kiss to her fingers. "I have every intention of doing that very thing, Elise."

>>><<<

WESTON SAW THE pained look on Elise's face and so he asked Claire, for the third time, "Are you sure you don't wish to go to my sister's?"

"No, Your Grace," the tyke said. "I want to stay with Maisy and Mark."

Elise bent next to the invalid chair and took her daughter's hand. "But it's Christmas, Claire."

"I know, Mama. But I get to see you all the time. I want to stay with my new friends."

Elise looked at him helplessly and he shrugged. "It might be for the best. The trip to and from might tire her out. This way, Mrs. Digsby will see that she gets a good meal in her. The children will look after her. And if she does tire, she can be brought upstairs to nap."

"Please, Mama," begged Claire.

"All right. I will miss you dreadfully, though." She kissed her daughter's brow.

"Don't worry, my lady," Mrs. Digsby said. "Lady Claire won't be in the way at all. Maisy and Mark will keep her plenty busy."

"You're sure she won't be too much trouble?"

"No, my lady. Lady Claire is a real angel."

Elise kissed her daughter once more. "Be good, my little love."

"Have fun with His Grace, Mama."

Weston led her downstairs and helped her into her cloak before they went outside and boarded the carriage. The rain of the past week had stopped yesterday. The roads were still atrocious, which had led to him deciding not to attend church in the village this morning. It was only a couple of miles to Colebourne Hall, though, and he was eager for Sam and George to meet Elise.

As the vehicle started up, he said, "I know Maisy and Mark well. They are very good children and will dote on Claire."

"She's never really been around any children other than her two cousins. They are all boy and don't have much to do with her. She takes her lessons alongside them but they don't really play with her. I spend as much time with her as I can but I know she is lonely. It will do her good to be around them today. Especially Maisy. They've already played with her several times as it is."

He casually took her gloved hand. "See, you already know it's the best thing for her. It will give you a brief respite, as well."

Reluctantly, he released her hand, wishing he could hold it the entire way. He didn't want her to skitter away, though. If she had any idea he had no plans to look for a gentleman to be her husband, she wouldn't have agreed to their arrangement. She already knew of his abominable reputation. A day without a story about the Duke of Disrepute in the scandal sheets was not a day at all. He would need to prove himself to her. That meant keeping his hands to himself.

Even if they longed to stroke her silky hair. Caress her curves. Show her exactly how pleasurable joining together could be. He suspected poor Ruthersby had muddled that up and Elise had no idea what making love was truly like. Weston very much looked forward to tutoring her in the art of love.

"Will any other guests be at Colebourne Hall?"

"Hmm. I hadn't thought to ask," he admitted. "It's been a while since I've spent Christmas in Devon."

Last Christmas, he had gone to three different women's boudoirs.

"My sister was still up north, living with her in-laws," he explained.

He couldn't go into the nightmare that had been Sam's life. "Now that she is nearby and wed to my closest friend, I hope to spend many holidays with her. I'd like to alternate hosting between Treadwell Manor and Colebourne Hall."

She chuckled. "You'll have to see if your duchess agrees to that plan."

"Why wouldn't she?" he asked, perplexed.

"The kind of woman you are interested in marrying is one who has a mind of her own, Weston," she said.

He liked hearing his name on her lips. It sounded . . . *right.*

It would sound even better when she cried his name in the heat of an orgasm.

"I don't see why she wouldn't want to spend a holiday with my only sister and best friend."

"She may have family of her own."

"Then she can invite them to Treadwell Manor," he said stubborn-ly. "A duke should be allowed to celebrate Christmas where he wants." He knew Elise didn't have any true family. It shouldn't be a problem in the future.

"You sound like a petulant child," she teased. "*A duke should always get what he wants,*" she whined.

He grinned. "If that is meant to be me, it's a poor imitation."

Elise laughed, full-throated and low. God, he wanted to kiss her so much.

"Very well. I agree that my future duchess will—and should—have a say as to where we celebrate Christmas. However, I must remind you, I plan for her to bear me numerous sons and daughters. She will want them at our home. Or next door, with all of their cousins. George and I grew up together. I expect his children and mine will become good friends. Play together. Learn to ride and hunt together. Even go off to school with one another. They'll look out for each other."

She sighed. "That sounds very nice. Though Joseph and Josiah are sweet boys, I doubt they'll ever have much to do with Claire. I suppose it won't matter. I'm going to be able to give her several brothers and sisters. At least, that is one of *my* requirements. You never did ask me what I wanted in a husband, Your Grace."

"Weston," he corrected.

"Weston," she echoed, a trace of a smile playing about her lips.

"Well, tell me," he urged. "I ought to know. It will help me as I conduct my search."

"Children are a must. I have a great love for them and want to wed a man who also feels the same. And . . ." she hesitated a moment and then added, "I want him to accept Claire."

"Claire is a delight. Any man would be fortunate to be her stepfather."

Elise shook her head. "Not many men look kindly upon the offspring from a previous husband. I understand that it will be difficult for my husband to love Claire. I only hope that he will treat her kindly and be fond of her."

Weston could tell her that he was almost as mad for Claire as he was her mother but chose to keep that tidbit to himself.

"What else?" he asked.

"I think I will borrow from your list."

"How so?"

"I would also choose to wed a man who is intelligent. Ruthersby was. I liked that about him. He didn't see me as merely ornamental."

He raised one brow. "You are very pretty, Elise. I'd even say beautiful."

The blush bloomed on her cheeks. "That's all well and good but I am more than my looks."

You certainly are.

"And I think I would like . . ." Her blush deepened. "I would like a man who could teach me how to kiss."

Weston disguised his shock. "Ruthersby didn't kiss you?"

"Well, he did. But I don't think either of us was very good at it." She sighed. "Frankly, we weren't good at much of anything regarding that. Oh, we knew enough to make a baby. Two, actually, but I want my next husband to know something about the process."

"You want a man who can teach you how to enjoy sex."

Now, her face flamed. "Yes. I suppose so."

"So, let me get this straight. You made no mention of a lofty title or wealth."

"I don't need a title, Weston. I married an earl before. He was, in the long run, but a man. If you find a titled gentleman you think suitable, that's perfectly fine. But if he's only a mister—a third or fourth son—I don't really care."

"All right then. A man who will give you multiple children and be affectionate to Claire. One with a decent intellect who will converse with you and not treat you as an object. And a man who will be a worthy lover."

"Yes," she said firmly. "That all sounds quite good, indeed."

The carriage slowed. He noted it had taken them longer to reach Colebourne Hall than usual and blamed it on the muddy roads.

"I am only sorry we are here. I would like for this conversation to continue because I find it fascinating, Elise."

She playfully punched him in the arm and primly said, "There will be no more talk of this, Your Grace. You have my specifications now and I have yours. You will look accordingly and so will I."

The carriage door opened and the footman set the steps down. Weston bounded down them and saw mud everywhere. As Elise gave him her hand to help her down, he ignored it, scooping her into his arms.

"What are you doing, Treadwell?" she asked, wriggling.

"I didn't want the hem of your gown or your slippers to get muddy, Lady Ruthersby," he said, matching her in formality.

The butler opened the door and Weston swept inside.

CHAPTER FIFTEEN

T HOUGH MORTIFIED AND certain her cheeks were as red as a ripe apple, Elise couldn't help but relish the feel of Weston's arms about her. He carried her as if she weighed no more than a piece of parchment. She inhaled deeply, adoring the spice of his cologne and that utterly unique smell that was simply Weston. The wall of his chest seemed harder than bricks as her palms pushed against it.

"Put me down," she ordered as he stepped into the foyer and the butler closed the door.

"Good afternoon, Your Grace," the servant said.

"Weston! What on earth are you doing?" a feminine voice called.

"Yes, what *are* you doing?" a masculine one asked.

Weston's gazed pinned hers for a moment and a rush of heat swept through her as she saw something in his eyes.

Desire . . .

No, that couldn't be. She blinked and it was gone. He grinned and set her on the ground.

"Sam, George, how good to see you," he said smoothly, kissing his sister's cheek. The he indicated Elise. "I would like to introduce you to Lady Ruthersby. My lady, please say hello to the Duke and Duchess of Colebourne."

Elise somehow maintained her composure and curtseyed to the pair. "It is a pleasure to make your acquaintance, Your Graces. His Grace speaks very fondly of you both."

"Oh, he does?" the duchess said, studying her. "I know you. I've met you before."

"Yes, Your Grace. It was over five years ago when I made my come-out."

"Was it a garden party?" the duchess asked. "I seem to have a picture of you in a violet dress. I thought how splendid it looked with your beautiful eyes." She glanced to her brother. "Lady Ruthersby has beautiful eyes, doesn't she?"

"She certainly does," the duke agreed affably. "But she is more than her looks," he added, causing Elise's face to flame once more.

"Come up to the drawing room," Colebourne said. "Everyone else is there. You might as well tell us all at the same time how Lady Ruthersby and you became acquainted." He offered Elise his arm and she took it. "We are happy to have you at Colebourne Hall, my lady."

"Thank you for allowing me to come to your Christmas dinner," she replied evenly, trying to breathe calmly and regain her composure.

She did so by the time they reached the drawing room, wondering what other guests would be present. Upon entering, she saw two gentlemen standing by the fire and two ladies seated nearby. All four looked up as they came in, curiosity on their faces.

The duke led Elise to them and said, "This is Lady Ruthersby. She's a guest of Weston's. My lady, this is the Duke of Blackmore. His sister, Lady Elizabeth. And the Duke and Duchess of Windham."

For a moment, she froze. It was overwhelming to be in the company of four dukes—but her trepidation went beyond that. It was being in the presence of the Duchess of Windham. This woman had also suffered as Elise had, made a widow by the same tragic accident. She worried how the duchess would react if she learned who Elise was. Ruining Christmas for this group was the last thing Elise wanted yet she had no way to gracefully exit.

Instead, she drew from the well of strength within her, managing a splendid curtsey. "I am delighted to make your acquaintances. Happy

Christmas to you all."

"Please, have a seat," the Duchess of Colebourne said. "My brother told me he was bringing guests. Is anyone else coming?"

"His Grace was referring to my daughter, Claire. She is but four and stayed behind at Treadwell Manor."

Blackmore assessed her with a friendly look. "How on earth did you come to stay at Treadwell Manor, Lady Ruthersby?"

"It's all thanks to a stingy earl and a rickety carriage," Weston replied smoothly.

Elise listened as he told the group about the accident and how the vehicle had been destroyed and she and Claire injured.

"You are very fortunate, Lady Ruthersby," the Duchess of Windham said. "That horrible vehicle alone could have done you in but to survive a burning tree crashing into your carriage?" She shuddered.

"His Grace was very brave," Elise said. "He got my daughter out quickly and then me."

"No, first was Claire. Then her doll. Then your satchel. Finally, came you," Weston corrected. "The satchel contained Ralph Rabbit, a treasured stuffed animal that Lady Claire simply cannot sleep without. A treasured book and atlas were also inside it. Who am I to argue when a lady asks for her satchel to be saved, and then herself?"

"Your wrist is better now?" asked Lady Elizabeth.

"Yes. Much better. Dr. Cherry said it was a mild sprain. Claire's ankle is still a bit swollen since her sprain was much more severe. She's been sitting in your invalid chair, Your Grace."

"I'd forgotten about that. I broke my leg," the Duchess of Colebourne said. "I was a tomboy, always following Weston and George about, thinking I could do everything they could. Actually, I did climb trees better than they could but I turned too quickly and hit my forehead on a limb that day. It caused me to lose my balance. I fell wrong on my leg when I hit the ground." She gazed fondly at her husband. "George carried me all the way back home."

"I felt awful," Colebourne said. "You were crying and looked miserable. Snot coming out of your nose. A nasty knot springing up on your forehead."

He took her hand and kissed it. She smiled and said, "Perhaps you need to make it up to me later this evening, Your Grace."

The look she gave him—and the one he returned—stunned Elise. The air between them crackled with an electricity that was palpable.

"Stop it, you two," Weston admonished playfully.

"Your Grace?" said the butler. "Dinner is served."

They went into the small dining room, which still seated twenty, and partook in a lavish meal. Weston kept his eyes on Elise, making sure that she was not only conversing with everyone but enjoying herself.

He turned to Phoebe when the conversation died down. "I noticed a special glow about you. When is your child due?"

She smiled radiantly. "Early April. That means no Season for me. We will remain at Windowmere instead."

"Congratulations to you both." He looked at his sister. "I suppose you'll be making a similar announcement soon. I find I am eager to become an uncle."

"We hope so," Sam said. "Of course, I expect you to teach your nieces and nephews the things you and George taught me. Except for fishing, that is."

"Why not fishing?" Elise asked.

Sam wrinkled her nose. "Weston has some sort of secret that he never shared with either George or me. When we fished in our pond, he caught double the number of fish that George or I did."

He laughed. "Why would I reveal my secrets to your children, dear sister? I will pass them along to my own. That way, when the cousins hold a fishing tournament, my offspring will win every time."

Everyone around the table laughed.

"I'm quite full," George announced. He turned to the butler.

"Please let Cook and the kitchen staff know how successful this Christmas dinner was."

"I will, Your Grace," the butler replied.

"I'm dismissing you and the footmen," the duke added. "You can clear these dishes away later. For now, you need to join your own Christmas celebration in the servants' hall."

"Thank you, Your Grace."

The butler and four footmen filed from the room.

"Shall we retire to the drawing room?" Sam asked. "I've got a few parlor games I need to set up for us."

Weston groaned. "Games?"

"Yes. Why don't you men sit and have a glass of port first? By then, I'll have everything ready."

The ladies rose and once they'd vacated the room, Weston turned to Jon and said, "Quit eyeing Lady Ruthersby. I plan to make her my wife."

Jon whistled. "Don't tell me the same bug which bit George has now decided to nibble on you." He paused. "Have you declared for her yet?"

"No," he admitted. "She's skittish. I didn't want to lose her so I convinced her to enter an agreement with me."

"What kind of agreement?" Andrew asked.

"She's to help me find a bride this coming Season. In return, I will use my connections to vet a husband for her."

Jon laughed. "And you will reject every woman she suggests, I suppose, while making sure you are the only candidate standing by Season's end?"

"Something like that," he said testily. Hearing it aloud made him question his judgment.

"Do you love her?" Andrew asked quietly.

"Love's got nothing to do with it," he declared. "I went down that path before and it proved disastrous. For now, I recognize that Lady

Ruthersby has all the qualities I would want in a wife and the mother of my children. That's enough for me."

"It may not be enough for her," George said. "If you don't love her, don't marry her, West. It wouldn't be fair to either of you."

"See here, George, you can't go thinking everyone can fall in love. Simply because you and Andrew are the rare exceptions and have both found a love match doesn't mean that the rest of us will. Or even want to. I like Lady Ruthersby quite a bit. I actually am lusting after her, truth be told. I'm doing my best to be a gentleman, however. I will present viable candidates to her but, in the end, I plan to make her my duchess."

Weston glanced back to Jon. "That means no pursuit of her on your part."

"All right. I'll agree to not vie for her hand but I will most certainly ask her to dance. It would be rude of me not to, now that we've been introduced. It will also keep another suitor from dancing with her."

"That's acceptable," he said.

"I still think you do both of you a disservice," Andrew stated. "I know how happy Phoebe and I are. I want that for you, too, Weston."

"I will be happy with Elise. She's a remarkable woman. I also am quite fond of her daughter. We will get along splendidly. I have no doubt about that. She's suffered through some difficult times. I plan to pamper her and always care for her." He paused. "Let's join the ladies."

The four men rose and Weston motioned to Andrew to wait a moment, allowing George and Jon to leave the room first.

As they fell into step behind the pair, Weston said quietly, "I need to tell you something."

"More than letting me know you are ready to wed the delightful Lady Ruthersby?" his friend teased.

"The carriage accident that killed Borwick and Nathan? Lady Ruthersby's husband also perished in it," he revealed. "I thought you should know in case Phoebe learns of this connection."

Andrew nodded. "I appreciate the warning, Weston. Does Lady Ruthersby know Phoebe was married to Borwick?"

"I told her."

"If I've learned one thing about women since I have wed, it is that they talk. About everything," Andrew said. "I'm certain they will discuss this matter but I do thank you for preparing me in case Phoebe grows upset when she learns of the connection."

⟫⟫⟪⟪

ELISE WENT WITH the others to the drawing room. She had enjoyed the meal very much, the conversation as much as the food. Weston had some very nice friends and she hoped she would see more of them when the Season began, the exception being the Windhams since they would be absent as they expected their first child.

"Weston told us of your carriage accident, Lady Ruthersby, but he didn't say where you and your daughter were headed," her hostess said.

"We were going home to Briarcliff. It's about ten miles west of Plymouth," she replied. "I continued to live there after my husband's death, which occurred almost three years ago."

"That must have been very difficult," the Duchess of Windham said. "I lost my husband—and my boy—in a carriage accident around the same time."

Elise decided she must reveal her identity to the Duchess of Windham, however unpleasant it might be.

"Was your husband Lord Borwick, Your Grace? And your son Nathan?" she asked, not wanting to abruptly announce her news, rather easing into it.

"Yes," the duchess said, tears misting her eyes. "I have missed my boy every day."

She took the woman's hand. "I lost Ruthersby in that same accident. A passing physician rendered aid to him but was unable to save him. I was carrying my husband's child at the time. I had a boy, Your Grace. I named my boy Nathan—after your son. Unfortunately, he only lived three days. It was like losing Ruthersby all over again, a pain that will never leave me."

Tears now streamed down the Duchess of Windham's face. "I also was with child. I lost my baby the same day of the accident. It is something I never speak of." She gripped Elise's hand tightly. "It seems we are bonded in tragedy, my lady. I hope, however, that we can bond in friendship, as well."

Elise was touched by the duchess' generosity. "I would like that very much."

The two women embraced and then the Duchess of Colebourne and Lady Elizabeth also hugged them. Suddenly, it seemed as if a burden had been lifted from Elise. She'd never really had anyone to share in her grief. She'd always tried to remain happy in Claire's presence, not wanting tragedy to mark her girl. Her own parents had been missing from that time in her life. Ruthersby's brother and wife hovered in the wings, waiting to see who would become the new earl and had never given her a sympathetic word or smile.

These three women, though, were the first who had truly made her feel that her sorrow wasn't hers alone. It was to be shared, thus lightening her burden.

"I don't recall you during last Season, Lady Ruthersby," Lady Elizabeth said. "Are you ready to rejoin society?"

"Actually, I am," she shared. "I have longed for more children, not wanting Claire to be an only child. That desire means I must find a new husband."

"You won't have any trouble at all doing so," the Duchess of Colebourne assured her. "You are beautiful and sweet and kind. Men will flock to you."

"I have no dowry, though," she said. "I don't want just any man. That is why I have entered into an arrangement with Treadwell."

That drew the trio's interest.

"Are you going to marry my brother?" the duchess asked.

Elise felt herself flush. "Of course not. However, the duke has made known to me his desire to wed. He is eager to put his past behind him and raise a family. He said he dreaded perusing the Marriage Mart for a bride and has asked for my guidance in helping him find a bride." She shook her head. "His list of demands of what he wants in a wife is rather long, though. I hope I will be able to find him a suitable mate. In exchange for my help, he is going to review eligible men in the *ton* and make a recommendation to me as to whom might be worthy to wed."

"Do you also have a list of characteristics you seek?" asked Lady Elizabeth.

"I do." It wasn't one she could share with them, so she said, "Since I have no dowry, it may prove more difficult. I don't require a title. I am not interested in looks or money. I realize that I will be competing with all the young, fresh-faced girls who will be making their come-outs. I will be practical and—"

"What about love?" the Duchess of Windham asked.

Elise's brow furrowed. "What about it? I didn't love Ruthersby. I liked him. He was a very gentle, scholarly man. He was an excellent father to Claire. That's another thing. I need a man who will allow Claire to live with us and treat her decently. I can't have her sent away from me. We will go together—or not at all."

"I didn't love Borwick," the Duchess of Windham said. "Now that I have found love with Andrew, I cannot imagine being married without it. I understand that you are looking to secure your future, Lady Ruthersby. I only hope that you will find love with your new husband."

"Since you haven't been in society for a few years, I can help,"

Lady Elizabeth said. "Once we're back in London, we must have tea. I will tell you all about the girls who made their come-out with me last year and the ones who will do so this year. That can help you narrow down which ladies to suggest to Treadwell."

"I must be a part of this," the Duchess of Colebourne declared. "After all, it is my brother we are talking about."

"We can also discuss unmarried gentlemen of the *ton*," Lady Elizabeth continued. "That way, you won't go into the Season blindly."

"Thank you. I would appreciate your help on my behalf and Treadwell's. He's declared with confidence that we'll both be engaged by the end of the Season."

She saw the two duchesses exchange a glance and wondered what it meant. At that moment, though, the men joined them.

Elise knew it would be far easier to find Weston a bride than her a groom. He was, after all, a duke, while she was a penniless dowager countess with a child. As they began a word game of their hostess' choosing, Elise couldn't help but wonder if it would be possible to find a husband at all.

The four dukes entered the room. Weston immediately looked to Elise to gauge her mood, feeling certain she would have sought out Phoebe and revealed the tragic way they were connected. He relaxed, seeing her smile as she listened to something Phoebe said. He might have known that Elise would win over these women. The four suddenly burst out laughing.

Weston turned to Andrew. "It seems all is well between them."

"I did not think Phoebe would blame Lady Rutherford in any way," his friend said.

"I knew she wouldn't but I feared the thought of remembering the tragedy would upset her." He paused. "I want a word alone with Samantha."

"To share your plans involving the lovely widow?"

"Yes. Go distract the others if you would. Let Jon and George help."

Weston caught his sister's eye as the three dukes joined the women and she slipped away, joining him on the far side of the room.

"I hear you are ready to find your duchess," Samantha said, slipping her hand into the crook of his arm as they took a turn about the room. "Lady Ruthersby shared with us how you and she are to aid one another as you look for spouses this Season. Frankly, I don't think you have to look at all, Weston."

Curious as to what she would say, he asked, "And why not?"

Samantha's eyes sparkled as she declared, "Because Lady Ruthersby is a perfect match for you."

"I think so, too."

She stopped. "You do?"

He nodded and continued their slow pace. "I will admit that I am quite taken with her—and I plan by Season's end to ask her to be my wife."

Samantha frowned. "Then why go through the pretense of each of you searching for a mate?"

"I believe she is extremely cautious. She puts Claire, her daughter, before everything. You, of all people, know my reputation is not the best. I want to change, Samantha. Show her I am a better man than what Polite Society thinks of me. I want to slowly win her over. Allow her to trust me. That will take time."

She squeezed his arm affectionately. "I will do whatever I can to help you in this endeavor. She is a lovely person."

"I think so, too. And I will admit I am also captivated by young Claire. Being around her has given me the desire to father children."

Samantha beamed at him. "It is good to see you so happy, Weston. It has been a long time since you were. I hope Lady Ruthersby will quickly recognize the good man you are and come to love you as much as you love her."

Weston didn't bother to correct his sister. He had not spoken of love—and didn't need any lectures from Samantha on the topic.

No, it would be enough to simply claim Elise as his when the Season ended.

CHAPTER SIXTEEN

WESTON LOOKED AT Elise and Claire, who sat opposite him in the carriage as they journeyed to Briarcliff. Claire was stretched out so that her ankle could be propped on her mother's lap. If he couldn't have Elise's warmth next to him, having his eyes rest on her was the next best thing.

The week after Christmas had passed too quickly. He'd spent as much time as he could with the pair, learning both their likes and dislikes. It amazed him how well-spoken Claire was for a child so young. Elise attributed that to how well the girl already read and the fact she'd never spoken down to her. He'd read to Claire and had her read to him. He'd played games with her and her mother, as well, usually indulging in a game of chess or cards with Elise after Claire had gone to bed.

He had dined with Elise each night, getting to know her better. She was extremely intelligent and, besides books, must have read the newspapers voraciously. She'd freely given him her opinions on a variety of topics, from the war with Bonaparte to crop rotation. They would sip on brandy after dinner and she would become slightly tipsy after a single snifter, which only endeared her to him even more.

It was becoming increasingly difficult to keep his vow not to kiss her again. He might not love her—but her certainly wanted to make love to her.

George had ridden over two days after Christmas. His guests had gone home and the two had gone for a long walk. They'd argued about the idea of needing to love Elise in order to wed her. Finally, George gave in, declaring that Lady Ruthersby could always tell him no if and when Weston finally offered for her. The thought of her turning him down wasn't acceptable. He wanted her as his duchess. No other woman would do. It would be imperative to see that she found something wrong with every bachelor of the Season that he might present to her.

Except him.

He hoped by Season's end that they would get to know each other well and that she would become comfortable with him—and the idea that she could be the Duchess of Treadwell. Of course, that meant her attending Season events, which he would be speaking to Lord Ruthersby about in the next few minutes once they arrived at Briarcliff. Weston had sent word to the earl that he would be escorting his guests home today.

"Do you really think you'll be able to convince my brother-in-law to allow me to participate in the Season?" Elise asked wistfully.

"It seems you have no faith in me, my lady. Granted, you have only known me as the Duke of Disrepute but being a duke, disreputable or not, I am expecting a spectacular welcome by Lord Ruthersby. He will be amenable to whatever I suggest."

"Don't call yourself that," she chided. "Disrepute. I don't care if that was your past. It's certainly not your future."

Not our future, he wanted to say but kept silent.

"How will you convince him?" she pressed.

He laughed. "Do you not think I can use charm on him? Or should I have brought George along for that?"

She pursed her lips. Her very kissable lips. Finally, she said, "You are quite charming, Your Grace. Perhaps that should have been your nickname instead of Colebourne's. I shall have to think of a new nickname the *ton* can call you. It would be good to see something agreeable about you in the gossip columns for once."

He chuckled. "They only write about the bad stuff. Like the Bad Dukes. Hopefully, two other new rakes will catch their eyes. With George happily married and me searching for a bride, I can't see where either of us will be interesting."

She studied him a moment. "You do realize that Polite Society will doubt your mission, don't you? Even if you proclaim you have changed, they will delight in knocking you off your ducal pedestal."

"I'm to be on a pedestal?" he teased.

Those violet eyes grew merry. "You know what I mean. They will watch your every step. There will be men goading you to behave badly as before. Women who will no doubt fling themselves at you, trying to tempt you into their beds again."

"You'll see. I am made of sterner stuff than they all imagine."

The carriage began slowing and he saw tension fill her. He leaned over and took her hand.

"Don't worry, Elise. I will take care of everything."

"Even a seamstress?" she reminded him.

He hadn't found one yet but he'd already sent a note to Sam, explaining what he needed. Weston knew by now that George and Andrew had told their wives of his plan to marry Elise and Jon must have spoken to Elizabeth, as well. Hopefully, none of them would divulge that information to Elise.

"I thought it best to wait until you go to London. I've found a modiste for you there. You will have more materials to choose from and she will be more informed as to what is in fashion."

"You don't have a seamstress," she accused.

Oh, she was too clever by far.

"Whether I do or don't, you'll be taken care of in London. My sister has recommended the perfect modiste."

Her eyes grew large. "I can't have you buying me a wardrobe. What would people think? That I'm a . . . kept woman?" She began turning red.

He almost choked. "No. It won't be like that."

"What will you say when we wind up in each other's company during the Season?" she asked.

"That we are family friends."

"Can a man and woman ever be just friends?" she asked pointedly.

"In our case, yes."

He did want to be her friend. He also wanted to be her lover. Her everything. The more time he spent in Elise's company, the more he wanted her. Weston supposed it was in the chase. The having to wait. That was what made her so delectable. So tempting. He told himself to remain calm. In a few months, he would make it obvious to her that they suited more than anyone else.

Then he could finally have her in his bed. As his wife.

The carriage stopped. Claire stirred and sat up, rubbing her eyes.

"Are we here, Mama?"

"Yes, darling."

"Do I have to go to lessons with Joseph and Josiah today?"

"No. We won't start those until tomorrow."

"Elise," Weston said, his tone warning her.

"Well, someone has to teach them until a governess can be hired."

He frowned at her as his footman opened the door. Weston climbed from the carriage, holding his hands out to take Claire. He swung her to the ground and she giggled. Then he reached for Elise. His fingers grasped her waist and he brought her to the ground, holding on for just a moment longer than necessary.

Turning, he saw not only several servants but the earl and countess awaiting them outside, despite the chilly day.

"Good afternoon, Your Grace," Lord Ruthersby said, bowing low.

His wife echoed the greeting and curtseyed deeply.

Weston looked at Elise and gave her a silent *I told you so*. She quickly glanced away, one hand coming up to hide her smile as she took her daughter's hand.

"Good afternoon," he told the couple and gazed at them pointedly. When they looked at him cluelessly, he cleared his throat. Still nothing. Finally, he moved to Elise and placed her hand on his forearm and said, "I am sure it is also good to see your sister-in-law and niece again."

"Oh, yes," the earl said, understanding finally penetrating his thick skull. "It is very good to have you back at Briarcliff, my lady."

The countess still didn't acknowledge Elise and said, "Won't you come in, Your Grace? It's terribly cold out here."

He allowed the pair to move ahead and led Elise and Claire inside the house. The butler took his greatcoat and Elise's cloak.

"Mama, I'm tired," Claire said.

Immediately, Elise picked up her daughter. As they moved up the stairs, she told Weston, "I will take Claire to our room and get her settled."

The countess turned, a tight smile on her face. "You can see to the boys, as well. They have been . . . a handful in your absence. Stay with them while we take His Grace in to tea."

By now, they'd reached the top of the first landing and Weston said, "No." His tone was calm. Firm. Brokering no objections.

Still, the idiotic current countess said, "Oh, don't trouble yourself, Your Grace. She always cares for our boys. Until she was gone the past two weeks. It really was a most inconvenient situation."

Anger stirred within him. "I'll help get Lady Claire settled," he informed the countess. "Send a maid up to stay with her so that Lady Ruthersby might take tea with us."

"But she never . . ." The countess' voice faded away as he stared at her intensely. "Oh. Certainly, Your Grace."

With that, Weston removed Elise's hand from his arm and lifted Claire, holding her close. She was a tiny thing, with skinny arms and legs and wonderfully large, soulful eyes the same shade as her mother's. He hurried up the next flight, sensing Elise behind him.

The earl called out, "We'll be in the drawing room, Your Grace."

He didn't bother answering.

"It's this way," Elise said when they reached the top floor, leading him down the corridor. She stopped at a door and opened it, indicating for him to go in.

It was incredibly small. A room meant for a governess, not the former lady of the house. A narrow bed. A table beside it with a wash basin. One chair. No wardrobe.

"This is your room?" he asked, his anger beginning to boil as he set Claire down.

"Yes."

"And you and Claire sleep together in that bed?"

She looked away, shame filling her face. "Yes," she said quietly.

Suddenly, a door burst open. Not the one they'd come through but one that he assumed connected this room to the schoolroom.

"Auntie!"

Two boys raced in, slamming into Elise, who wrapped her arms about them.

"Hello, Joseph. Josiah."

"We missed you," the taller boy proclaimed.

"Joseph read to me every day," the shorter one said. "But he didn't do any sums."

"We went riding. Lots! Just like you said we would It was fun."

They hugged her again, their arms clinging to her legs. She ruffled each boy's hair and said, "Claire and I missed you, too."

"Why were you gone so long?'

"Did your mama die? Did she go to Heaven?"

"Who is he?"

Elise laughed and Weston wanted to hear that sound every day. Her laugh was rich and bubbly when it erupted. He feared she hadn't done much laughing the past few years.

She pried the boys from her and had them stand straight. "This is His Grace, the Duke of Treadwell. Do you remember introductions?"

"Yes, Auntie," both boys said in unison. Then they turned to Weston and said, "Pleased to meet you, Your Grace."

They bowed to him.

"It's excellent to meet you both," he replied.

"How do you know a duke, Auntie?" the oldest asked. "Is he your friend?"

"I am a great friend of your aunt's. And of your cousin, as well."

He glanced over and saw Claire had climbed onto the bed and was already fast asleep.

"Come to the schoolroom, boys," he told them.

He led the way as they followed him. Elise didn't appear and he figured she was removing Claire's shoes and clothes and placing her in a nightdress.

"Your auntie has been teaching you," he began.

The smaller boy nodded enthusiastically. "I'm learning how to read. And Joseph does Latin and we all look at the atlas and find faraway places. Auntie tells us about them. We're going to go to Africa and China someday with her. Even America."

"I'm glad you've learned so much from her but she's going to step aside and let a governess teach you until you go away to school."

Sadness filled their faces.

"She doesn't want to be with us anymore?" Joseph asked.

"Oh, I'm sure she'll still teach you things. Just not in the classroom anymore. She's going to be helping me."

"You need a governess?" Josiah asked, his face obviously baffled.

"I do. I believe your aunt is the best person to help me. As a duke, I always want the best. I have a lot to learn and she's going to help me. That means you'll have someone new come to teach you. You must be respectful to her and learn everything you can so you can do well when you go away to school. I will be asking your aunt about your progress. I want to hear good reports on not only what you learn but how well behaved you are. Is that understood?"

"Yes, Your Grace," both said, wide-eyed at the prospect of a duke receiving reports on them.

"Good."

A maid entered with a tray. "I've got milk and bread for you, little lords. And I'm to stay with Lady Claire."

"Very good," he said. To the boys, he added, "I will visit your townhouse when you come to London and if your parents agree, I'll take you to the park. We'll fly a kite."

"Yes!" cried Josiah.

Weston turned and saw Elise standing in the doorway. At that moment, she looked like an angel watching over him and these boys. A rush of warmth flooded him and he went to her.

"Are you ready to go speak to your in-laws?" he asked.

A radiant smile lit her face. "I am. And for once, I'm not afraid. Because you will be with me."

Elise allowed Weston to escort her downstairs to the drawing room, where her in-laws immediately sprang to their feet, a welcoming smile on their faces. She didn't think either had smiled at her once since they'd arrived at Briarcliff. Of course, the smile was not for her. It was for the duke. She held her head high as he brought her to them and again, they bowed and curtseyed to him.

A full tea was laid out and the countess invited them to take a seat, saying, "We are so grateful for your presence in our humble home today, Your Grace."

"I wouldn't be here without having made the acquaintance of the delightful Lady Ruthersby," he said smoothly, causing Elise to bite the inside of her cheek to keep from laughing aloud.

"I'm sure she owes a great deal to you, Your Grace," the earl said. "You took her in after her carriage broke down. Called in a doctor to tend to her injury."

"Oh, it was more than that, Lord Ruthersby," Weston said. "For some abominable reason, Lady Ruthersby was given an inferior carriage. One wheel came off and two others almost did. Then lightning struck a nearby tree, setting it ablaze. It toppled onto the carriage, crushing it."

The couple gaped at Weston. Elise found she had to lower her gaze to her lap to hide the mirth she knew was in her eyes.

"I find it horrifying her ladyship and daughter had to suffer to this extent. However, it did give me the opportunity to get to know her. I have grown very fond of Lady Ruthersby."

She grasped her hands tightly. Though Weston meant well, these words—coming from the Duke of Disrepute—would give her brother-in-law the absolutely wrong idea about their relationship.

"I see," the earl said smugly.

"I don't believe you do, my lord," Weston said. "Meeting a woman of Lady Ruthersby's elegance and refinement has convinced me that the time has come for me to settle down and seek a bride of my own. Her ladyship is mature and wise. I have asked her to help guide me through the swirling waters of the Marriage Mart and help me select my new duchess."

Elise glanced up to see their startled looks.

"That means that Lady Ruthersby will need to come to London for the Season and participate fully in social events."

The countess began shaking her head. "I am afraid that wouldn't be possible, Your Grace. You see, she cares for our boys and—"

"And now a governess will, as would be expected," Weston interrupted. "While I know of the deep affection between your boys and Lady Ruthersby, it would be inconvenient for *me* for her to be tied up with something hired help should attend to." He smiled. "Of course, I would expect you and your husband to escort her to all of these affairs. Since I will need her advice on a daily basis, this means you will be invited to an immense number of events, hosted by the highest echelons of Polite Society. Would that be possible, my lady?"

Elise saw the glee break out on both of their faces.

"We would be most delighted to escort my sister-in-law to what-ever events you wish her to attend, Your Grace. We certainly would never want you to be inconvenienced."

"Good," Weston said and then studied the pair. "If you wish, Ruthersby, I'll give you my tailor's name. I'm sure since you will be running in high circles that you might want to replenish your ward-robe. As for the two ladies, my sister, the Duchess of Colebourne, has an excellent modiste in London. She's very particular about the clients she takes on but is willing to dress both ladies for the upcoming Season. Since I am asking for Lady Ruthersby's advice and want her by my side, I will need her to be turned out especially well. I will pay for this wardrobe and that of your wife's."

The earl waved a hand. "Oh, that won't be necessary, Your Grace. You are already doing so much for us. I cannot put you in such a position."

"Very well. See that your wife and sister-in-law are outfitted in the finest of gowns."

"Yes, Your Grace."

"You'll need to return to London early. Shall we say a month be-fore the Season begins? That would give me time to introduce you about my various clubs and the modiste will have the time to work her magic. I'll also give a dinner party, inviting my closest friends—Colebourne, Blackmore, Windham—and have you meet them before the Season begins."

The countess' eyes nearly popped from her head. "Four dukes at a dinner party? And us?" She smiled with glee. "Your Grace, you are a most generous man."

"I try to be. As for Lady Ruthersby, you must treasure having her while you can. I've promised her in exchange for helping me find a wife, I will also help her to find a husband. That means she will no longer be living with you in the future. Another reason to hire that governess as quickly as possible." He paused, pretending to think, but he didn't fool Elise. "It would also be a good idea to hire a nursery governess for Lady Claire. Your boys will need the full attention of their governess to prepare them for when they leave for school."

"We will do so at once, Your Grace," declared the earl.

"Good. Very well then. I must get back to Treadwell Manor. I will see you in London."

He rose and the Ruthersbys leaped to their feet. She also rose to bid him goodbye. Tears began to sting her eyes and she blinked rapidly.

"Will you walk me downstairs and see me off, Lady Ruthersby?"

"Of course, Your Grace."

He placed her hand on his arm and they departed the drawing room. Once in the corridor, she tried to remove it but he placed his hand over hers.

"If they renege on anything, you must write to me at once. Gently threaten them first and then if you see them lagging, I'm to know at once."

"I will but you were very convincing. I'm sure they'll promptly do as you suggested."

"You've been taken advantage of by them, Elise. They are awful people."

She cocked her head. "Yet you're going to introduce them all about society to your friends."

He shrugged. "A small price to pay to get you to the Season. Besides, just because I introduce them does not mean my friends will take to them."

They reached the foyer and the butler helped Weston into his greatcoat.

"I will miss you," he said, his voice low and rough.

"And I will miss you," she replied, the moment she'd dreaded finally here.

He took her hand and raised it to his mouth. His lips tenderly grazed her knuckles.

"Write to me anyway," he urged. "Even if all is going well."

She nodded, not trusting herself to speak.

Weston left and Elise stood there, cursing silently in her head as his carriage left. She had done the most foolish thing imaginable.

She'd gone and fallen in love with the Duke of Treadwell.

CHAPTER SEVENTEEN

London—Two months later . . .

W ESTON HAD ARRIVED in London last night and fallen into bed. He awoke and lay in bed lazily, thinking of everything he wanted to do to Elise in that bed. His thoughts put a smile on his face.

Wilson entered. "Good morning, Your Grace. My, what a broad smile. You must be happy we've returned to London."

"I am," he told his valet. "Dress me with care this morning. I have an appointment at my tailor's. I always like to look my best when I see Mr. Whipple."

"You would have to be his favorite customer, Your Grace, because you wear his clothes so well."

Still, Weston noticed that Wilson took extra care in selecting a waistcoat and tying Weston's cravat to intricate perfection.

The valet stood back and admired his work. "There. You are the best-dressed man in London and certainly the most handsome. The ladies will fawn over you come the Season."

"I only need one to do so, Wilson. Lady Ruthersby."

Wilson looked a bit startled and then smiled. "Her ladyship is very kind. Always had a nice word for everyone while she was at Treadwell Manor. She is very well liked." He paused. "Does this mean Your Grace is thinking about settling down?"

"No thinking is involved. I've already made my decision to do so. With Lady Ruthersby. I'll just have to make sure she accepts my offer when the time is right."

The valet snorted. "Of course, she will. She will be a duchess—and have the most eligible man in England."

Weston laughed and went downstairs for breakfast. He perused the newspapers, ascertaining who was already in town. He didn't know exactly when Elise would arrive. Based on her last letter to him, she should have come to London a few days ago. Sam and George were already here and he knew his sister planned to take Elise and her horrible sister-in-law to a modiste in order for all three ladies to be outfitted properly for the Season.

He left and went to Mr. Whipple's shop, where the tailor dropped everything he was doing to spend an hour with Weston. The tailor advised him on materials and various coats. In the end, as always, he gave Mr. Whipple free rein to pull together a new wardrobe for him.

Next, he went two doors down and visited his shirt maker, followed by a trip of two blocks to his bootmaker. Having gotten all of that out of the way, he decided to walk along the Serpentine instead of going to White's. He wasn't in the mood to talk to anyone there, much less see the sly smiles and listen to the innuendos in conversation. A big task awaited Weston. He had to change all of Polite Society's perception of him. Though only Elise's opinion mattered to him, he felt a need for the ton to see him as the man he would be from now on, not the one they'd known for almost a decade.

He reached Hyde Park and proceeded to the Serpentine. Not many people were out for this first week in March. The day was chilly and the winds blustery. Still, he'd never let weather stop him from walking. It was one of the simple pleasures in life he enjoyed year-round. He moved briskly, lost in thought, until he heard the shouts of children ahead. Weston glanced up and even from a distance, he recognized Elise. She had all three children with her and a kite in her hand. As she ran, holding the kite in one hand and her skirts in the other, they chased after her. She got the kite in the air and handed the ball of string to her older nephew. The younger one also put his hands on it. She stood behind them, watching to see if they could control the kite in the strong wind.

His heart skipped a beat at the sight of her. His entire body came alive. Suddenly, it was clear as a bell to him.

He loved her.

He'd allowed Juniper the power to govern his life for too long, vowing he would never fall in love again after his one, disastrous experience. Having finally put aside the control she had over him, he'd never wanted to relinquish it to anyone else. Especially another woman. But Elise wasn't just any woman. She was the antithesis of Juniper in every way. Warm to her cold. Kind and giving to Juniper's selfishness. Humble instead of haughty.

Why guard his heart against a woman so wonderful?

Weston started toward them. Claire spotted him and ran to him. He knelt and she flung herself into his arms.

"Your Grace!" she cried. "You came to see us."

"I did." He rose, lifting her with him. The feel of this child in his arms tugged at his heartstrings. He loved the girl. He loved her mother. He would love all the children they made together.

Carrying Claire, he reached Elise. She wore her spectacles, which he'd never seen on her. She'd mentioned she only wore them to see things in the distance.

"Mama! His Grace is here."

As he set Claire down, Elise turned. Her luminous smile made him feel as giddy as a schoolboy who'd just stolen his first kiss. Oh, how he wanted to kiss this woman. And much, much more.

"Good afternoon, Your Grace," she said.

He started to correct her and then decided it wouldn't do to have the children hear them address each other more intimately.

"Lady Ruthersby, I am delighted to have run into you." He glanced about. "Are you here with the boys' new governess? Or Lady

Claire's nursery governess?"

She'd written to him that both positions had been filled.

A sheepish look crossed her face. "They stayed behind. They've been very good with the children but you know the boys are quite energetic. I didn't think it would hurt to give both women a brief respite. Besides, the children are used to spending a great deal of time in my company."

"*I* need to spend a great deal of time with you," he said, causing her to blush.

"I remember our arrangements, Your Grace," she said. "In fact, I am having tea tomorrow afternoon with your sister and Lady Elizabeth. We are going to discuss the eligible ladies who will be in attendance this Season."

So, Sam was inserting herself into the process. Weston would have her act as his spy and report back to him on all that was said. His sister had already declared Elise a perfect match for her brother. He wondered what schemes Sam might come up with to push the two of them together.

"Are you free for tea today?" he asked.

"Yes. Though Lord and Lady Ruthersby already have plans away from the house."

"Even better. Then I will get you all to myself."

"Help!" Joseph cried. "It's getting away."

He turned and saw the two boys struggling to hold the ball of twine and rushed to them, taking it in hand.

"Let's bring it in," he suggested. "There are some days that are too windy to fly a kite. This is one of them. Here, help me."

Slowly, he turned the twine, aided by Joseph and Josiah, until the kite came back to earth. Joseph ran to fetch it.

"I thought you were going to wait for me before you went kite flying," he said.

"We didn't know how," Josiah said. "Auntie Elise said we could practice."

"We didn't want to be embarrassed," confessed Joseph.

He knelt so he could look both boys in the eyes. "There will be many things you won't know how to do. That's what life is all about, learning how to do new and different things, no matter what your age. Don't ever be ashamed. Always go in with an open mind and learn as much as you can. Try your best."

"Will you come with us and help us fly our kite again?" Josiah asked.

Weston doubted the boys' father ever played with them and said, "Of course. We might even learn to make a sailboat and sail it along the Serpentine."

With that statement, the boys cheered.

Claire clutched his trousers. "When will you read to me again?"

"How about this afternoon?" he suggested. "I'm coming to tea. We can read afterward."

She hugged his leg. Warmth filled him. Claire had also given him an idea.

"I will see you in two hours' time, Lady Ruthersby," he said.

"Very well, Your Grace. Children, it's time to go home."

They parted ways and Weston stopped at the first bookstore he came along. It had been years since he'd read on his own and he realized he'd missed doing so. The slightly musty smell of books filled his nostrils as he inhaled deeply.

"May I help you, my lord?" a clerk asked.

"Where are your children's books?"

"Right this way."

He perused the section and selected a book Claire would like and then added two more for each of her cousins, not wanting the boys to feel left out. The clerked lingered nearby and he handed the books to him.

"I'd also like to take a look at your atlases."

The clerk led him to the far side of the store and said, "I'll have these at the front for you, my lord."

Weston spent a good half-hour looking over the various atlases. He finally decided on which to purchase, eager to see the look on Elise's face. He had the clerk wrap the books in brown paper and then headed home. He would take the books with him to tea today.

He couldn't wait to finally be alone with Elise.

ELISE MADE SURE the children were settled upstairs. Claire had asked her three times when His Grace would arrive. She had combed through her books, trying to decide which one he should read to her. Josiah had come to help, making suggestions. He asked if the duke would also read to him. Joseph declared that he wanted to read to His Grace.

She shook her head, leaving the children in the hands of the two governesses. She didn't really think Weston wanted to spend time reading to Claire, much less her two nephews. He was a duke. Dukes had better things to do with their time than read to other people's children.

Or take tea with widows.

She returned to her room and went to the small mirror. It was too late to change her gown. She saw color flushing her cheeks. She seemed to turn all shades of pinks and reds whenever in Weston's company. He was bound to tease her about it, pointing out that it might be hard to find her a husband if she blushed all the time. She was glad that Lord and Lady Ruthersby had a prior engagement. They'd gone to spend the afternoon and evening with friends and had told her they wouldn't return until late. Because of that, she would have Weston all to herself. Not that it was a good thing. Being around him, as she would be during the next few months of the Season, was inevitably a bad thing. It would only make her want him more than she already did—and she didn't think that was possible.

With a last glance in the mirror, she hurried downstairs to the drawing room and went to look out the window. She saw his carriage pull up. Her breath caught as he stepped from it.

Was there a more handsome man in England?

She doubted it.

Elise took long, slow breaths as she continued to stare out the window. She could picture him knocking at the door. Being admitted. Coming up the stairs. Her body tingled with anticipation.

"My lady? His Grace, the Duke of Treadwell, has arrived."

She thanked the butler and then Weston entered the room. He seemed to fill any room from the moment he stepped into it. Today, he wore buff breeches and a hunter green coat. His shoulders looked impossibly broad in it and the breeches hugged his muscular legs, leaving little to the imagination. Suddenly, she wondered what he looked like sans clothes and found the idea terribly appealing.

"Good afternoon, Your Grace," she said politely. "Tea will be here shortly." She nodded to the butler, who left the room, knowing he would see that the teacart came with all haste.

Alone now, Weston came toward her, making her heart pound something dreadfully. She feared it would draw his eyes to her chest and he would see her gown move with each beat.

He took her hand and raised it to his sensual lips and gave her fingers a lingering kiss.

"Good afternoon, Elise," he said huskily, causing her belly to tighten.

"Won't you have a seat?" she managed to get out.

She indicated a settee, one where once upon a time she'd sat with Norwood and had tea. She pushed the thought from her mind. She shouldn't compare her late husband to Weston because he would fail to measure up in every way. So would any other man. The thought of the duke finding her a husband suddenly held no appeal. Yet she knew it was a necessary move on her part. One that would ensure her and Claire's future. Living with Lord and Lady Ruthersby had become more unpleasant, especially since they'd been forced to hire care for their children. She knew the countess, in particular, was unhappy having to pay for a nursery governess for Claire because she'd mentioned it several times. Marrying at Season's end was a way to escape having no control over her life and give her daughter a father figure.

"Are you going to stand throughout tea?" Weston asked, a teasing light in his eyes.

Elise sat. "I'm sorry. I was woolgathering."

He leaned and placed a few packages on the nearby table.

"What did you bring?"

"Books. I thought if I am to read to Claire, she might enjoy something new. I didn't want her cousins to be left out."

"That is very thoughtful of you."

His eyes gleamed. "Oh, I can be quite thoughtful. It's one of my good qualities. Of course, the *ton* isn't aware of that. They've painted me the rake for so long, they don't truly see me."

Though his tone was light, Elise detected hurt in it. "How awful for everyone to think the worst of you. I know you aren't anything like what they say."

One eyebrow rose. "I'm not?"

She clasped her hands together. "Well, perhaps you were. To some extent. But they will see you differently now this Season. You will still be charming but you will show them that you have many good qualities to offer." She chuckled. "I hate to say it. Even if you were four decades older, ugly as sin, and hateful to everyone, you would still have eligible women vying to be your duchess."

"That's why you have to help me find a woman who doesn't care about my wealth. Who looks beyond my titles." His gaze penetrated her. "Who sees me for who I am."

Elise grew warm under his stare. "We—your sister and I—will certainly do so."

Weston smiled. "I can't imagine leaving my future in two more capable hands."

CHAPTER EIGHTEEN

A MAID ROLLED in the teacart and Weston watched as Elise busied herself for a few minutes, making sure that he had plenty to eat and pouring out for them both. She remembered that he liked two lumps of sugar and prepared the tea to his satisfaction. They talked mostly about the children for several minutes and what they had been up to ever since Elise and Claire had returned to Briarcliff.

"Would you like a second cup?" she asked when he'd finished and placed his saucer back on the table.

"No, thank you. I think we need to talk more about the Season."

"Why? You've given me a list of your requirements," she pointed out. "I also told you mine." Elise lowered her eyes, resting her saucer on the table and fiddling with her hands.

Weston reached over and placed a hand atop hers. Immediately, she looked up, nervously licking her lips.

Driving him wild.

Now that he had her attention, he removed his hand. "Speaking of your requirements. You mentioned wanting a husband who could teach you how to kiss."

"That's correct," she said primly, color rising in her cheeks.

"Being a widow, most men will assume you already know how to do so. In fact, because of your experience, they are more likely to attempt to kiss you than when you made your come-out." He paused. "Did you manage to kiss any other gentleman besides Ruthersby during your Season?"

Her blush intensified. "No. Mama warned me not to kiss any man else they'd think I was fast. In fact, I didn't kiss Norwood until our wedding day."

Weston groaned inwardly, thinking what an innocent she truly was. Then again, it would be to his advantage—and pleasure—to teach her all she needed to know.

"That's all well and good for a young debutante, Elise, but I'm telling you—men will try to kiss you. You'll want to do so. With several."

"Why?" she asked guilelessly.

"You need to see which ones you enjoy kissing. If they kiss well, they'll most likely do other things well."

Her face flamed at his words and she started fidgeting again. She bit her bottom lip in thought and he was proud he restrained himself from leaning over and doing the same.

"Weston, I . . . well, what I mean is . . . I really don't know if I'll enjoy kissing anyone or not. Norwood gave me very . . . perfunctory kisses. When we were . . . about to come together. I think there is more to it but I'm not sure what. How will I even know if a man is a good kisser?"

This was exactly the realization he wanted her to come to.

"Kissing is a fine art. It takes lots of practice to become good at it."

"Then I am certain you are an expert," she murmured, rolling her eyes.

"I heard that," he said, grinning. "True. I have experience in it. You don't. I think in order for you to be able to choose a man who will suit you in that area, you'll need to know more about it. I'm perfectly willing to teach you."

"What?" she gasped.

"You heard me, Elise. You don't know what you're doing. You'll be kissing a few men come the Season. You're trying to find the one who best suits you."

"I won't marry a man strictly because he can kiss well," she insisted.

"No, but it is a huge part of enjoying what goes on in the bedroom. If you are better prepared, I believe you'll make a wiser choice." He smiled at her. "What do you think?"

"About kissing you?"

"About kissing me."

She thought a long moment and he was almost afraid he'd pushed her too far. But by God, she needed a little pushing. He was dying to kiss her. He needed to make an impression on her now, before the Season began, before all those lusting gents started sniffing about her skirts.

"Very well," she said formally. "I will allow you to teach me." Then she rose and went to stand before the window, her back to him, her arms wrapped about her protectively. "But you must promise not to make fun of me since I won't know what I am doing."

Weston rose and went to her, gently turning her gently by her shoulders until she faced him. "There is nothing to be embarrassed about, Elise. No one is born knowing how to kiss."

He allowed his hands to remain lightly on her shoulders, wanting to reassure her and have her get used to him touching her.

"May we begin our first lesson?"

Those large, violet eyes flickered with interest, mixed with doubt. "Yes," she whispered.

She had said the Ruthersbys wouldn't be back until this evening. No one should interrupt them. He had time. He didn't want to rush anything. He would pace himself. Lifting his hands to her face, he cradled it, looking at her for a long moment. He thought she might be holding her breath. Slowly, he bent until his mouth touched hers. Gently, he brushed his lips against hers. He could feel her trembling. He kept up the slow motion, allowing his fingers to glide to her throat, then using his thumbs to caress her face.

Weston kept this up for a few minutes, feeling her start to relax. He lifted his lips and kissed the tip of her nose, moving to the bridge. He kissed her brow. Her temples. The sides of her face. Along her jaw. Back to her mouth. This time, he pressed his lips against hers, moving one hand to her nape to hold her steady while the other went around to the small of her back. He pulled her closer, continuing to kiss her. Her ample breasts brushed against his chest, the nipples teasing him. Maintaining his composure, he lightly nipped at her full, bottom lip. She drew in a quick breath and he noticed her breathing more rapidly now.

With his years of practice, he gently coaxed her lips apart and slipped his tongue inside her mouth. Elise stiffened in his arms and then tried to pull away. When he continued to hold her next to him, she broke the kiss.

"What are you doing?" she asked, her tone accusatory.

"Kissing you."

"Like that?"

He smiled. "Like that."

"That's allowed?"

"Anything is allowed between a man and a woman, as long as they both consent."

She frowned. "I don't give mine."

"Ruthersby never kissed you like that?"

"No. Never," she said firmly.

"Could we at least try?" he pleaded. "It is a very pleasurable way to kiss." When doubt flickered in her eyes, he said, "Trust me. You said I am the expert. If you try it and don't like it, we can stop."

"Truly?"

He nodded.

"All right," she agreed.

Weston lowered his mouth to hers again and kissed her for a few minutes, trying to persuade her to relax again. Then he used the tip of his tongue to outline her mouth. She didn't pull away in protest so he continued. He urged her to open to him and she did, though he felt her tense again. Going slowly, he stroked her tongue with his, teasing her. Her hands, which had clutched his shoulders, slid to his chest.

Breaking the kiss, he asked, "Can you feel my heart beating?"

"Yes. It's very fast."

"That's because of you."

He swept her into his arms and carried her to a large chair in the corner. After he sat, she squirmed, her beautifully rounded bottom teasing him.

"Elise. Be still," he commanded.

She stopped moving.

Weston returned to kissing her. Soon, she was making beautiful little noises in her throat, which told him she was enjoying herself. He certainly was. He couldn't remember the last woman he'd taken such time with. He couldn't remember any woman. Just Elise. Here. Now.

"Kiss me back," he murmured against her mouth and was pleased when she began mimicking his actions. She learned quickly and, soon, his body heated, the blood rushing to his ears, swooshing as loud as waves crashing against the rocks. He broke the kiss and let his lips move against her throat, nipping and licking it, delighting in her coos and moans. Her pulse beat wildly against his tongue. He thought of other places he'd like to taste and began to grow hard.

This wasn't about him, though. It was about her. Teaching her to kiss and learning about her body. He had an image of Elise and Ruthersby making love in the dark, fully clothed, and imagined that was fairly accurate. This woman deserved so much more than what she had been given.

Weston's mouth returned to hers except, this time, one hand cupped her breast. She sighed and he began squeezing it gently, dragging his nail across the nipple. She moaned into his mouth.

God, he wanted more. Just a little more. A small taste.

He kissed his way down her throat again to the curve of one breast and allowed his tongue to follow that curve. Her skin was slightly salty and like velvet against his tongue. Pushing her gown down, he lifted a breast from her corset and suckled it. His teeth grazed her nipple, causing her back to arch. He kissed and laved and wanted more. He couldn't let his desire cloud his judgment, though.

Removing his mouth, he pulled her gown into place and kissed his way back up to her swollen mouth. She now kissed him hungrily and he knew desire rose within her. Knew he had put it there. He smiled against her mouth and then broke the kiss. Her eyes remained closed a moment longer and she sighed aloud.

"That was an excellent first session," he praised. "You are an apt pupil, my lady."

She blinked several times. "I had no idea. No idea at all, Weston. It was like having a candle lit after spending my entire life in the dark."

He kissed her again, long and slow. "You now know a little about kissing."

"A little?" she snorted. "How much more could there be? Why, you even kissed . . ." Her voice trailed off and her color rose.

"Your breast. Yes, I did. I wouldn't advise you to allow any of your suitors to do so, however."

"Then why did you?" she demanded softly, her eyes studying him anew.

"I wanted you to see that there are different ways to kiss besides on your mouth."

"Where else?" she asked.

He chuckled. "That is for later." He stood, bringing her to her feet. Fortunately, her hair was still pinned into place. If he'd had his way, he would have removed all the pins and run his fingers through it. "Why don't you ring and have the children brought downstairs? I'll read to them a bit from their new books."

Her fingers came to her lips. "Do I look different? As if we've been kissing?"

"Well, your lips are a bit swollen. Summon a servant and go wash your face. I'll ask for the children to be brought here."

"All right." Her hand fell but her gaze met his. "You were right. Using our tongues made it very pleasurable."

If only she knew how much more pleasure could be found. All in good time.

She pulled the cord and then excused herself. Weston wandered about the room until a servant appeared and he requested the three children come to see him. By the time they arrived, Elise had returned, her lips still slightly swollen but not as noticeable.

They greeted him and Elise dismissed the governess who had accompanied them downstairs, asking her to return in an hour, and then said, "Come and see what His Grace has brought you."

Eagerly, they rushed over and clapped their hands as he distributed the packages to them, leaving the last one on the table.

"May we open them?" Joseph asked and Weston nodded.

Immediately, all three ripped into the presents with glee, holding up the books to show Elise.

"Read mine first," Claire demanded, placing the book next to Weston and then crawling into his lap.

He reached for the book and opened it, liking the feel of this little person in his arms. He read the story to her and then Josiah asked to be next. Weston read the second book aloud as the boy also sat in his lap. When it came to Joseph, he said he would sit next to the duke. He also would read his book aloud to His Grace and not be read to.

By the time Joseph finished, the hour had passed and the governess returned to collect her charges. Elise had the children thank him and they left to have their dinner.

Weston lifted the final brown parcel from the table and handed it to her. "I also came bearing a gift for you."

"You didn't have to do so."

"I wanted to. Open it."

She placed the package in her lap and untied the string before ripping at the paper. When she'd removed enough to see what lay inside, she paused, growing very still. He saw tears fill her eyes and cursed silently for thinking to replace the atlas her husband had given her.

Then Elise looked up, her violet eyes a darker shade than normal, thanks to the tears brimming in them.

"You couldn't have given me a more perfect gift," she told him. "I used to look at my atlas every day, dreaming of all the places to go."

"Where would you go first?" he asked.

"Paris," she said dreamily. "It's supposed to be the best city in the world."

"I only hope you have that opportunity. Bonaparte has escaped and is said to be marching toward Paris. Hopefully, England and her allies will defeat the little monster and lock him away for all time. My friend, Sebastian, is part of the forces who better bring the dictator to heel." He thought a moment. "Perhaps you could go there on your honeymoon if Bonaparte has been put down. It's supposed to be the most romantic city. Where after that?"

She shrugged. "So many places. The Swiss Alps. Tuscany. Sailing along the Rhine or Nile. Or across the ocean to America." She stroked the book in her lap. "Even if I never go to any of those places in person, I can always look at them in these pages and go to them in my mind."

Weston vowed he would take Elise wherever she wanted to go.

When they were husband and wife.

CHAPTER NINETEEN

E LISE BRUSHED HER long hair and smoothed it, winding it into her usual chignon. She hadn't had a lady's maid since her sister-in-law became the new Countess of Ruthersby and laid claim to everything in the household, including Elise's maid. When she dressed every morning, she did so with the help of a parlor maid who did her best. The girl knew nothing about doing hair, however, and so Elise had to forego any fashionable, elaborate hairstyles. It would probably make for a bit of gossip among some of the women in the *ton*. Her dress made up for it, however.

Samantha's modiste had been a dream to work with, encouraging Elise to be bolder in her color selections and even more daring in the cut of her gowns. She'd praised Elise's figure, especially her breasts, declaring them meant to be seen. Though she was self-conscious about putting them on display, glimpsing into the mirror told her the dressmaker had been correct.

She looked divine.

Opening a small box, she withdrew the sapphire earrings that her father had presented to her on her sixteenth birthday. He'd told her to wear them on special occasions and hoped she would remember him when she did so. Tonight was one of those nights. She put them on and admired her reflection in the mirror. Satisfied with what she saw, she slipped from her room and sneaked up the stairs. Though the children were supposed to already be in bed, she'd arranged with the two governesses to keep them up a bit so she could come and show them her dress.

She entered the room that had been the one she shared with Claire when they were in town and was now solely her daughter's. It had taken some explaining for Claire to understand why her mother now slept downstairs instead of with her daughter. Elise had bragged on what a big girl Claire was becoming and how she would be like her cousins and have a bed all to herself.

Claire now sat in bed, the pillows propped behind her. Joseph and Josiah perched at the foot of the bed. All three children gasped as she came in.

"Mama! You are beautiful."

"Auntie Elise, you look like a princess," Josiah said.

"No, a queen," Joseph corrected.

She hugged each of them. "Thank you very much. I hope everyone at the ball will also think the same."

Claire reached up and touched the earrings. "These are pretty, Mama. Where did you get them? Why don't you wear them?"

"My papa gave them to me years ago. One day, I will give them to you," she promised.

"Do you have a necklace to match them?" Josiah asked innocently.

"No, I only have the earrings."

"You need a necklace. I'll bet all the ladies will wear one," Joseph said. "Should I go ask Mama if she'll loan you one?"

"No. Your mama is busy getting ready and shouldn't be bothered," she told her nephew.

It did sadden her to think of the jewelry she'd once had when she was the Countess of Ruthersby. Although Norwood had given her a piece on every birthday and Christmas, as well as when Claire was born, the new countess demanded they be returned. Elise had explained they were personal gifts from her husband and not part of the Ruthersby collection of jewels to be worn to social events. It hadn't mattered. What the new countess wanted, she got. In this case, it was every bit of jewelry Elise had.

Except for these earrings.

It didn't matter. She was going to a ball tonight. She might even dance with her future husband. Though she didn't long for jewels to wear, he still might give her some after they wed. She couldn't wait for the day she and Claire could leave this place and begin a new life together.

"All right, my darlings, into bed with you all."

She tucked Claire in and kissed her and then went to supervise her nephews getting into bed.

"Remember, keep my visit to yourselves," she said, not wanting the boys to get into trouble for being up past their bedtime.

"We will, Auntie," Josiah promised solemnly.

Elise returned to her bedchamber and collected her reticule and a filmy wrap, placing it about her shoulders. Easter had come early this year, which meant the Season started sooner than usual. The March winds were still strong and brisk. Word had come that Napoleon had entered Paris two weeks ago. She supposed that would be the talk of the ball tonight. Or perhaps not. With it being the first social event of the Season, people might be more interested in fashion and flirting than discussing a long-term war.

She went downstairs to the foyer, knowing Weston was coming for them in his carriage. It surprised her to already find him standing there. As she descended the stairs, his face lit up.

Taking her gloved hand as she reached the bottom, his admiring glance told her all she needed to know.

"You are simply breathtaking, my lady."

"It's the gown. Actually, the modiste who created the gown. Samantha told me she was a genius."

Weston had been right about believing she and his sister would become fast friends. Though Elise hadn't thought a duchess would want to have anything to do with a widow who had no social connections, she'd been wrong. The Duchess of Colebourne hadn't a mean bone in her body. She'd insisted they be on a first-name basis. They'd had tea several times and gone shopping together, often with Lady Elizabeth in tow. They'd also discussed possible candidates for Weston's bride-to-be.

Elise had also struck up a correspondence with the Duchess of Windham since their shared Christmas Day dinner. The fact both women had lost their husbands in the same accident, as well as losing babies, had been the foundation of their friendship. It had grown well beyond that, though, and they wrote to one another weekly. Elise couldn't wait since she felt the next letter she received from Phoebe would be news of her baby's birth.

"Madame might be a genius but you are fulfilling her vision of the dress rather nicely," Weston praised.

She looked at his dark evening clothes and snow-white shirt and cravat. "Your tailor has also done quite well, Your Grace. I don't believe I've ever seen you looking more handsome."

"Not even the night we first met?" he teased. "I was younger then."

"Some men age particularly well. You will be one of them," she said. Glancing to the stairs and finding them empty, she added, "I have three names of women that you are to ask to dance with tonight. You may partner with as many as you choose but these three are ones I think you'll find particularly interesting."

"Name them," he urged.

Elise did, adding their immediate family connections and telling him a little about each one.

"It sounds as if you've been thorough. I look forward to meeting these women."

"What about me?"

He frowned.

"You told me you've been looking at your clubs for men to introduce me to. Which particular ones do you have in mind?"

Weston laughed. "I will introduce you to plenty of men this evening. I will not be giving you the names of individuals, though."

"Why not? I've been carefully evaluating eligible women the last couple of weeks. You were to do the same. Don't you recall our agreement?"

He reached for her hand. The feel of his fingers, even though they both wore gloves, brought heat to her.

"I don't want you to go into this with preconceived notions. Dance with several men tonight. Then we will discuss the ones you found interesting when I visit you tomorrow afternoon. If you like a man and I can recommend him to you, I will do so. If I believe you should be warned away, I'll voice my opinion then."

"Hmm. That doesn't seem quite fair. You know exactly what women to dance with while I'm going in blindly to this first ball."

Weston chuckled. "I know Sam and Lady Elizabeth and you haven't just been talking about ladies for me. They've also told you about various men."

She shrugged. "They may have. Still, I will look to you for guidance before I commit to any suitor."

"You said suitor. Don't think you must fixate on one. I say let a variety of men call upon you. In fact, I may be here most afternoons to help you cull through them."

"No, you should be calling on the woman—or women—you are considering making your duchess."

"I plan to visit you daily to seek your advice, Elise. I will also make my own calls. The world of Polite Society is small and, fortunately, most of them live close to one another. It won't take me long to get from Ruthersby's townhouse to another one in Mayfair."

"Oh, Your Grace, you're here!" cried Lady Ruthersby, coming down the stairs on her husband's arm.

"Yes, my lady. I'm nothing if not punctual."

"I thought you were always late to *ton* affairs," Elise said out of the side of her mouth before the pair joined them.

"I used to be," he said quietly. "This is the new me."

The two men shook hands and Elise watched her sister-in-law bat her lashes at Weston. It caused a queasy feeling inside her. She wondered if they'd been together.

"Thank you for stopping by for us," Lord Ruthersby said.

"Delighted to," Weston replied. "I see my tailor has had his way with you. You look splendid, Ruthersby. You are also turned out very well, Lady Ruthersby."

The countess gave him a flirtatious smile. "Why, thank you, Your Grace."

"Shall we? My carriage is just outside your doorway."

Weston took her arm and held her back as her in-laws eagerly rushed ahead.

"I've never touched her," he said. "She did flirt with me last Season. Right in her husband's presence. Even the Duke of Disrepute had some rules he lived by, Elise. Discretion was one of them. I never considered her for a lover. In fact, I have never spoken publicly about any woman I've bedded. It's my one-time lovers who weren't as discreet and made public our liaisons."

"I suppose it's a good thing you haven't slept with my sister-in-law," she said lightly. "Although not from lack of trying on her part. You might want to emphasize to her again that you are looking for a wife this Season."

He smiled, his even, white teeth gleaming at her. "I'll do so."

Leading her to the carriage, he handed her up and joined her, sitting across from her in-laws.

"We've never been in a ducal carriage," Lady Ruthersby fawned. "It's so very plush."

"Thank you. I quite like it. As to this evening, I thought we should have supper together. Unless you have made other plans?"

"No, none," Lord Ruthersby confirmed. "We would be delighted to dine with you, Your Grace."

Weston turned to Elise. "That means you should reserve the supper dance for me since we'll all sup together."

"That's not necessary," she told him.

"Yes. It is."

"Then I will save it for you, Your Grace."

The rest of the ride was taken up with the countess chattering nonstop. Elise stopped listening since her sister-in-law never directed a question to her or ever included her in any conversation. Instead, she enjoyed the nearness of Weston. They sat close together, the right side of his body pressed against the entire left side of hers. He radiated heat, which filled her. With every breath, she caught the whiff of his cologne and that beautiful, masculine scent that was all him. She wondered if dukes smelled better than other men.

They arrived and went through the receiving line. He was doing a good job of including the Ruthersbys, both tonight and in the past few weeks. The four went to join the Colebournes in the ballroom.

A footman handed Elise a programme and Weston promptly took it, scrawling his name by the supper dance. Then he wrote his name again beside the last dance and returned the card to her.

"You can't do that," she said quietly. "Scratch through your name."

"Why?"

"Even the former Duke of Disrepute must know if he dances with a woman twice, it indicates his interest in her. We don't need to set the tongues of the *ton* wagging on the very first night."

He shrugged. "I merely thought it would be easier to locate you to go home if we danced the final number together."

She gave him a pointed look. "I won't be that hard to find."

"Look at it this way. If a duke is interested in you, it will cause other eligible men's interested to be piqued. I am doing you a favor by dancing twice with you."

"You have a ready answer for everything, don't you?"

"I like getting my way. And crossing my name out seems so . . . gauche." He looked around. "Ah, here comes the horde. I will introduce you around but you'll need to decide which men to accept as partners. The way you look tonight, you really don't need my help at all."

Quickly, Elise was surrounded as Weston made introduction after introduction. The names and faces blurred. She hoped by engaging gentlemen as partners that she would get enough time with them to distinguish them from one another—and see if they were husband material.

As her dance card quickly filled, she leaned to him and said, "You need to go find your three lovely ladies and sign their programmes before it's too late."

Weston grinned. "It's never too late for a duke to request a dance. I will do as you ask, though." Then he winked at her, causing laughter to bubble from within her as he sauntered away.

CHAPTER TWENTY

WESTON DID AS Elise had requested and found the ladies she had recommended to him. All three were very attractive. Two were widows in their mid-twenties and one of them had a daughter. The third candidate was making her come-out but she had a maturity about her that most young women didn't share. They eagerly made room for him on their programmes. He decided to dance the first three dances of the evening with them in order to be free the rest of the time.

To watch Elise.

The ball opened and he partnered with a widow first, a brunette with lively brown eyes. The second dance was with the other widow, a blond with a perfect complexion and almost icy beauty. The debutante, his final dance, had light brown hair and danced the best of the three. For her age, she was quite self-assured. If he didn't already have his heart set upon Elise, he might have considered the girl to be his duchess.

None of these women held a candle to Elise, though. Her incandescent beauty was only one of many things that attracted him to her. Her sterling character made her as beautiful inside as out. The fact that she came with the most delightful child in England was merely icing on the cake.

Weston returned his partner to her formidable mama and excused himself. He got something to drink and then watched as the next dance began, a lively country reel. He spied Elise and watched her, her steps sure and full of energy, her face glowing with happiness. Suddenly, the urge came over him to go out and claim her now, in front of everyone. Why wait for weeks, especially when some handsome nobleman might sweep in and steal her away?

As he started forward, someone grabbed his arm and tugged him back.

George.

"What do you want?' he asked grumpily.

"For you to stop staring at Elise like a hound in heat," his friend replied drolly. "You are mooning over her."

"I am not mooning," Weston snapped. "Merely observing."

"Have you fallen in love with her?" George asked softly.

"Yes," he muttered. "And no I-told-you-so from you," he warned.

"You won't get one from me. I'm merely happy for you. But you need to wait."

"Why?"

"Weren't you about to rush out to the dance floor and declare for her?"

"How did you know?"

George smiled. "How could I not know? We've been together three decades now, West. I know you better than you do yourself."

"What is your point?"

"I think you should let Elise enjoy a small bit of the Season. You've told me how difficult her life has been. Look at her. She's happy. Truly happy out on that dance floor. Let her giggle and flirt a bit. Claim attention from a few good-looking swains."

"What if one of them offers for her while I stand idly by?" he asked.

"Then let her have a week," George said sagely. "No one will declare for her that quickly. She certainly wouldn't accept any man that fast. Let her bask in the sunshine. Go buy a special license. Then in a week's time, after she's had a bit of fun, tell her that you love her. That she is your entire world. She'll say yes to you. Then you can wed and let her continue the rest of the Season as your duchess. She'll thrive, knowing she has your love. Polite Society will fall to her feet. And you can show everyone how the beautiful and elegant Lady Ruthersby tamed the Duke of Disrepute."

Weston's eyes continued to follow Elise but he said, "When did you become so wise?"

George laughed. "Perhaps it was always in there somewhere. Sam seems to have brought out an innumerable amount of good qualities within me."

He turned. "You're happy with my sister?"

His friend's smile told his story. "Indubitably. As you will be with Elise. Do you have any more dances scheduled?"

"No. I danced with the three women she wished me to. I've claimed the supper dance from her, though. And the last one."

"Then you have time to come to the card room with me. No sense in standing on the sidelines, yearning for her." George grinned. "Or seeing her in another man's arms and punching him out."

The thought of Elise held close by another man angered him.

"Come along, Your Grace," his friend urged. "Let's keep you out of trouble."

He did as his friend advised and they left the ballroom. Weston played several hands of cards and won all but one. He circulated, talking to old friends he hadn't seen in months since he'd been in Devon. The time passed quickly until George found him.

"The supper dance is two away. I thought it wise to return to the ballroom. Have you kept yourself occupied?"

Weston nodded. "It was good advice. I might have thrashed someone if I thought he danced too close to Elise."

They made their way back to the ballroom and found Sam returning.

"Where have you been, my love?" George asked, taking her hand and kissing it before tucking it into the crook of his elbow.

"The retiring room. It's very crowded." She glanced to Weston. "Have you danced yet with the women assigned to you?"

"All three," he said smugly. "How much a part did you play in their selection?"

"Some," she said vaguely. "Although I have been good in talking you up. Subtly, of course. Oh, I do like Elise, Weston. She will make for a perfect duchess and can be my best friend. We'll live next door to one another and raise our children together." She gazed at her husband. "I never knew I could be so very, very happy."

George kissed her and Weston heard a few whispers and tittering.

"I say, Charm, you better save that for your bedroom," he teased. "Wouldn't want to cause a scene here on the first night of the Season."

"He won't," Sam assured him. "However, he does cause quite a scene in our bedchamber on a nightly basis."

Weston laughed. "I'm sure he does, little sister."

They went inside and he gazed across the room, looking for Elise. Spotting her, he cursed aloud.

"What is it?" George asked, glancing about the room. "Oh."

He hadn't asked any individual to dance with Elise tonight, despite what she thought. He knew with her beauty that she would attract a bevy of men. Any that she asked him about, he would find something wrong with them. Unfortunately, he should have thought to warn her away from certain gentlemen, including the one she danced with now.

Lord Ivy.

Anger surged through him. Weston took a step forward and was immediately pulled back, George's fingers tight on his arm.

"Let go," he ordered quietly.

"No. Listen to me and cool your heels, West," George insisted. "I've already escorted you out of London once over Ivy. You don't want to storm out onto the dance floor and cause a scene in front of the entire *ton*. You're trying to show what a good man you truly are. Punching Ivy in the middle of a ballroom would be the kiss of death in your pursuit of Elise."

George relaxed his hold and Weston took a deep breath.

"You're right," he agreed. "As usual." He took another calming breath. "Thank you. For keeping me from making an idiot of myself and ruining any chance I have with Elise."

George smiled. "That is what friends are for."

ELISE HADN'T HAD time to catch her breath since the ball began. Her programme had filled quickly. She had glanced about and seen Weston dancing twice with women she'd suggested he partner with. She knew what each of the three looked like, thanks to Samantha and Elizabeth. One had visited the same modiste and Elise had even been introduced to her in the shop. The woman was a widowed countess with a young daughter. She'd met the second woman in a bookstore she'd visited with Elizabeth, who had known the girl since childhood. The third woman, a childless widow and dowager viscountess, had been standing nearby when they arrived tonight. Samantha pointed her out and Elise planned to speak with her before she left this evening.

All three women were very beautiful, so much that it hurt to see Weston dancing with them. She hadn't seen him lately, though, and hoped he would return to the ballroom in time for their dance. She supposed he was in the card room, a place her father enjoyed going so he wouldn't have to see his wife flirt shamelessly. Elise still found it hard to believe that Papa had loved Mama so much and had allowed her to hurt him as much as she did.

The dance ended and the tall baron she'd partnered with led her from the dance floor.

"Might I call upon you tomorrow, Lady Ruthersby?" he asked

casually.

"Yes, you may," she said.

She'd given permission to every man who'd asked to call. It was hard to decide which ones were worth knowing. Conversation was impossible with some dances and limited with others. She would keep her dance card and go down it tomorrow with Weston, seeking his opinion on the men who'd claimed a dance with her this evening, as well as discuss the ladies she'd suggested to him. It pained her to think of this time next year. She would arrive at the first ball of the Season, a married woman, and see Weston from across the room with his duchess. Perhaps he would speak to her. Most likely, they'd merely make eye contact and he'd nod. The closeness they'd discovered as they'd been thrown together these past few weeks would be gone. They would be wed to others. He might have even forgotten her name by then.

But she would never forget him. Never forget his kiss. His scent. The way her body tingled with anticipation anytime he came near. He wasn't her first love. He would be her only love, a man she worshipped from afar. Still, he'd proven to be right. She hadn't lacked for dance partners tonight. Everyone had been very kind and pleasant to her. Elise knew without a doubt that she would be able to find a husband. She would throw herself into her new marriage and try never to think of the Duke of Treadwell.

"My lady, I believe I am your next partner."

She turned and saw a man just under six feet. Fair-haired with pale blue eyes. Attractive. Oozing self-confidence.

She consulted her card. "Lord Ivy?"

He laughed. "If I weren't Ivy, I would claim to be. All to have a dance with you, Lady Ruthersby."

Elise smiled. "Are you merely charming or are you flirting with me, Lord Ivy?'

He cocked his head. "Perhaps a little of both. Shall we?"

His offered his arm and she took it as they went to the center of the dance floor. The orchestra struck up the next song and their dance began. He was very smooth on his feet.

"What do you wish to know about me?" he asked. "I already know about you."

She sensed her cheeks heating. "How do you know about me? We were only introduced this evening."

"I make it my business. Especially when a beautiful woman who hasn't been involved in the past few Seasons turns up on the arm of the Duke of Disrepute."

"I am helping His Grace," she said. "He seeks a wife and hasn't always been a good judge of character. I suppose it's hard for a duke to know if people like him for himself or merely like his title."

"And your role in this?" Lord Ivy asked.

"Since I am a widow, His Grace believes I am more mature and I know what a good marriage should entail. I have worked on drawing up a list of eligible ladies for him to consider. He plans to be engaged by Season's end."

Lord Ivy frowned. "And what do you get out of this, my lady?"

"I am also considering marriage again, my lord. I lost Lord Ruthersby three years ago. My daughter needs a father. I would also like to have more children. Attending the Season is a way of meeting prospective mates, wouldn't you say?"

"It can be."

"Have you ever been wed, my lord?"

His eyes darkened. "No."

Elise read people well and knew this man was hurting. "Did you lose someone you loved?" she asked.

"I did." His jaw tightened. "It's in my past, however." He smiled down at her. "I am open to the prospect of finding a wife of my own. I've recently come into my title. My father passed away last October. It was his fondest wish that I settle down and begin a family."

"I am sorry. I lost my own father last year."

A light came into eyes. "Then we have sorrow in common. Might I call upon you tomorrow, Lady Ruthersby? I won't hide the fact that I would like to get to know you better."

She smiled. "I would very much like that, Lord Ivy."

The music came to a halt and he escorted her from the floor. Weston waited for her, a dark scowl on his face. George stood next to him, looking tense. Samantha shrugged, indicating she hadn't a clue what went on.

Lord Ivy released her and bowed. "Until tomorrow, Lady Ruthersby." He glanced at Weston and then walked away.

Elise looked at Weston. "What's wrong?"

"You're not to see or speak to that man," he said in his most haughty ducal tone. "Ever again."

"Why not?" she asked.

Without answering, he took her hand and placed it on his arm. "Dance now. We'll talk later."

Frustration built within her. She wanted answers now, not silence.

Then the strains of a waltz began and Weston took her hand in his. His arm came about her, pulling her close. Much closer than she thought appropriate but she didn't complain. He swept her away, their steps perfectly matched. Elise didn't think she'd ever danced so gracefully or felt so alive. Warmth flooded her as the colors swirled by. Without her spectacles, anything beyond Weston was a blur. It almost made it seem as if only the two of them danced, in a world of their own making. Her blood rushed through her veins, pounding loudly in her ears, almost blocking the music. She felt her breasts brush against his hard, muscled chest and began to grow hot and faint.

She wanted this man. She wanted to kiss him and hold him and love him for the rest of her life. How was she to push aside her foolish notions and pledge herself to another when he dominated her every thought? He'd ruined every other man for her. She had no choice but to wed after this Season. She couldn't go on living in the Ruthersby household, treated like an inferior in every way. Yet how was she to do so when her body and soul cried out for Weston?

The music ended. He didn't release her. Others began moving toward the doors.

"Let me go," she urged, unsure why he held her in place. Worried that others might start to notice and question his behavior—and hers. After all, he was the Duke of Disrepute to everyone present. They would merely think her his latest conquest. What man would want her after he'd left his mark?

He did as she'd asked, his gaze never leaving hers. He placed her hand on his arm and ever so slowly, began leading her from the ballroom. So slowly that by the time they reached the doors they were the last couple to exit.

When Elise tried to continue through the doors, Weston pulled her back into the empty room.

And kissed her.

He hadn't done so since that first lesson a few weeks ago. They'd never found themselves alone, constantly surrounded by family, friends, or the children. She'd lain in bed at night, thinking of his kiss, her body burning for him.

But now? Here? Why?

She started to protest but his mouth silenced it. His arms went about her, holding her close. He didn't waste any time. He eased her mouth open and his tongue stroked hers. Chills raced through Elise, a good kind that signaled excitement. Her body sprang to life. Her arms went about his neck, her fingers pushing into his hair. He groaned into her mouth. Her breasts felt full and heavy, aching for his touch, the nipples tender. He tugged her head back, deepening the kiss, stirring the fire that now raged within her.

Then he broke the kiss, resting his forehead against hers as they both breathed heavily.

"What was that?" she asked, her voice shaking.

Weston lifted his head from hers. "That was to show you what you seek with a man. That man will never be Lord Ivy. Is that understood?"

"Yes," she said meekly, still reeling from the kiss.

"Good." His hands encircled her waist and pulled them apart, pushing her slightly away. He took her hand and placed it on his arm. "Shall we go into supper, Lady Ruthersby?"

"Yes, Your Grace," she managed to say, clutching him tightly because her legs shook like jelly.

Elise knew now was not the time to go into it, especially with all of Polite Society surrounding them as they made their way to a table where the Colebournes and Ruthersbys sat—but she would get the truth from Weston about Lord Ivy.

Soon.

CHAPTER TWENTY-ONE

W ESTON WATCHED AS another gentleman left the Ruthersby townhouse. That made four in the last quarter-hour. Who knew how many were still inside fawning over Elise?

He'd avoided any conversation regarding their kiss. Last night, he'd escorted her into supper, where they sat with her in-laws and George and Sam, knowing she wouldn't bring it up in front of the others. She and Sam had departed for the retiring room after they ate and he'd made himself scarce until the final dance of the evening. It was another waltz and Weston had relished the feel of Elise in his arms.

They merely enjoyed dancing together and hadn't bothered with conversation. He'd collected the Ruthersbys and Lady Ruthersby had dominated all conversation the entire way home. Weston had informed Elise he would call on her the next afternoon but she had told him it was imperative to go visit the three ladies he'd danced with. He'd compromised, agreeing to do so if he could come to tea afterward. Before Elise could answer, both the earl and countess enthusiastically replied that His Grace would be most welcomed.

Weston hadn't visited any woman today. Instead, he had his driver drop him at his club and spent a few hours there. He had read the newspapers, which made much of the Duke of Charm now being happily married and how it was rumored Disrepute would soon follow. He'd also eavesdropped as club members spoke about last night's ball, hearing Elise's name mentioned several times. It took great restraint on his part not to smash his fist into the nose of any man who spoke about her. She may not have made much of an impression during her come-out but now she'd grown into her beauty. The gentlemen of the *ton* were now panting after her, much to his chagrin.

When he couldn't take any more gossip, he left White's, dismissing his driver and walking the streets for an hour before taking a hansom cab to see Elise. He had the driver stop a half-block away, paying for his time as Weston watched the stream of men leaving. His anger grew and he had to remind himself of what George had said. Elise had never received attention. She needed this time to see how worthwhile and deserving she was.

It didn't make him like what occurred, though.

Finally, he paid the driver and went to Ruthersby's front door. The butler admitted him as three more bachelors departed. All turned, gazing at him in curiosity, and he heard one fellow ask another why they'd been made to leave when Treadwell was only arriving.

"Because he's a bloody duke, you fool," his companion uttered as the butler closed the door on the trio.

"Right this way, Your Grace. Lord and Lady Ruthersby are expecting you."

As the servant led Weston upstairs, he asked, "Were you very busy today?"

"Quite," the butler replied. "It did my heart good seeing so many nice gentlemen call on Lady Ruthersby. She deserves a little happiness in her life. It was hard to see her lose Lord Ruthersby. And now . . ." The servant's voice trailed off.

He realized this man had seen Elise come to the household as a young bride and now witnessed how the new earl and countess behaved toward her.

As they reached the drawing room door, Weston asked, "How do the Ruthersbys treat her?"

The butler looked surprised and then said, "Abominably, Your Grace. My hope is she and Lady Claire will find a good man to take them away from this place."

The servant's honesty surprised him yet it confirmed what he believed.

"Forgive my indiscretion, Your Grace," the butler added. "It's just that everyone in the household adores Lady Ruthersby and her daughter. To see how her life has changed is very hard."

"I am sure Lady Ruthersby will make an excellent match very soon," he said. Left unsaid was he planned to be her fiancé.

The butler nodded and then announced him. Weston entered the drawing room and the three occupants rose. Pleasant greetings were exchanged even though he had a bad taste in his mouth regarding the Ruthersbys. He would never speak to them after his marriage to Elise.

The teacart arrived and they made small talk as Lady Ruthersby poured out. The conversation continued in that vein until he finished what was on his plate.

Looking at Elise, Weston said, "Might we go for a drive in the park, my lady? I would be interested in discussing the group of ladies you encouraged me to meet last night."

"Is that wise?" she asked. "You do know how the park is full of people at this hour of the day."

"I feel like getting some air," he replied. "I daresay you need some, too, being trapped all afternoon with so many visitors."

"Go ahead," Lord Ruthersby urged and then looked to Weston. "You will be at tonight's musicale, Your Grace?"

"Of course. Would it be convenient if I stopped for you and the ladies on my way there?"

The earl looked pleased. "That would be delightful, Your Grace."

Weston rose and the three followed suit. Both he and Elise left the drawing room.

"We shouldn't be seen together in the park," she reiterated as they moved down the corridor.

"Well, I certainly don't want to discuss matters of an intimate nature in front of those two. I doubted they would be leaving anytime soon, which is why I suggested we take a drive."

"You know Hyde Park is the place to be seen at this time of day," she accused.

"Is it?" he asked innocently. "I've never taken anyone driving in the park."

"Oh."

Elise remained quiet as the butler handed her a shawl. Weston helped place it about her shoulders and they stepped outside.

"Damnation," he uttered, under his breath.

He'd forgotten that he'd dismissed his driver and had no carriage here.

He took her hand and tucked it into the crook of his arm. "Would you mind a walk through the park instead?"

"That would be nice. I know you enjoy walking."

Weston turned toward Hyde Park. He pointed out a few houses he liked as they strolled along.

"I didn't know you enjoyed architecture," she said.

"I like classic lines. I helped design new stables at Treadwell Manor when I had just completed university. I plan to be spending more time there and will need to add to my current crop of horses. Do you ride?"

"I did all the time before my marriage. I told you I was Papa's shadow. We used to go about on horseback visiting our tenants. My husband wasn't fond of horses, though. He'd fallen from one as a child and never quite conquered his fear of them. I gave it up at his request."

"You do enjoy riding, though?"

"I do. Actually, I've missed it. I've gone down a few times with Joseph and Josiah as they started their riding lessons. I wanted to place Claire on a horse at an early age." She paused, her mouth turning downward. "The earl said it was a poor idea and forbid it."

"I think Claire would take to riding very well because she is so spirited. I will teach her."

Elise stopped. "Quit being so affable, Weston. You're a duke, for God's sake. You don't have to be nice to me or my daughter."

"What if I wish to be?"

She blew out a breath. "Then you can be nice by finding me a husband. Let's talk about that and the women from my list."

They started up again and soon reached the park. Entering, he saw so many carriages, it looked like traffic was at a standstill.

Spying a bench off to the side, he said, "Come sit. I don't want to get caught up in that."

They took a seat and she said, "Tell me what you thought of my choices. I put a great deal of thought into the process. Did you have a particular favorite?"

She peppered him with questions about each woman and her displeasure grew with his responses.

"I don't understand you at all," she proclaimed. "I thought I did. I believed I had gotten to know you fairly well since we've been acquainted. You've found something wrong with every one of them."

"Can I help it if I am choosy? After all, this will be a woman I spend the rest of my life with."

Her brow wrinkled in frustration. "Yes, you should be careful in your selection, Weston, but you are being finicky." She gave him a haughty look. "That one is too tall. This one too short. This one is stern. This one giggles too much. She is a featherhead, while she is a bluestocking. This one can't form an opinion. This one is so opinionated, it's frightening."

He laughed. "Your imitation of me is quite good." He shrugged. "I cannot help it."

"You can. You don't want to," she accused. "I spent many hours culling through eligible women. Those three came as close as possible to the list of characteristics you wanted in your duchess. They are all beautiful. Charming. Clever. Good-natured. No one is perfect."

You are.

"You'll just have to keep looking, Elise," he said firmly. "I'm not saying those ladies are out of the running but nothing about them struck me as being duchess material. Enough of that. Let's talk about the gentlemen you found interesting. Did any of them stop by for a visit with you today? Or were any responsible for the myriad of bouquets scattered about the drawing room?"

"Yes and yes," she said smartly.

"Who? I want to hear how discerning you are. After all, you had a list yourself."

She reeled off half a dozen names. He was pleased Lord Ivy wasn't one of them. Four of them were actually good choices and would have made excellent husbands for her—if he didn't want her for himself. The other two had definite things wrong with them. He went through each one, elaborating on the faults of the two who were totally unsuitable and inventing reasons why the other four wouldn't be appropriate.

When he finished, she shook her head. "I thought I was a good judge of character but it seems I'm not."

He hated that she doubted herself and said, "Of course, I am being quite picky for you, too. A couple of those fellows wouldn't be awful. I believe we can do better for you, though."

"You found something wrong will all six of them, Weston. Surely, one or two of them have a few redeeming qualities."

He finally gave in and told her a few good things about two of them but cautioned her that it didn't necessarily mean they would make for a good husband.

She sighed. "I wish Papa were still alive. If so, he could simply arrange a marriage for me. Perhaps finding Ruthersby was a stroke of luck and I won't be able to repeat it again."

"Was everything perfect with Ruthersby?"

"No," she admitted. "But we suited well enough. He didn't try to change me, nor I him. Who knows if the marriage would have been successful, though? He died so young. We never were confronted with any serious problems. Perhaps we would have drifted apart."

He took her hand. "Your next husband will not drift away. He will be a perfect match to you in every way."

"You sound so certain."

"I am."

She tried to pull her hand from his. "Let go, Weston. Someone might see. It's already going to cause gossip enough us being seen in the park together."

"You seem to think that's a bad thing."

Elise twisted her hand and it came free of her glove. He continued holding it.

"Please give it to me."

"Let me put it on you."

"No!' she cried and then looked around to see if she'd drawn attention. "I know you mean well but I don't think we should be out in public anymore. People will start to think we are a couple."

Weston returned her glove. She unbuttoned a few buttons and slipped her fingers into it. He fought the urge to button it back as he watched her struggle to do so. Finally, she gave up, letting her hands rest in her lap.

"I do need to know one thing," she said quietly.

Weston steeled himself.

"About last night. The kiss."

"What about it?"

"Why did you kiss me?"

Because I couldn't help myself.

"I needed to remind you that passion—and desire—will be an important part of the choice you make. Did you kiss anyone last night?"

She looked startled. "No. Only you. No opportunity presented itself. If it does, I will certainly try it. I agree that I should find a man I enjoy kissing." She paused. "Why did you warn me about Lord Ivy?"

He'd struggled on how much to tell her and then decided she deserved nothing less than the truth.

Even if it made him look bad.

"It's a number of things. On the surface, he's polished. Handsome. He recently came into his title and fortune. Beneath the veneer, however, he is cruel. Not the least bit clever."

"And you know this how?" she demanded.

"We were at school together. He was behind me by a few years. Still, he was stupid and a bully and a snob." He swallowed. "There's more. He was tupping his stepmother."

Elise gasped.

"She is younger than he is. Married the dead Lord Ivy for his money. I have a problem with a man who lacks scruples. Coming from Disrepute, I know that sounds odd, but it's true." He faced her. "Elise, the young Lady Ivy was someone I coupled with once."

She grew very still. "I know you have had countless lovers."

"Her husband was old and infirm. It was according to my rules. Only once. In secret. Frankly, if I would have known she was bedding her stepson, I never would have touched her."

Elise stood and he rose, tucking her hand through his arm. They began walking.

"I can see why Lord Ivy would be unsuitable for me. You are right, Weston. He has a handsome face but little substance. Certainly no scruples. He is not a man I would want around Claire."

"Ivy has threatened to kill me."

She stumbled and he caught her. "Tell me."

"Apparently, Lady Ivy told her stepson that she preferred me as a lover, enraging him. He wanted to challenge me to a duel or some other nonsense. I left London with George, hoping he would cool off. In the meantime, his father died. He assumed full control of the estate and moved his stepmother to the dower's house at his country estate. She is not in London this Season since she is in mourning. I'm hoping he's forgotten all about it. From what I gleaned at my club, he has bedded several women since then."

"So you think you are safe?"

"I believe so. We haven't come face to face yet. If we do, I'll be able to see the truth in his eyes. Since he's dropped his pursuit of his stepmother, I doubt he'll come after me. It would only dredge up old gossip. I think he's well on his way to becoming London's leading rake."

"Still, you should be careful, Weston," she said, her face full of worry. "I wouldn't want anything to happen to you."

"It won't. I just wanted to warn you as to the kind of man Lord Ivy truly is."

Elise smiled, causing warmth to radiate through him. Of all the women he'd been with, she was the only one who touched his heart.

"Shall we head back?" he asked. "I know you'll need time to dress for tonight's event. I cannot wait to see this evening's gown."

She smiled, her dimple showing. "It is a rose color. I'm very partial to it."

"Sit with me tonight," he said. "The gathering is small. We can take a spot on the back row in order to see the room clearly. It will allow us to talk about those present. Maybe even revise our lists."

Her violet eyes drew him in. If they weren't on a busy street, he would give in to the urge to kiss her. In fact, Weston didn't care what George had said. He tired of the games. He wanted to ask Elise for her hand in marriage.

Tonight.

CHAPTER TWENTY-TWO

E LISE THANKED THE parlor maid for her assistance in helping her dress this evening and went to her dressing table. Her chignon had stray tendrils, most likely from her walk in the park with Weston. She removed the pins and combed it out, redoing the hairstyle and securing it again until it was smooth.

She had no intention of sitting with him at tonight's musicale. Frustration built within her. She feared that he wasn't looking for a wife at all. That being back in London had awakened his rakish tendencies and he would find fault with any woman she suggested. She had carefully vetted the three she had presented to him. They were all beautiful and charming and would make for an excellent duchess. Weston seemed determined not to like any of them. She hadn't asked him how his afternoon calls seeing them went. She knew merely dancing with someone at a ball wasn't a good way to get to know a person. Surely, though, all three visits hadn't gone sour.

At least two of the women would be present at tonight's event. Lady Millicent, who was making her come-out this Season, would be attending because her parents were close friends with the hosts. Lady Morrow, the widow with the two-year-old daughter, had also mentioned to Elise last night that she'd been invited. It would give Elise an opportunity to watch Weston with both women and see what might be the matter. Perhaps he was scared. Although she didn't think anything could frighten him, the possibility of marriage for the next several decades might be making him uneasy without him realizing it. That could be why he hesitated and found reasons he didn't want to pursue them.

She wondered why he'd also found fault with every gentleman she'd mentioned having an interest in. Suddenly, she realized why. She didn't have any brothers but her friends had told her how protective they could be, especially older ones. Elise and Weston had formed a close bond during the time she'd spent at Treadwell Manor. It had grown over the last month during his many visits. No wonder he didn't seem to approve of any of her potential suitors. He most likely never would. Knowing this, she decided she would speak to him tonight regarding the situation.

She stood, allowing the gown to billow about her and smoothing it into place. She had fallen in love with the bolt of rose silk and knew once it was made up, the gown would become one of her favorites. Again, the neckline was too low for her tastes, though she'd seen many in the same style at last night's ball and decided it must be the latest in fashion. She certainly looked different now than when she'd made her come-out. Her clothes then had all been selected by her mother, who made sure they were all girlish and prim at the same time. No wonder Elise hadn't attracted many men that year, as compared to last night and today's flood of suitors. It hurt that her mother had seen her as competition, which was ridiculous. Mama had been married to the most wonderful man in the *ton* and had never acknowledged it.

Elise claimed her reticule and went downstairs. As on the previous night, she found Weston waiting in the foyer. His appreciative smile let her know the gown was a success.

"You look ravishing, Elise. Men will admire you and grovel at your feet."

"Speaking of that," she began and took a deep breath before proceeding. "I will no longer require your opinion regarding my suitors."

His eyes narrowed. "Why not?"

She decided to test her theory. "I have no father or brother and I believe you have assumed the role of an older, protective sibling. You are trying to watch out for me. No man will ever be good enough for me in your eyes and that is why you dislike every name I mentioned to you. Since I am of legal age—and have already chosen one husband—I believe I have the maturity and experience to do so again. Without any comments from you. I know what I need in a husband and what Claire needs in a father and will make my selection accordingly."

Before Weston could reply, her in-laws arrived, the countess cooing, "Oh, there you are, Your Grace. Always so prompt. I wouldn't have thought a duke would be aware of time or so considerate of others."

"I think the way we treat others speaks volumes about ourselves," he replied. "Take for instance, your sister-in-law. I know you value her as a member of your family. I'm sure you treat her with the utmost kindness, especially knowing how your boys love her so."

Lady Ruthersby blinked rapidly several times, speechless.

Her husband quickly said, "Well, this musicale was the talk of White's this afternoon. The guest list is quite exclusive. I must thank you, Your Grace, for seeing that we were on it."

"Shall we?" Weston held his arm out and Elise took it, glancing down at her feet to hide her mirth.

As they went out the front door, she murmured, "You can be very wicked at times, Your Grace."

He chuckled. "You haven't seen the half of it, my lady. There are times I wish to eviscerate that woman."

In the carriage, she sat as far from him as possible. Which wasn't far enough. She could still feel the heat of his body, which made her think of last night's kiss when he'd held her close. The subtle spice of his cologne filled the air. She really had to stop allowing him to fill every thought in her head. This man was a duke, one of the most powerful peers in Great Britain. He never had and never would consider her for his duchess.

Elise was determined to find her own husband without his help. She wasn't the naïve debutante from several years ago. Tragedy had forced her to grow up. She was a mother and her first duty would always be to her daughter. She would trust her instincts and marry a man she deemed worthwhile. It really didn't matter if he kissed well. If he were honest and kind and good to her and Claire, that would be more than enough. It would help them leave her brother-in-law's household, where every day had been a challenge. She had been the one in charge once. She had planned the menus and entertainment and dealt with the servants. She saw the pity in their eyes as Lord and Lady Ruthersby treated her as a poor relation. It was important to move on and make a new life for herself and Claire. She was grateful to Weston for giving her the opportunity of another Season for she truly believed she could find a spouse.

They arrived and Elise saw Samantha alighting from a carriage and rushed to join her. They linked arms and headed inside the town-house, her party and Colebourne trailing behind them.

"That gown is utterly divine on you," her friend proclaimed. "So perfect with your coloring. Did you have anyone call on you this afternoon?"

"Several gentlemen. None of whom your brother thought good enough for me. I fear he's decided I'm a sister to him and he plans to shoo every last suitor away because none of them live up to his impossibly high standards."

Samantha chuckled. "I'm not so sure about that."

"Well, I am. He was most disagreeable. Not only about the men I was interested in but also the women on our list."

"Weston didn't like any of the three women we decided upon?"

"Not a one. He found fault with each one of them," she revealed.

They greeted their host and hostess and continued on.

"My brother is very selective. Not just any woman will do as a duchess, especially for him."

"I don't know if he even plans to wed. I fear the temptations of London are calling to him."

Samantha shook her head. "You are wrong, Elise. I know him. He is most serious about finding a wife and settling down."

"Then he'll have to prove it to me."

"Prove what?" Weston asked, joining them.

"I'm going to find George," Samantha said.

"Coward," whispered Elise. Then she looked at her companion. "You never said how your afternoon calls went, Your Grace."

"Because I didn't make them," he said flippantly.

"Why not? You cannot assess a woman's worth by a single dance with her. You must get to know her. The three women I suggested to you are gracious and quite beautiful. I know two will be present this evening. I want you to speak to each of them. In my presence."

"Why?" he asked testily.

"Because I want to see how you engage with one another. I believe you are being far too particular, especially since you haven't gotten to truly know any of them. You've snapped to a judgment of their character when you don't know anything about them at all."

"And you do?" he challenged.

"Yes. I have learned quite a bit about each of them. Sought the opinions of others. Spoken to all three myself. Let me see you with each of them. I demand that you give them a chance."

"None made a good first impression on me."

"Then you will be magnanimous and allow them the chance to make a second, more delightful one on you," she insisted. "Only if I see there is no hope will I go back and find another three for you to consider."

"Why is it I am required to take your advice when you no longer wish for my guidance?"

"Because you've never searched for a wife before, much less been married. You may have more experience in many things, Your Grace, but I know what I'm talking about in this instance. The kind of woman you have sought before and engaged in casual affairs with is not the type you want as your wife."

Weston arched one eyebrow. "Is that so?"

"It is. You will need to trust me on this. Come. Take me about the room. I see Lady Morrow. We'll speak to her first. She is the one who was wed to a man forty years her senior and has a young daughter."

"I remember," he said grumpily.

"Behave," she said sternly. "Stand up straight and be charming. I know you know how to do so."

"Yes, my lady. I am at your service," he said dutifully.

"And if you feel like kissing one of them, do so," she added, mirroring his advice to her. "I know it's the one requirement you'll have a say in. I'm sure you know all about how to create that kind of opportunity."

He gave her a rakish smile. "I did so last night, didn't I?"

"Quit being impossible," she admonished, feeling her cheeks heat. "I believe you enjoy testing me."

Weston sighed. "You're on to me. And you sound like a governess chastising me."

"Maybe you need one to do so," she said. "I'm sure you were impossible as a little boy since you're wildly inappropriate as a grown man."

"But I am a lot of fun." He waggled his eyebrows and she began laughing.

They made their way to where Lady Morrow stood. Elise had enjoyed conversing with the widow last night. She was very animated and had warm, lovely eyes that showed her interest in a person. Fortunately, the couple she spoke to turned away just as she and Weston arrived.

"Lady Morrow, how nice to see you again," she said. "I am Lady

Ruthersby. We met last night. The Duchess of Colebourne introduced us. I'm sure you remember His Grace, the Duke of Treadwell?"

The widow smiled brightly. "I remember you both, my lady. His Grace is certainly a fine dancer. I have a tendency toward clumsiness but His Grace made me feel as if I were graceful."

When Weston didn't say anything, she dug her nails into his forearm.

"I would never have guessed so, Lady Morrow," he responded politely. "I thought you a superb dancer from the beginning."

Elise eased her hold on him. "Would you excuse me? I see someone I must speak with."

She left them and then went a short distance to where she could study them. Elizabeth joined her.

"What are you doing?" Her gaze followed Elise's. "Oh, His Grace is with Lady Morrow. She made the list, didn't she?"

"She did and I like her quite a bit."

"But does Treadwell like her?" Elizabeth asked as Weston bowed to Lady Morrow and stepped away.

"Blast," Elise muttered. "Would you excuse me?"

Elizabeth laughed merrily. "Of course. Do let me know how it comes out."

Elise followed Weston as he weaved through the crowd. He stopped in front of George and Jon and she joined them.

Slipping her hand through his arm, she said, "If you'll excuse us, Your Graces, your friend has someone I'd like him to become reacquainted with."

She could hear them chuckling as she pulled Weston away and asked, "Why did you leave her?"

"Because I didn't want to stay. I told you. Lady Morrow is not for me."

"Very well. I will allow you one pass. No more. Though I do believe you are making a mistake. Lady Morrow is refined and friendly, two assets a duchess should possess."

"How do you know so much about what a duchess should have?" he asked.

"Quit being impossible," she ordered.

Unfortunately, they weren't able to find Lady Millicent before they were asked to take a seat. Being that she stood next to Weston, she would have to sit with him. He led her to the back row and had them take the two chairs on the end. The evening's entertainment was a noted soprano, an elegant redhead with an amazing range. Knowing Weston, he had most likely bedded the woman. Thinking that, she had trouble even looking at the songstress. It was a good thing that Elise wasn't going to marry him, else she'd be jealous of every woman he came in contact with. That would be no way to live, always uncertain that her husband was slinking off to make love to another woman.

Clapping startled her and she came out of her reverie and joined in.

"Where were you the past hour?" he asked.

"I had things on my mind," she said loftily. "Trying to decide which gentlemen to encourage and which ones to discourage."

He frowned. "Elise, I—"

"There you are, Your Grace," Lady Ruthersby said. "Wasn't that divine? I am so pleased that you thought to have us accompany you tonight. And after supper, we will hear more."

Elise hadn't known the concert would be extended. She spied Lady Millicent, though, and said, "Oh, you must excuse us. His Grace has been most desperate to visit with Lady Millicent."

She dragged him away and in the direction of the debutante.

"Desperate? Dukes aren't desperate, Elise. We can be charming. Disreputable. Wealthy. Arrogant. But never desperate. Unless we wish to escape from a matchmaker."

They reached a group of five, which included Lady Millicent, and Elise managed to ease them into the circle. Pleasantries were exchanged, including everyone singing the praises of the soprano.

"I heard that you sing rather well, Lady Millicent," she said encouragingly.

The young woman smiled. Elise liked her smile. It wasn't ingratiating. It reached her eyes. She had lovely eyes, a moss green, and thick hair curled high upon her head. She was slender but had an ample bosom. She was also one of the most beautiful women in the room tonight.

"I enjoy playing the pianoforte and singing, Lady Ruthersby. I began lessons when I was only five years of age and continue to this day."

"I know His Grace would enjoy hearing you perform sometime."

"Would I?" he asked drolly and then smiled. "Of course, I would, Lady Millicent. I am sure you are most talented."

"There is a small parlor off the ballroom which has a piano," Lady Millicent said, her eyes bright and full of confidence. "I have played it many times since my parents and I are frequent guests here. Would you care to hear a song before supper begins, Your Grace?"

"That would be amusing, my lady," Weston said. "I'm sure the others would care to join me."

By now, Elise saw two couples had joined them, one being Lady Millicent's parents. The young woman's mother almost salivated at the thought of a duke listening to her daughter play.

"Oh, yes, Millicent, you must play a song for His Grace. Come along, everyone," the proud mama said, nudging her husband.

The group moved away—but Elise remained behind. Weston became surrounded by others and she was able to relax a moment, happy that he would see Lady Millicent at her best. She might be young but Elise could tell that Lady Millicent had a strong enough personality to stand up to Weston.

She joined Samantha and George and went in to supper with them. About a quarter-hour passed before she saw Weston and the small group enter. They all sat together at a table, with Lady Milli-cent's mother maneuvering everyone so that her daughter sat next to the duke.

When they had finished with supper, Samantha said, "Would you accompany me to the retiring room? I'm feeling queasy."

Her friend did look awfully pale. "Of course."

Elise took Samantha's arm and they left the room. When they reached the retiring room, Samantha hurried behind a curtain and was violently ill.

"Are you all right?" she called.

"I will be."

Minutes later, Samantha emerged, still pale and looking shaky. She rinsed her mouth and sat for a moment.

"I must be," she murmured to herself.

Elise realized what was happening. "You are increasing?"

Samantha nodded wearily. "I believe so. It was like this before."

"Before?"

She rose. "I was with child when wed to Haskett. I lost the baby after four months. I remember the sickness and feeling tired all the time. It came upon me suddenly this morning. I didn't think anything of it until now. I thought it was because we were out late last night because of the first ball of the Season. It's the same as before, though."

Elise hugged her. "You must see a doctor tomorrow. I also think you should go home now. There's no sense staying for more of the same."

"You're right." Samantha sat again and sighed. "Would you go and find George?"

"I will. Stay here."

As she left the retiring room, Elise decided this would be a way to avoid Weston for the rest of the evening. It might even allow him additional time with Lady Millicent. She returned to the supper room and saw Weston engaged in conversation with the debutante.

Hurrying to George, she leaned close and whispered, "Samantha is feeling ill. She would like to go home."

George sprang to his feet. "Where is she?"

"The retiring room," she said. "If you don't mind, I'd like to leave with you. Just to see if she's all right."

"Of course. I'll go call for the carriage."

"We'll meet you outside."

The duke hurried off and she went to her brother-in-law and said, "My lord, my friend, the Duchess of Colebourne, has taken ill. I am accompanying her home. I will see you tomorrow morning. Please make my excuses to His Grace and Lady Ruthersby."

"I will."

Elise hurried away, sensing Weston's eyes on her and deliberately not gazing in his direction. She found Samantha leaving the retiring room and slipped her arm about her friend's waist.

"George is having the carriage brought around. I will ride with you to make sure you don't need anything."

"George can help me if I need something," Samantha protested.

"No. I've heard enough of the gifted soprano," she said firmly. "And if I'm gone, Weston won't be worried about whom I speak with. It seems he may be intrigued by Lady Millicent after all. I'd like for her to have his full attention."

With that, Elise took Samantha's arm and led her outside.

CHAPTER TWENTY-THREE

WESTON BURST INTO George's breakfast room, a jumble of emotions running through him.

George, ever unflappable, said, "Have a seat, Your Grace. Coffee or tea?"

"Coffee."

As he sat, a footman appeared with a cup and saucer, while a second one poured the brew into the cup. Weston added his own cream and sugar and stirred, the motion soothing him. He took a sip and placed the cup down.

Sam entered the room and didn't seem surprised to find him there. Quickly, the footman brought her tea and a plate of food, though Weston noted there wasn't much on it.

"I came to see if you are feeling better," he said, noting she was a tad pale and had dark circles under her eyes. "You don't look it. Shouldn't you be in bed?"

She glanced to her husband. George placed a hand over hers and nodded. Sam turned back to Weston. "I am with child. It's early yet so we won't be sharing our news for several more weeks."

"Congratulations," he said with sincerity, knowing she had lost another baby and how she must be worried about the same thing happening again. "Is that why you left the musicale early?"

"Yes. Though I've heard it referred to as morning sickness, it seems to strike me more in the evenings."

"I assume Elise knows about this."

"Yes," Sam confirmed. "She was with me in the retiring room when I was violently ill last night. It was her suggestion that I leave the event early and come home to rest."

"Was it your idea that she accompany you?" he prodded.

"No. She was worried about me, though, and wanted to tend to me in the carriage."

"George could have done that," Weston pointed out. "Did she leave to avoid me?"

Sam shrugged. "She did mention that you were intrigued with Lady Millicent and had gone to listen to her play and sing a few songs. I saw you supping with the lady and her parents. Elise believed if you weren't worried about her, you could focus more attention on your companion."

"I was going to ask Elise to marry me last night," he revealed.

George chuckled. "That special license must be burning a hole in your pocket."

"What?" Sam exclaimed. "You've bought a special license."

He nodded. "I purchased it yesterday. George wanted me to wait a week before I spoke to Elise. I can't."

"You love her," Sam said, wonder in her voice. "You *do* love her."

"Yes," he confirmed. "I don't see why I should waste time pretending to court other women when all I want is to be with her. I even went to St George's after leaving Doctors' Commons to see what dates the chapel was open. Since the Season has just begun, their calendar is wide open."

"You think Elise will want a big society wedding?" George asked.

"I don't know. Especially with it being a second marriage for her. If she does, the chapel is available. If she prefers a more intimate affair, we will do that."

"We will host the wedding breakfast for you. I insist," Sam said. "And if you do decide upon a small gathering, you are more than welcome to hold the wedding here."

"Thank you. Now, all I have to do is ask her. I'm actually nervous about doing so."

George chuckled. "Afraid to give up being a bachelor?"

"No—afraid she may turn me down."

"Why would she?" his sister asked. "Just be sure to tell her you love her. Elise is not interested in the things women usually want from a marriage. She needs to know that you love her. The rest will take care of itself."

"How do you feel about her already having a child?" George asked.

"I'll admit that factored into my decision. I adore Claire. Gaining a wife and a child at the same time is merely a bonus."

"That's good to know," his friend said. "Not every man would be so generous. So, tonight is the night then?"

"Yes." Weston rose. "I'm off now. Thank you."

"For what?" Sam asked.

He smiled. "For just being you." He went and kissed her cheek. "I am very happy for you and George. I hope that Elise will soon be in the same state. Nothing would please me more."

Weston left and decided to avoid his usual haunts. He didn't feel like seeing anyone else. He needed to figure out how to ask Elise to marry him.

And then he hit on the perfect idea.

ELISE HEARD THE clock chime four and rose.

Addressing her visitors, she said, "Thank you for calling on me today, my lords. I hope to see all of you at tonight's ball."

Immediately, Viscount Dorsley said, "You must save the supper dance for me, Lady Ruthersby."

The three other gentlemen protested and Elise shushed them.

"No, my lord. You must sign my programme as all the others do. I won't play favorites and reserve a dance for you."

He grinned. "Then I shall arrive half an hour before the ball starts and be first in line."

The others grumbled good-naturedly and she nodded at Smithson, who'd just stepped inside the drawing room. The butler asked for the visitors to follow him. Almost immediately, however, he returned.

"May I speak with you a moment, my lady?" the butler quietly asked Elise.

"Of course," she replied.

"Is Treadwell here yet, Smithson?" her sister-in-law asked.

"No, my lady."

"Hmm. I wondered what's keeping him. He's usually so very prompt," the countess said.

"I do not know if His Grace is coming this afternoon," Elise told her sister-in-law. "I've received no note from him indicating he would be here."

The countess looked peeved. "Then what about arrangements for tonight's ball? Surely, he will come and escort us there."

"We do have a carriage, my dear," the earl said. "It can convey us to the ball."

"I want Treadwell to take us," she whined.

Elise didn't say anything more and indicated for Smithson to leave with her. In the corridor she paused.

"What is wrong?" she asked.

"It's Lord Ivy," he said.

She'd forgotten to tell the butler yesterday that she wouldn't be home to Lord Ivy and he had been one of her callers. Fortunately, he'd left before Weston arrived so there'd been no confrontation between the two. The viscount hadn't been at the musicale last night so she hadn't needed to avoid him. She had since instructed Smithson not to allow him in.

"Did he show up this afternoon?"

"He did, my lady. Pushed his way past me, he did. He's waiting in the small parlor. I told him you weren't at home but he told me he would wait until you arrived and speak with you then."

"Very well. I'll see him and make it clear to him that in the future he is not to call."

Smithson followed her downstairs and said, "I'll be waiting outside the door if you need me, my lady."

"Thank you."

Elise took a deep breath and then entered the small parlor off the foyer. Lord Ivy stood by the window, his hands behind his back. He cut a graceful figure but knowing what she did about him, she had no wish to be in his company.

He turned and said, "Ah, Lady Ruthersby. You are now home. I suppose all those suitors I saw leaving waited in vain."

"Good afternoon, my lord. I felt I needed to speak with you in person. I would prefer that you no longer call upon me."

"At whose request?" he demanded.

"Mine."

He crossed the room and stood in front of her. "I'm sure Treadwell is behind this. That man is a liar and a scoundrel. Whatever he told you about me, don't believe it."

"In my experience, I have found His Grace to be very truthful and he assures me he has reformed from his former days."

"Your experience," he said, his gaze boring into her.

Elise felt her cheeks blaze and said, "It is not what you think. I am merely friends with His Grace."

He studied her a moment. "Have you kissed him? No, don't answer that. I can tell you have." He grasped her elbows. "You need to know what a proper kiss is."

His mouth came down hard on hers. Elise struggled to get away and knew he was too large and overwhelming to succeed. Instead, she became as a dead fish, not moving. He thrust his tongue into her mouth. She remained motionless, not responding, even though disgust rose within her. He broke the kiss.

"I would like you to leave."

He glared at her. "Oh, I'll do more than leave. A few well-placed words tonight in a handful of selected ears—and you'll be ruined, Lady Ruthersby. Even Treadwell won't want you anymore."

Panic filled her. If gossip spread about her, she wouldn't be able to counter it. A man's word would always be believed above a woman's. Lord Ivy's lies would spread like wildfire and she would have no chance of securing a husband.

Unless she could do so tonight. Of all the men who'd called upon her, Viscount Dorsley seemed the most interested—and had the most to gain. A widower, he'd been left with two small girls and was eager for an heir. If Elise could speak with him tonight and let him know she would be happy for a quick match between them, it wouldn't matter what gossip Lord Ivy let loose.

That wouldn't be fair to Lord Dorsley, though. If she didn't inform him of the potential gossip, he might make and then quickly break their engagement. A broken engagement was always the kiss of death for a woman in Polite Society, no matter which party ended the arrangement. She decided she would speak to the viscount at tonight's ball and let him know malicious things were being said about her and then let him decide if he still might be interested in pursuing marriage with her. If not, she couldn't imagine what would happen to her and Claire.

She looked up at the viscount. An evil smile spread across his handsome face. "Of course, I wouldn't have to say anything at all."

"At what price?" she asked, knowing whatever he said she'd be unwilling to pay.

"Why, you could wed me," he said smoothly.

"Get out," she ordered brusquely.

He released her, his expression now grim. "You've dug your own grave, my lady." He brushed past her, leaving Elise alone, her throat thick with unshed tears.

Smithson came in. "Is everything all right, Lady Ruthersby?"

She nodded, too emotional to speak, and left the room. Going to her bedchamber, she lay on her bed and wept.

Suddenly, someone shook her shoulder.

"My lady, you must rise and dress for the ball."

It was the parlor maid who had helped ready her the past two nights. Elise sat up, feeling groggy, realizing she must have fallen asleep.

"Which gown tonight, my lady? This one?"

"The midnight blue," she said, rising and going to her dressing table. One glance told her she would need to repair her hair and so she began removing the pins.

The maid helped her from her day gown and into the one for the ball.

"I thought the rose gown was lovely but you're a sight for sore eyes in this, my lady," the servant proclaimed. "Better hurry with your hair, though. Lady Ruthersby's as mad as a hornet and causing all kinds of trouble tonight. If you're not downstairs in time, you'll be left behind."

Elise quickly wound her hair into place and secured the pins in it. She added her sapphire earrings to finish off the look and hurried downstairs. Her in-laws were walking out the front door. Thank goodness she'd been in time. Quickly, she fell into step behind them and a footman helped her into the carriage. Inside, the tension was thick.

"I don't know what you've done to alienate Treadwell," her sister-in-law said. "Things are a disaster now."

"His Grace is looking for a wife," she said. "He may have formed an attachment with Lady Millicent last night. He has been most generous in securing you and Lord Ruthersby invitations to events you usually do not attend. Those won't be rescinded. You will still have a full and busy Season."

"But he's dropped us," the countess complained. Her eyes narrowed as she gazed at Elise. "I know it's your fault." She turned to her husband. "Ruthersby, this woman has caused me unbearable grief. You're to send her and that brat of hers back to Briarcliff tomorrow."

"If that's what you wish, dearest," the earl said, glaring at Elise for making his wife out of sorts.

That meant she only had tonight to find a husband. If Lord Dorsley turned her down, she would have to act quickly—and still reveal to whomever she spoke to that untruths were being spread about her. Fear filled her, knowing she had a limited time in which to ensure her future.

And Claire's.

Elise would do whatever it took to make a good life for Claire. Anything.

As their carriage pulled up and the footman opened the door, her sister-in-law scowled at her.

"If we would have been closer to home, I would have had the coachman turn around and leave you there. Don't speak to me tonight. Don't even look at me. I can't have you hanging about me as I try to undo whatever harm you've done to our social standing. I can only hope Treadwell will not blame us for your shortcomings."

The earl and countess proceeded inside without her. Elise followed at a distance. She avoided the receiving line and went straight to the ballroom in a daze, accepting a programme from a passing footman and staring down at it.

Someone touched her arm. She saw it was Elizabeth. "Are you all right, Elise? You look ill."

"What's wrong?" Samantha asked, hurrying up, George in tow.

"I am being sent back to Briarcliff tomorrow. My sister-in-law wishes to wash her hands of me," she said dully.

"What?" Samantha hissed. "No. They cannot."

"They can," she said. "I am a penniless relation. The countess has always despised me. She's never even given me leave to address her by her Christian name. The earl has no use for me. I have no choice."

"You will come stay with us," George said. "It won't be for long."

"That is very kind of you, Your Grace." Elise pushed aside the hurt that filled her. She couldn't sleepwalk through this ball. "I must find a husband. Tonight. Viscount Dorsley seems to be the likely choice. I will speak to him tonight regarding a match between us."

"No," Samantha said. "Elise, I beg you to—"

Suddenly, she found herself surrounded by gentlemen, all clamoring for a dance. Dorsley was at the forefront.

"I'd like to claim the supper dance, Lady Ruthersby," he said eagerly.

She rewarded him with a brilliant smile and offered him her dance card. "That would be lovely, Lord Dorsley. I have something quite particular I wish to discuss with you during supper."

He scribbled his name on her programme and returned it to her. "Until then."

Quickly, her card filled—leaving no room for Weston. She didn't even know if he would attend tonight's ball. It didn't matter. He had a plethora of women who would be willing to wed him. She'd done her best to suggest three that would make for a good duchess. If none of them suited him, then he would have to find a bride on his own.

Samantha tugged on her arm. "Please, Elise, we must talk."

She took her friend's hand as she heard the musicians finish tuning their instruments. "I know that you married for love and you would wish the same for me. It's not meant to be, Samantha. I must do what I can to acquire a fiancé tonight. Lord Ivy has already threatened to bring me to ruin this very night with falsehoods."

"He . . . what?" George demanded.

"It doesn't matter. I must go." Elise smiled as the marquess who had requested her first dance approached. "Good evening, my lord."

"Are you ready to have your toes trod upon, Lady Ruthersby?" he asked. "Come along then. I'm your man."

The marquess led Elise onto the dance floor.

CHAPTER TWENTY-FOUR

WESTON DELIBERATELY WAITED until well after the ball had started before making his appearance. He didn't want to sign any other woman's programme or make conversation with them. He wanted Elise. Period. There would be no wasting time pretending otherwise.

He entered the ballroom, pausing in the doorway as he tried to locate her. The musicians were between numbers and guests were milling about. Then a signal was given and couples started toward the dance floor. He caught sight of Elise, her gown a deep blue, the same sapphire earrings as before dangling from her ears. They must be the only jewels she possessed. He would shower her with jewels. Clothing. Whatever she desired.

But first, he must ask for her hand in marriage.

It didn't matter that she already had a partner. Weston strode onto the dance floor, moving between couples. He passed George and Sam and winked at them. Three couples past them he found Elise dancing with Viscount Dorsley. The man looked besotted as he gazed upon her. Without hesitation, Weston stepped forward and tapped Dorsley on his shoulder. The viscount turned and stumbled, coming to a stop.

"What do you want, Treadwell?" he asked, his confusion clear. "Can't you see that I'm dancing?"

Weston glared at the man. "You are. With my fiancée. I need you to stop. At once."

Dorsley released Elise, apprehension filling his face. "I didn't know, Your Grace. Please, forgive me." He hurried away.

Turning, he saw Elise standing there, dumbfounded. He slipped an arm about her and took her hand as he guided her into the steps of the waltz.

"What is going on?" she asked, recovering from her stupor. "Why would you tease poor Lord Dorsley by telling him that we are engaged? The viscount is most interested in me."

He pulled her closer. "I am more interested in you."

"Enough, Weston," she said, a chill in her voice. "I am being sent to Briarcliff tomorrow. Tonight is my one chance at finding a husband. Lord Dorsley has paid a great deal of attention to me. I was hoping to ask him if he wished for us to settle upon a more permanent arrangement."

"No."

"No?" Color spotted her cheeks. "You cannot tell me what to do."

He chuckled. "No, I supposed I'll never be able to. It's one of the things I love about you."

Her feet stopped moving. He didn't try to force her to continue.

"What did you say?"

He grinned shamelessly. "It's one of the things I love about you," he repeated. "There are many things that make me love you, Elise."

His voice now carried across the dance floor. Other couples around them came to a stop, curiously listening in on their conversation.

"I . . . surely . . . I mean . . ."

Weston pressed a finger to her lips. "No more talking. Listen."

Even the music died away as the musicians eagerly leaned toward them. Weston took her hands and laced his fingers through hers.

"I love you, Elise. Madly. Deeply. Passionately. Maturely. That is what matters. I thought once, long ago, that I was in love but after knowing you, I finally know what true love is and that I could only love you. I asked you to help me find a wife this Season—when all along I knew *you* would be that woman. Every characteristic I gave you to search for in my future duchess was one you already possess. Intelligence. Compassionate. Kindness. Humor. I wanted a woman who loved children. No one is a better mother than you are to Claire. I need you to be my friend. My conscience. My everything."

He saw tears brimming in her eyes as she began to smile.

Weston leaned in until his lips brushed her ear, his next words meant only for her. "Most of all, I want you as my lover. My God, I so want to be with you physically. We've built a relationship on the bonds of friendship but my desire for you grows every day. I long to be physically intimate with you. We have never made love, Elise, but I know a passionate woman lies within you. I've bedded many women—but you will be the only one I will ever make love with."

His eyes met hers and he raised her hands and kissed them tenderly. "Please, love. Say you'll marry me. Be my companion and lover. The mother of my children. Grow old with me, Elise. I promise that our lifetime will be an adventure."

He kissed her hands again and lowered them.

"Yes. Yes, Weston," she said, tears streaming down her cheeks. "Yes, I love you. Yes, I want to be your wife. You are my everything, now and always."

He cradled her face and kissed her tenderly. It was their first kiss after confessing their love for one another. It would be one of thousands. Hundreds of thousands. Millions.

Breaking it, he swept her off her feet. Her arms went around his neck and they stared at one another a lingering moment. He kissed her once more and then marched from the stunned ballroom. As they moved through the parting crowd, the stunned silence turned into loud applause. He grinned shamelessly at his fiancée.

"I have a special license," he confessed.

"You do?" Joy filled her face. "When can we wed?"

"Tomorrow will do if you want a small wedding. If you desire a large one, you better give it a week or more and turn the planning over to Sam."

"I want what you want," she said breathlessly.

As he crossed the foyer and a footman quickly opened the door, he stepped into the night and said, "What I want now, more than anything, is to have our wedding night tonight."

"Now?" she squeaked.

"Now. You know I will marry you, Elise. I proclaimed my intentions in front of all of Polite Society. What I need now is time for just the two of us."

They reached his waiting carriage. "What do you say?"

She kissed him. "I say yes. To now—and always."

"Home," he told the coachman and carried her up the steps the footman had placed beside the open carriage door.

Inside the vehicle, he sat, keeping her on his lap. They kissed the entire way home, long, drugging kisses that branded her as his. When the carriage came to a halt, he said, "We're home."

Weston slid Elise from his lap and threw open the door, bounding from the carriage. He held his hands out to her. She moved toward him and he captured her waist, swinging her to the ground.

"What will your servants say?" she asked. "Will they be shocked?"

"They will say their master is in love," he replied. "And they will be shocked because I have never had a woman in my own bed."

Surprise filled her face and he swept her into his arms again, heading into the house.

"Oh, yes. George and I had quite a few rules during our heyday as Charm and Disrepute."

Her fingers toyed with the hair at the back of his neck. "And what might some of those rules be?"

He started up the staircase. "One, never bed a woman and then fall asleep. Waking up next to her makes her more possessive. We will sleep together every night, however."

"I won't have my own rooms?" she asked playfully.

"You will. They'll be for your extensive wardrobe that I will lavish upon you. But you will be in my bed—our bed—every night. Waking up with you will be the best way to start my day."

"Any other rules?"

"George and I specified age limits, both on young and old ends. You fall nicely into that range. I also only engaged in intercourse with a woman once before moving on. We'll make love repeatedly, several times a day, for decade upon decade."

"I like the sound of that. Any more rules?"

"Bathing after being with a woman was imperative. I had to rid myself of her smell. You, on the other hand, will linger on my skin as a reminder of how much I adore being with you."

He reached his bedchamber and opened the door, taking her inside and closing it. Lowering her to her feet, he captured her hands in his and nudged her backward against the door, raising her hands above her head and pinning her wrists together with one hand. His other hand caressed her cheek.

"Finally, no lover was to ever grace my bed. It was to be my sanctuary." He kissed her. "Now, it will be our sanctuary. I plan to spend hours—days—in it. With you."

"Your Grace, that sounds . . . most interesting."

Weston kissed her thoroughly as his free hand roamed her body. He found her breast and kneaded it, tweaking the nipple as she squirmed. His lips caressed her throat as his hand hoisted her skirts, his fingers gliding up the satin skin. He reached her nest of curls and teased the seam of her sex as she moaned.

"Have you ever been touched here, Elise?" he asked hoarsely.

"No. Not like this."

He pushed a finger into her and she groaned. Stroking her with it, he feasted on her mouth. She began writhing. He added a second finger and she whimpered. He let his fingers make love to her, enjoying all the sweet noises coming from her.

"Weston," she murmured against his lips. "Something's happening."

"It most certainly is. I want to watch your eyes as it does."

"It's . . . oh! It's . . . I have no words."

"None are needed, love. Just ride the wave. Give in to it."

He brought her to orgasm and enjoyed the darkening of those violet eyes and his name coming from her lips. She shuddered violently and then became limp. He released her wrists and she lowered her arms, wrapping them about his neck as she kissed him with enthusiasm.

Finally, breaking the kiss, she said, "I don't know what that was but I like it. Very much."

"Then we'll have to do it again. Can you walk to the bed or should I carry you?"

"Carry me. If you weren't already holding me up, I would have collapsed long ago. I still may."

He lifted her in his arms and crossed the chamber to the large bed. He eased her onto it and removed her slippers and stockings. Then slowly, he freed her from her layers of clothing until she lay bare. Weston gazed down upon her.

"You are so very beautiful." He placed his palm against her belly and lightly stroked it with his thumb.

"I'm nervous," she said quietly, worry in her eyes.

"Why?"

"Because although I was married, I have no true experience with this. I've never lain in a bed with no clothes on. You've done so with countless women. I have no idea how to please you."

He kissed her softly. "You already please me. Just by being you, Elise. Yes, there have been other women but none of them come to mind now. You are what fills me. My mind. My heart. My soul." He smoothed her hair. "I am nervous, too."

"You? Never."

"Yes. I am. Because this will be the first time I've truly made love in my life. It's the start to our life together. I want it to be right for you. I want to please you and pleasure you."

She reached up and took his hand, bringing his palm to her lips and kissing it tenderly. "I have much to learn. Teach me, Weston."

Elise watched as Weston stood and stripped off his clothing. Her eyes followed his every move until he was bare to his waist. His muscled chest looked like a sculpture from one of the Greek masters. He sat and removed his boots and trousers, tossing them aside. His stockings followed. She looked at the broad back and shoulders and couldn't help but reach up to stroke the smooth, warm flesh.

He turned toward her and lay next to her, their limbs entwining as they kissed deeply. His kisses stirred a fire within her, her body's heat matching his. Desire filled her. She kissed him with all the love in her heart, still reeling that this man loved her as she did him. She nuzzled his throat and nipped at it as he'd done to her. His groans and hands tightening on her body let her know he enjoyed it.

Weston kissed his way to her breasts and then labored over each one, devoting equal time to both as he licked and sucked and fondled them. Boldness filled her and she kissed his chest, her hands moving over hard muscle. His nipples were flat, so unlike hers, but she found them tender to her touch and her tongue. Elise became another person, courageously touching and tasting him. Her heart pounded fiercely and her blood sang as it poured through her veins. Still, they kissed, his hands gliding along the curves of her body as if they were meant to always do so.

His fingers returned to the place between her legs, pushing inside her and driving her into a frenzy. The intense feelings drove her to new heights and she felt as if she climbed a mountain and touched the sun as warmth explode through her and the waves crested and fell, over and over. Then Weston hovered above her and Elise knew he was ready to join with her. It had always been something she endured with Norwood but this time was different.

He pushed into her, kissing her deeply, filling her until she didn't know where she ended and he began. Then he began moving, teasing, convincing her to join in the dance. She worried she didn't know how but as on the dance floor, Weston proved to be the ultimate partner. Soon, Elise soared high again as they moved in the ancient rhythm as old as time. The sensations built within her again and as she toppled into the abyss, he cried out hoarsely.

Her name. Hers. In that moment, she knew she was his and he was hers and nothing would ever change that.

He collapsed atop her, breathing hard, and she held on to him tightly, never wanting to let go. Weston rolled to his side, still inside her, and kissed her.

"I love you, Elise. I love what my life will now be like with you and Claire in it. I love that I've found my best friend in my duchess. I love that we'll have children together and be parents. I may never be happier than I am in this moment."

"I love you, Weston. Love for you is spilling from me. I know it will continue to grow. You're wrong about this being your happiest moment. I believe every day when we awaken, we will be happier and more in love than the day before."

"You're right." He kissed her. "I know to listen to you. You are a woman of substance." He stroked her back.

"I am a woman in love," she said, confidence brimming within her. "With the most wonderful man in the world."

"When will you marry me, Elise?"

"Now?" she laughed. "Though I doubt we could find a clergyman to do so. Especially with us in a state of undress."

"I will wait if you want a ceremony at St. George's Chapel. We can have all of Polite Society attend it."

"I only want a few people at our wedding. Something simple. And soon."

"Sam offered to host the wedding breakfast. We could wed at her and George's townhouse."

"Let's do so. What about the day after tomorrow? Tomorrow is already here and I need to tell Claire about us."

"She'll be pleased," he said with confidence.

"She likes you a great deal."

"She will come to love me. Just like her mama." Weston kissed her. "I hope we just made a baby."

Elise laughed. "Actually, I do, too."

He relaxed his hold on her and climbed from the bed. "I suppose I should return you to the Ruthersbys' place."

She frowned. "I told you I am supposed to leave for Briarwood in the morning."

"What?"

She explained how put out Lady Ruthersby was and that she'd ordered for Elise and Claire to be taken from town and returned to the country.

"I don't want you or Claire under their roof any longer," he said and began dressing. "You'll leave there tonight. I'll take you and Claire to Sam's."

"In the middle of the night?"

"I don't like them. I don't trust them. I know it will disrupt Claire's sleep but I insist."

Weston helped her to dress and they went downstairs where his butler awaited.

"I need a favor from you, Caldwell," he instructed. "Lady Ruthersby and her daughter are moving to my sister's now. For a night. Then they will come here. She is to be my duchess." He thought a moment. "In fact, we should bring their trunks here. I wish for you and Mrs. Caldwell to accompany us now to the Ruthersby townhouse.

Mrs. Caldwell may pack for Lady Ruthersby and you and the coachman can bring the trunks downstairs. Have a wagon hitched for the luggage. You can drive it."

"Shall I also send a footman with word to Her Grace to be expecting you?"

He chuckled. "You think of everything. Yes, do so."

He turned to Elise. "I can have whatever gown you wish sent over for the wedding." Looking back to his butler, he added, "And don't forget Miss Molly and Ralph Rabbit. They are Lady Claire's favorite doll and stuffed animal. You must pack them before anything else."

"Yes, Your Grace," Caldwell said with enthusiasm. "I shall rouse Mrs. Caldwell now and have your coach readied and horses attached to the wagon." The butler left.

Within minutes, both carriage and wagon stood in the street and Mrs. Caldwell had joined them.

"Let's go get Claire," Weston said.

As Elise entered the vehicle, she decided she'd fallen even more in love with her fiancé.

CHAPTER TWENTY-FIVE

WESTON TOOK ELISE'S hand as they went to Ruthersby's front door. It was half-past three in the morning. He assumed the earl and countess would have arrived home recently from the evening's ball but hoped he wouldn't have to see them. He rapped on the door and a sleepy footman answered, his eyes bugging out.

"Your Grace!" Nothing else came out of the man's mouth.

"We are here for Lady Claire," he said and swept by the servant. The Caldwells and his coachman followed. "Show them your bedchamber," he told Elise, "then we'll go and claim Claire." To the footman he said, "We'll need light."

The servant fumbled but lit candles and distributed them.

Elise led them up two flights and directed the three servants to her room.

"Pack what you can and be quick about it," he directed. "Anything left behind can easily be replaced."

He guided Elise up another flight of stairs. When they reached the landing, she stopped.

"Should I see if Mrs. Dandridge wants to come? She is Claire's nursery governess."

"All right."

She paused in front of a door and knocked. A woman in her mid-thirties answered it.

"Lady Ruthersby! Is something wrong with Lady Claire?" the governess asked frantically.

"Claire is fine," Elise assured the servant. "I am going to wed His Grace the day after tomorrow and we feel it best to get Claire out now. I know you were to return to Briarcliff with us. Would you like to come—"

"Oh, yes, my lady," the governess interrupted. "Lady Claire is an angel. I adore her. If I stay here, I will be out of work."

"Then pack quickly," Weston told her. "We'll leave shortly."

"I have already done so, Your Grace. I will dress now and meet you downstairs." Mrs. Dandridge closed her door.

He turned and saw another door open across the hall. A woman in her early forties stood there in her dressing gown. He assumed it to be the boys' governess.

"Your Grace, might I wake Joseph and Josiah so they can tell Lady Ruthersby and Lady Claire farewell?"

He knew how much the two boys cared for Elise. "Go ahead."

"Thank you, Your Grace."

Elise moved down the corridor and opened a door. They stepped into the room and crossed to the bed. Candlelight fell upon Claire and his heart stirred. Soon, this little girl would be his.

Elise set the candle down and perched on the bed. She gently shook her daughter, urging her to awaken. Unlike most children, Claire came wide awake quickly.

"Mama? What's wrong?"

"Nothing, my little love."

Weston went and knelt next to the bed. Taking Claire's hand, he said, "Your mama and I are going to get married. That means you'll both come live with me."

Claire's face lit with joy.

"I know you had a papa and your mama will always tell you everything you want to know about him so you won't forget him."

"I know," the girl said, her voice small.

"But since you'll be living with me, I wonder if I could also be your papa?"

"Yes!" she said with enthusiasm and threw her arms about his neck.

Weston lifted her from the bed and said to Elise, "Pack her things."

"It won't take long," she assured him.

"Your Grace!"

Joseph and Josiah bounded into the room and each wrapped their arms about his legs.

"I'm going to live with His Grace," Claire announced. "He's my new papa."

"Could we come live with you?" asked Josiah solemnly.

"No, you have parents," he said gently, seeing their faces fall.

"They don't like us," Joseph proclaimed. "They never come see us. We like you."

"And we'll miss Auntie Elise and Claire," Josiah added, sniffling.

"Then you will have to come visit us at Treadwell Manor this summer," he told them.

The boys cheered.

"I'll speak to your parents about it."

"Promise?" Joseph asked.

"I promise."

"I'm done," Elise said, holding up a small valise.

"Mama, get Miss Molly and Ralph Rabbit," Claire said.

"We won't forget your special friends," Weston told her, collecting the stuffed animal from the bed and placing it in her arms as Elise tucked the doll close.

"Go back to bed, boys," he instructed.

"Yes, Your Grace," they chimed in unison before hugging his legs again and then embracing their aunt.

They started out the door and Elise said, "The book!"

Weston paused as she darted back into the bedchamber and

glanced around. She found it and joined him and Claire.

"I couldn't leave the book you gave Claire. It means too much—to the both of us."

He gazed at her, love for this woman filling him, threatening to spill over. He brushed a quick kiss upon her lips and found her fingers, lacing his through hers.

"Are we ready now?" he asked.

Elise smiled. "We are."

As they ventured into the corridor, Mrs. Dandridge awaited them, her valise in hand. They went down two flights of stairs and then came across the earl and countess on the next landing. Weston supposed the footman had awakened the butler to let him know what was going on and the butler had decided the matter important enough to wake his employer.

"What's going on?" the earl asked, his hair askew.

"Elise and I will be wed tomorrow. She and Claire are going to stay at my sister's to help prepare for the wedding."

Their jaws dropped.

"I'd also like for your boys to come visit us at Treadwell Manor for the summer once the Season ends," he added. "I've grown quite fond of them and I feel it important for Claire to continue to be friendly with her cousins."

"Of course, Your Grace," Ruthersby said. "We are humbled by your invitation."

"What of us?" Lady Ruthersby asked. "Are we invited to the wedding? And for the summer?"

He glanced to Elise and they seemed to communicate without words.

"You may stay the night once you drop the boys off and another night when you return for them," he said to the countess. "As for the wedding, I would have to see a remarkable improvement in your attitude, Lady Ruthersby. Elise will outrank you when she becomes my duchess. I would hope you would exercise kindness toward her." He paused. "A kindness that has been noticeably lacking on your part for some time now. Do you understand?" he asked, his tone brokering no excuses.

The countess appeared flustered but said, "I will be gracious to Her Grace in all future dealings."

"Very well. You may expect an invitation to the wedding then. Bring the boys. It will be a small, intimate affair but they should be a part of it. Goodnight."

He continued down the stairs, Claire in his arms. They reached the carriage and he saw Caldwell and the coachman loading a trunk into the wagon bed. Mrs. Caldwell and Mrs. Dandridge went to the wagon while Weston placed Elise and Claire inside his coach. The three sat together, Claire already asleep again in his lap, Elise resting her head against his shoulder. He took her hand and felt not only her warmth but satisfaction filling him. They were a family now.

"I have a new nickname for the *ton* to use," Elise said. "You are no longer the Duke of Disrepute. You are my Duke of Grace."

ELISE WOKE, ENVELOPED in warmth. She lay nestled against Weston.
Her husband . . .

A week had passed since their wedding and sometimes she still felt as if she were living in a dream. Her duke was attentive. Interesting. Charming. Handsome. And a phenomenal lover. He had already taught her so much in the art of lovemaking and promised her they had only scratched the surface. She didn't know how it could get much better but trusted he was right.

She also liked that he listened to her. Since Norwood's death, she had been so isolated. Her parents had offered no support. Neither did her in-laws. They'd kept her from her friends and society in general.

With the Season in full swing, Elise was enjoying participating in so many social events, renewing old friendships and coming alive. Weston had taken her to the theatre. Riding in Rotten Row. To a bookstore.

He'd also spent time with Claire each day, sometimes in Elise's presence and sometimes without her. They'd gone walking in the park and had ices at Gunter's. He bought Claire a new stuffed animal. Claire had taken easily to calling Weston *Papa* and he beamed with pride every time she did so.

They'd also been the subject of the gossip columns. The topic of their quick wedding, so soon after the Season began, had been second only to stories written about Weston's romantic proposal in front of hundreds of ballroom guests. How he'd scandalized Polite Society by kissing her in public and physically carrying her from the ballroom. Old stories of his and George's rakish adventures were brought up but most of the gossip centered on the fact that the Duke of Disrepute and the Duke of Charm had been tamed by beautiful widows. Speculation occurred regarding the possibility of the Duchess of Colebourne being with child and the columns said it was only a matter of time before the new Duchess of Treadwell found herself in the same condition.

She'd mentioned to one rather talkative friend how she liked to call her husband the Duke of Grace and the nickname had spread. Weston teased that she'd reformed his roguish reputation overnight.

As Elise lay beside Weston, she couldn't help but be grateful for this man coming into her life. He'd rescued her and Claire from an impossible situation and brought love and laughter into their lives. As much as she was enjoying their time in London, though, she couldn't wait to head back to the country. Weston was also eager to return to his estate. He was brimming with ideas of what he wanted to do for his tenants. He also planned to teach Claire how to ride once they returned to Devon.

On their way home after the Season ended, they were going to call upon Phoebe and Andrew. Her friend had given birth to a son on the same day Elise wed Weston. The Windhams wanted the Treadwells to be godparents to the boy and Robby would be baptized during their visit to Windowmere.

Weston stirred and his hand glided down her back, cupping her bottom.

"Are you awake?" he murmured softly.

"I have been forever. Waiting for you to awaken," she teased.

He pressed a kiss to the top of her head. "Don't let sleep ever interfere with any wicked intentions you have regarding me, Your Grace. Sleep is highly overrated. Especially where love is involved."

He tilted her chin up and pressed his lips to hers. Soon, their kisses heated up and they made love in a frenzy, as if they couldn't get enough of one other. Elise had become addicted to her husband's drugging kisses and skilled hands. Need for this man poured through her and she doubted she would ever be able to get enough of him. As he filled her and she cried out his name in ecstasy, she knew she would never be able to live without him.

Afterward, Weston cradled her in his arms, stroking her unbound hair, murmuring to her how much he loved her. He told her so multiple times a day but each time was like hearing it anew, causing a warm glow to fill her.

"What are you going to do today?" he asked.

"I'm taking Claire to the modiste at eleven. It's time she had some new clothes. Not too many since she's growing so fast but she does need a few gowns. And perhaps a riding habit for when we return to Treadwell Manor."

"Buy her whatever she needs. Double what she needs." He kissed her temple. "I want nothing but the best for my daughter."

"You are so good to her."

"I know she's Ruthersby's child but I can't help but feel she's also mine."

"He died when she was but sixteen months. I know she doesn't really recall him. You will be her true father." She kissed him. "Most men wouldn't care for another man's child."

"I am as besotted with Lady Claire as I am her mother." Weston kissed her soundly. "Do you have plans after visiting the dressmaker's shop?"

"I think we'll go for a walk in the park if it's a nice day."

He kissed her fingers. "I may join you. I need to visit with my solicitor first."

"We'll be close to where the boys enjoy flying their kite if you have the chance to meet us."

"Look for me. We can go to Gunter's after our walk."

She stroked his cheek. "You're spoiling us, Weston."

He kissed her. "That's what dukes do. Spoil the women they love."

He tossed back the bedclothes and rose. Coming around to the other side of the bed, he pulled Elise to her feet and kissed her soundly and then swatted her bottom playfully.

"You'd better go and dress in your chamber, Your Grace, else I might keep you in our bed all day."

She wiggled her fingers in farewell and returned to her room, ringing for her new lady's maid and dressing for breakfast.

Today was going to be a lovely day.

CHAPTER TWENTY-SIX

WESTON DROPPED ELISE and Claire at the modiste's shop, promising to hurry his solicitor along so that they could meet up near the Serpentine. As the carriage pulled away, Elise thought about how thankful she was that her selfish cousin had insisted she journey home in a broken-down carriage. It had led her to Weston's door—and lasting happiness.

As she reached to open the door, it swung open, revealing Samantha in the doorway. Her sister-in-law stepped outside.

"What a pleasure meeting you both here." She smiled at Claire. "Are you going to have some new dresses made?"

"Yes, Auntie Sam."

Claire had taken instantly to Samantha when Weston had brought them to his sister's home in the middle of the night. Claire had allowed her new aunt to hold Miss Molly and the three of them had held a tea party. When Claire stumbled over Samantha's name, she told Claire to call her Auntie Sam. Seeing the two together told Elise how wonderful a mother her friend would be.

"I was also seeing about some new gowns," Samantha said. "Might I come in with you?"

Claire's face lit up. "Yes. You can help Mama and me."

Madame greeted them as they entered the shop and took Claire's hand. "Lady Claire, we are going to measure you for many new outfits." Then with a conspiratorial smile, she added, "And I do believe a riding habit is also something you need?"

Claire looked to Elise. "Mama? I get to ride?"

"Yes. Your papa said he will teach you when we return to Tread-well Manor in a few months."

Her daughter clapped her hands gleefully and then spun in a circle.

"Careful, Lady Claire," Madame admonished. "You mustn't get dizzy. Come along with me. Let's get you measured and then your mama and aunt can help choose fabrics for your gowns."

Claire took the dressmaker's hand and waved as she was led to a back room.

Once she'd left, Elise asked, "Are you getting new gowns because of your condition?"

Samantha nodded. "I spoke with Madame about it. I usually use a dressmaker in Exeter and she's quite good but I thought I would take advantage of being in London to have at least a few things made up for when I grow larger."

"You've been so good with Claire. I know you are looking forward to a child of your own."

"I am. We both are. George is eager to have as many as possible."

She laughed. "Weston has said the same thing although he seems to favor us having girls."

Samantha chuckled. "Claire does seem to have my brother wrapped about her tiniest finger." She took Elise's hand. "I am grateful that Weston has married such a wonderful woman and that we will live close by. I lived far too long without friends of any kind and look forward to the years ahead of us."

"I feel the same. And Phoebe is less than a day's carriage trip from us."

"I cannot wait to see Robby," Samantha said.

"Weston has promised that we will stop and call on them when we return to Treadwell Manor."

An assistant came with fabric samples and said, "Madame asked that you begin looking these over. She will have suggestions, of course."

"Of course," Samantha said. To Elise, she added, "I would go along with whatever Madame suggests. She is quite right about everything."

"I know. Look at the gowns she made for me. I have never received such attention in my life."

"As a duchess, you will set fashion trends. Madame will help guide you. Both of us, actually. Sometimes, I feel as if I must pinch myself," Samantha confided. "I am a duchess. Wed to my best friend. Soon to have his child."

"I think the same thing when I awaken every morning next to Weston."

Madame returned with a chattering Claire and they looked over various materials, deciding which bolts of fabric should be used to make up particular dresses for Claire.

As they left the shop, Elise said, "I see your carriage waiting for you. Do you have plans?"

"None. Why?"

"Claire and I are going to go walk in the park. Weston may join us and take us to Gunter's afterward."

"Gunter's?" Samantha and Claire said in unison. Samantha added, "I would love to come. Let's drive over in my carriage."

She gave her coachman instructions and he took them to the park. Claire insisted on riding beside her aunt and Elise sat across from them. They disembarked and Samantha dismissed her driver, saying Weston could drop her at home after they had their ices.

The park wasn't busy at all this time of day. Elise had learned that most nannies and governesses brought their charges in the mornings, reserving afternoons for napping. After tea would be when all the fashionable carriages drove through the park, with people stopping and chatting, looking about to see who rode with whom and gossiping about new couples who had formed attachments. They walked to the

Serpentine and Samantha and Claire went and sat on the bank, watching a family of ducks swimming past. Elise sighed, thinking how wonderful it was to have Samantha as both friend and family.

Without warning, something hard pressed into her back as someone latched on to her elbow.

"Enjoying an outing with your daughter?"

She glanced over her shoulder and saw Lord Ivy standing closely behind her. She tried to pull away but his grasp tightened.

"I want you to come with me," he said, and pushed against her back again. "Else I'll shoot you."

Fear flooded her. It was a gun he held to her back.

"Why would you do that?" she asked, surprised how calm her voice sounded as she stared straight ahead, worried that Samantha or Claire would turn around and see something was amiss.

"It's nothing personal," he said. "I rather like you. In fact, I was disappointed when you chose to turn down my offer of marriage. Now, come along."

Elise stood her ground. "You won't shoot me in public," she hissed.

"Look around," he said. "I don't see anyone. And if you don't accompany me, I'll shoot your pretty little girl."

She sucked in a quick breath, tears springing to her eyes. Whatever this man wanted, he was desperate enough to abduct her in broad daylight. She would make any sacrifice to keep her child safe. "No. Don't. I'll come."

"Good."

Elise turned and he took her arm, his fingers digging into her flesh. The pistol still rested against the small of her back. They walked toward a carriage with only a driver and no footman. The door stood open. As they reached it and Lord Ivy pushed her inside, she heard Claire call out to her. Elise's heart broke as the door slammed and she saw Claire running toward them, Samantha standing and chasing after her niece.

Lord Ivy sat across from her, the pistol in his hand, pointed at her.

"What do you want?"

"You'll write to Treadwell in a week and tell him you no longer care to be with him. That you want to be with me."

"Are you mad?" she hissed. "Why would I do something like that? I would never choose you over my husband."

A smile of pure evil twisted his handsome features. "That seems to be a recurring theme in my life. It's time Treadwell paid for making my life miserable. It's obvious to everyone how he treasures you. He's a proud man. Too proud. I want him stripped of what he loves most."

Elise recalled how Weston shared with her that Lord Ivy was having an affair with his stepmother and how she'd made it known she preferred Weston as a lover over Ivy. Could this be what had driven Ivy over the edge?

"He won't believe such a note. Weston knows me." Then she realized he'd said a week. "Why wait a week?"

"Because by then I will have thoroughly debauched you," he said candidly. "You will be ruined—as I told you I would do to you. A debased woman, even a duchess, will never be able to hold her head up in society."

Terror filled her yet Elise bravely asked, "And what of the man who would rape me? You think society will look kindly upon you?"

Worry creased his brow. She realized he hadn't thought of that. He'd only wanted revenge upon Weston.

"Society need never know," he finally said. "I'll keep you a week and do as I please to you. No note from you will be necessary. I'll merely drop you at Treadwell's doorstep and send him a note of my own. How I enjoyed the pleasures of your flesh. Touched you everywhere. Had my way with you over and over. He'll never want to touch you again. He certainly won't want Polite Society to know his wife is a whore. He'll be miserable, just as I have been."

"He will kill you," Elise said, her gaze direct. "If you take what is his. If you violate me. Treadwell will never stand for that, even if he decides never to touch me again. I promise you, Lord Ivy, my husband is powerful and vindictive and he will take you apart with his bare hands—and enjoy every moment of it. It's your choice. Do you lose your life trying to claim some type of petty revenge? Or do you stop the carriage and let me go?"

Alarm, mixed with trepidation, filled his eyes, which darted back and forth in indecision. Suddenly, he rapped on the roof and called, "Halt."

The vehicle slowed and came to a stop.

"Get out," Ivy declared. "And don't you dare say a word to Treadwell."

"You want me to remain silent? After you've kidnapped me? Threatened me with rape and ruin?" she accused.

The door to the carriage flew open.

Elise saw Weston standing there, fury filling his face.

WESTON LISTENED AS his solicitor went over the papers he'd drawn up. Elise had told him she was penniless but he had doubted it. He knew her father must have negotiated the contracts before she wed Ruthersby. His gut told him the new Lord Ruthersby had neglected to inform Elise of what was due to her, most likely at the suggestion of his greedy wife. Though he longed to call out the man on such deception, Weston knew it was important to keep peace in the family. Lord and Lady Ruthersby were Claire's aunt and uncle. He didn't want her alienated from them, or rather, from Joseph and Josiah. They were good boys and he believed he could lend a guiding hand to help mold them into being good men.

He did want Elise and Claire to be taken care of in case anything should happen to him before they could produce an heir. The dukedom would go to a distant cousin that Weston didn't think much of. Hence, his instructions to his solicitor to create legal documents to see his family protected. Satisfied, he signed the papers and thanked the man for doing such speedy work.

"It is an honor to serve you, Your Grace."

Weston left the offices and instructed his driver where to go in the park. As they entered, he noted how open the road was. In a few hours, it would be clogged with carriages and people jockeying for position to see and be seen. Now, though, it was easy to navigate the path.

The carriage stopped and as he climbed out, he saw his sister, her arms around a crying Claire, comforting her. He glanced about and didn't see his wife anywhere.

Rushing to the pair, he asked, "Where is Elise?"

Sam looked perplexed. "She was here. And then I saw her riding off in a carriage." She pointed at a vehicle in the distance. "That one."

Alarm filled him. Without a goodbye, he ran to his own vehicle and leaped into the box next to his driver.

"Go! Now! Follow that carriage."

Thanks to the skill of his driver and the speed of his horses, they closed the gap within minutes. Suddenly, the vehicle they were chasing came to a stop. Weston leaped from the box and hurried forward, flinging open the door.

Shock filled him as he saw Lord Ivy with a pistol trained on Elise. Weston hurled himself into the carriage, wanting to block Ivy from shooting her. His hand flew up and grabbed the viscount's wrist, driving the gun upward. It went off, the noise deafening inside the small area.

His ears ringing, Weston forced the gun from Ivy's hand and struck blow after blow, seeing red. Then from a distance, he heard his name being called and someone shaking his shoulders.

"Weston! Weston! Stop—or you'll kill him."

That had been his intention but reason prevailed. He quit pounding Ivy's face and collapsed on the opposite seat. The viscount curled up, a bloody mess.

He looked at Elise, who said, "He was going to let me go. I'd convinced him you would kill him if he didn't."

"I may still," he said angrily, seeing Ivy flinch at his words. "I should've allowed you to challenge me months ago when you wanted to. I would have killed you then and been done with it."

But Weston wouldn't have met Elise if he'd done so. And if he killed Lord Ivy now, it could ruin her reputation—and that of their children. Only for that reason would he show this bastard any kind of mercy.

"Where is your country estate?" he growled, tightening the rein on his temper.

"Cumbria," Ivy spit out, blood and two teeth coming out as he responded. "Near the Scottish border."

"You will go there and remain. Never return to London. Never speak of this to anyone. If you do, I will come for you. I will destroy you. Then I will see you are committed to an asylum and spend whatever days that are left to you locked up with the insane. I am a duke, Ivy. You know it is within my power to do as I say."

He saw fear fill the viscount's face and Ivy visibly trembled.

"Nod if you understand. If you agree to my terms."

Ivy nodded his head vigorously.

Without another word, Weston exited the vehicle, capturing Elise's waist and bringing her out, as well. He slammed the door.

To the driver, he said, "Lord Ivy wishes to go home now. He is eager to return to Cumbria."

The coachman said, "Yes, Your Grace."

Weston slipped an arm about Elise and led her to their carriage. "Take us back to Lady Claire and my sister," he ordered the driver.

Inside the carriage, Elise took his face in her hands. The rage that filled him seemed to disintegrate with her gentle touch.

"I love you," she said and brushed her lips softly against his.

She broke the kiss and lifted one of his hands, battered from pummeling Ivy's face. Kissing it tenderly, she did the same to the other and then held it against her cheek.

"What do we tell Claire?" he asked hoarsely. "I don't want her to know of such evil in the world at her tender age."

"Leave it to me. Follow my lead."

Their carriage stopped and they got out. Claire came running toward them, flinging herself into her mother's arms. Sam followed closely behind, not bothering to mask her anxiety. Weston shook his head imperceptibly, hoping she would understand they would talk of the matter later.

"Where did you go, Mama?" Claire asked, confusion and worry mingling on her face.

Elise kissed her daughter. "I'm so sorry. Mama had to go help someone who was hurt. I rushed off and forgot to tell you goodbye."

Claire looked to him and frowned. "Papa has blood on him."

"Yes," Elise said soothingly, smoothing Claire's hair. "Papa came to help me. A man was hurt in his carriage. He had blood on him and Papa got some on his clothes. He's fine, though."

"I'm fine," Weston seconded and Claire stretched her arms out to him. He took her in a loving embrace. "Let's go home."

His daughter pursed her lips and gave him a look. "But Papa, you said we were going to Gunter's for ices."

Something told him he would see that look many times in the years to come. And give in to it every single time.

"I'd forgotten, Claire. I'm so glad you reminded me."

"Ices?" asked Samantha. "That's one of my favorite things."

"Will you buy Auntie Sam one?" pleaded Claire.

"I will," he promised.

He released Claire and she scampered to Sam, taking her aunt's hand and leading her to the carriage, chattering away. Weston reached for Elise's hand, their fingers entwining.

"May I buy you an ice, Your Grace?"

His wife's smile melted away the last of the tension that flowed through him.

"I may want two, Your Grace," she said, mischief filling her face.

Weston pulled her into his arms. "Then two it shall be, my love," and he kissed her.

EPILOGUE

Paris—April 1820

E LISE AWOKE AND felt the familiar wave of nausea hit her. She lay still, hoping it would pass.

She was with child again.

Weston's arm was draped over her. Even in sleep, he held her possessively to him. He would be delighted at the news. They had been hoping for another child ever since their baby daughter had died from crib death over two years ago. She had been born two weeks early, very small but so very pretty. She had resembled their son, born eleven months after they'd wed and the spitting image of his handsome father. Claire had taken instantly to her new baby brother and though there were five years between them, the two were close.

Her husband stirred behind her and she knew he would awake soon and make love to her. Time had not diminished the tremendous desire between them and their passion flared to new heights every time they coupled. Weston had been an ideal husband and father, spending enormous amounts of time with her and the children.

He had also taken her several places, understanding her wish to travel and see new sights. They had visited each of his ducal estates, scattered throughout England, and while in the far north they'd ventured into Scotland. Elise had loved the rugged beauty of the country, from the valleys of the Lowlands to the mountains of the Highlands.

Later, they'd gone to Gibraltar, on the southern tip of the Iberian Peninsula, and visited the Rock of Gibraltar, one of the Pillars of Hercules, and then traveled south into Spain, a country of sun and wine. He had promised future trips to Egypt and America but those would have to wait, especially now that she was with child again.

His lips began nibbling her neck lightly, sending a rush of heat through her.

"Good morning, Your Grace," he said lazily.

"Good morning, Your Grace," she echoed as he turned her to face him.

Before she could tell him about the baby, he kissed her and she became lost in a sea of want and need that only her magnificent duke could fill. Half an hour later, they lay panting, tangled in the sheets.

"What would you like to see today?" he asked, bringing her hand to his lips and tenderly kissing her fingers.

"Is there anything left to see in Paris?" she asked. "We have seen the stained glass and gothic architecture of Sainte-Chapelle. Been to the highest point on Montmartre at Sacre-Coeur. Seen the towers and spire of Notre Dame. Strolled the Champs-Élysées and admired the Arc de Triomphe."

Continuing to kiss her fingers, he added, "Don't forget cruising along the Seine and seeing the Egyptian collection at the Louvre. I hope that whetted your appetite for going to Egypt. I think that should be our next venture."

"About that," she began as the door flew open and their son bounded in.

"Mama! Papa! I ate a croissant!" he proclaimed as he scampered up the bed, evidence of the croissant obvious from the chocolate smears on his face.

Elise pulled the sheet higher and tucked it behind her.

Claire appeared. "Rhys, I told you to leave Mama and Papa alone."

"But they weren't sleeping."

"But they might have been," Claire said in her wisdom. "Good morning, Mama. Papa."

"Good morning, my love," Weston said. "Would you mind playing with your brother today? I have somewhere I need to take your mother."

"Of course, Papa. You have taken us all around Paris. It's only fair you and Mama should get to spend a little time together."

"Can I have another croissant?" begged Rhys.

"Only after you get dressed," Elise declared. "Go with your sister now."

The boy gave her a sloppy kiss. "Yes, Mama," and climbed from the bed.

"Where is mine?" asked Weston, causing Rhys to dash over and smack his father's cheek.

The children left and Weston kissed her. "We have got to start locking that door."

She chuckled. "You act as if it's my fault that we didn't."

"It is. We arrive at our bedchamber and I take one look at my lovely wife—then all rational thought flees my head." He kissed her soundly. "Including remembering to lock our door."

He rose, his sleek, naked physique still giving her a thrill.

"We should both dress and then have the day to ourselves. After all, we leave tomorrow."

Elise blew him a kiss. "I will see you soon."

She would tell him about the babe once they left the house and had privacy.

Her maid arrived with a tray of chocolate and the wonderful croissants that their son had fallen in love with. She preferred them plain but Rhys liked the chocolate ones. After a quick breakfast, she washed and dressed and came downstairs where Weston awaited her.

"Ah, you look quite lovely, Your Grace," he said, his admiration obvious by the look in his eyes. He offered her his arm. "Come. The

City of Lights awaits us."

As they left the house they had rented for the past month, Elise said, "I see you have a basket. And a blanket under your arm."

"Yes. We'll need both."

They made stops for fresh bread. A pungent cheese. Strawberries. Wine.

"It looks like the makings of a picnic," she said.

"You have found me out. Yes. I thought a picnic for two in the *Jardin des Tuileries* would be a nice respite after all our recent sightseeing. Don't worry, though. Tonight, we will dine on herb buttered snails. I know how you've grown fond of them."

The thought of snails suddenly seemed vile though she'd devoured them ever since they'd arrived in France.

They continued walking until they reached the gardens. Weston found a secluded spot of grass with a wonderful view of colorful tulips. He placed the basket on the ground and spread the blanket out.

"Come, my love. Settle yourself."

She did and watched as he withdrew their purchases from the wicker basket. Soon, he was feeding her, kissing her between bites. Love for him stirred within her and she prayed she would have decades to love him.

Finally, they finished their feast. Elise was so full that she lay down. Weston slipped her head into his lap and gently stroked her cheek. She knew now would be the time to tell him.

"Weston, I have something to tell you."

Those aquamarine eyes gazed down at her. "Another bill from a Parisian modiste? Though I must say, you look ravishing in your new gowns."

"No, not a bill. Something you will look forward to, though."

"More than seeing you in that déshabillé?" His fingers traced her lips. "That sheer bit of wonder stole my breath away. You should wear it again tonight."

She captured his hand and threaded her fingers through his. "I am with child, Weston. We are going to have another baby. Sometime in mid-October."

Elise would never forget the smile on his face.

"A baby?" His free hand moved to her belly. He placed his palm against it. "A baby," he sighed and he stroked her.

Then he lifted her head from his lap and brought his head next to her belly. His hands framed it as he said, "We know you are in there. We are your mama and papa and we love you so very, very much."

Weston kissed her belly and then brought them to their feet. He wrapped Elise in his arms, where she always felt secure.

"I love you," he said and kissed her tenderly.

She knew he did. He always would. And they would love this child and any others they were blessed with.

About the Author

Award-winning and internationally bestselling author Alexa Aston's historical romances use history as a backdrop to place her characters in extraordinary circumstances, where their intense desire for one another grows into the treasured gift of love.

She is the author of Regency and Medieval romance, including: Dukes of Distinction; Soldiers & Soulmates; The St. Clairs; The King's Cousins; and The Knights of Honor.

A native Texan, Alexa lives with her husband in a Dallas suburb, where she eats her fair share of dark chocolate and plots out stories while she walks every morning. She enjoys a good Netflix binge; travel; seafood; and can't get enough of *Survivor* or *The Crown*.